# The Survival Guide to
# Suburban Warfare

## Book One of

GRA

## Breaking All the Rules

Rule #1: Even kings need an enemy to rally against.

## RICK GRASINGER

# Chapter 1

(**2:00 PM Sunday, June 8, 2010**) Somewhere at the end of a long dark hallway, in one of the most prestigious private schools on the east coast, sits a ten year old boy staring out the window, wondering what lies in wait for him and his classmates this summer. He taps his number two pencil on the side of the desk, impatiently waiting for that glorious sound of the school bell signaling the end of his last class, on the very last day before summer vacation begins. He looks across the empty row of seats at his best friend James who sits intently reading the comments handed out by the teacher from his previous class. Wandering around the classroom, speaking with each student on an individual basis is an odd-looking teenager with long black wavy hair and a thinly built body that's over exaggerated by his extreme height.

He's clearly out of his element, the ten year old boy thought, too young for next year's teacher, but way too old to be a student. Suddenly the quiet room is interrupted as a sharply dressed man sporting a thick beard enters the room. The odd-looking older teen hastens to the back of the room to take a seat.

The boy leans over on the open desk and whispers to his best friend James, "Who the hell is this fool?"

"Shhh! How the hell am I supposed to know?" James quietly replies, "Just shut up and let him talk. The last thing we need today is detention."

"Yeah, I hear you.  I just can't wait to get started on our summer vacation," The boy replies as he quickly sits up at attention.

The bearded man slaps his yard stick across the top of the podium. "Quiet please! My name is Professor Chapman.  I will be your writing teacher next year, assuming all you illiterate children managed to pass fourth grade English." He pauses a moment to place a piece of paper on the first desk. "Please fill out this contact form, including your names, addresses, emails, et cetera." The Professor paces up one row and down the other trying to size up each and every student. "I have a fun and exciting project planned for you this summer."

A low groan rumbles through the classroom as each child realizes that their summer plans of swimming pools and slumber parties will be constantly interrupted by the dreaded summer homework assignment!

The Professor begins by handing each student a single sheet of paper, including the odd teenager in the back. "If you intend on passing my class next year, you will need to write a short story to these specifications over this summer break.  The failure to do so…" He softly chuckles into a closed fist, "Well, let's just say, no one graduates fifth grade without first passing my class."

Three of the boys sit there with dumbfounded expressions on their faces until one of them snaps out of it and turns to face the other two. "This is bullshit!" His voice rises just above a whisper, "I don't want to write during the school year.  What makes this dumb ass think we want to write during our summer vacation?"

The Professor stops between the three boys and looks down. "Son, it is by sheer luck that I don't know your name at this time and I most likely will have forgotten that comment by next fall.  However, I can assure you I won't stand for talking in my class next year and swearing will obviously not be tolerated! Do you understand?"

The dark skinned boy stands up, and at ten years old, he's nearly as tall as the teacher.  "Sss…sorry Sir," The boy shouts as he snaps to attention, then he smiles a boyish grin. "I've just got one...one question... Www...would it be alright if I ask two cute girls to help me with this fffun and exciting project you've bestowed upon me...? Sss...Sir...!"

"Great question, Young Man," the Professor responds enthusiastically as he gestures towards the boy's chair. "And after you sit down I'll gladly answer. If you look at rule number ten, it clearly states that you can and should get help. But the most important rule is rule number one which states that your short story must be consistent with your summer activities. Oh, and one more thing, your student teacher's email address and cell phone number is at the bottom of the page. Consider him at your beck and call, twenty-four seven. Please take full advantage of him as he comes to us touted as the very best our Ivy League has to offer."

The tall gangly young man from the back of the room attempts to slide out from the small desk and chair but realizes he's stuck. "Ummm... Professor Chapman is it?" He softly clears his throat. "I think there's a small mistake here."

"Mistake? No, I think not," the Professor shoots back, while spastically tapping his right hand into the side of his face. "There's no mistake!"

"It's just that..." The young man mutters.

"Well? Speak up boy!" The Professor cries out as he loses his patience.

"I'm your student teacher for next year, not one of your students."

"And that means what to us," the Professor snaps out. "Well?"

"It's just that... You handed me a sheet of rules as if I had to do this assignment as well," he explains hesitantly.

"Student… teacher…" The Professor shouts to the back of the room where the lanky teenager still sat in one of the small student chairs. "You're a student first and foremost, which means if you want to work under me in the fall, you'll do the assignment just like the other students. In my mind there's no better way to learn!" He steps back behind his desk.

A skinny little girl with long golden curly hair, sitting at the end seat of the last row stands up. "Mr. Professor? Sir, would you like me to return your contact form?"

"Could you please hand it to our student teacher on your way out," he asks her politely. "I'm looking forward to seeing all of you in the fall." Just then the school bell rings out. "That's all boys and girls. Class dismissed."

The three boys watch as the little girl with golden hair dashes to the back of the room.

"This child right here," she murmurs while pointing at a boy's name half way down the contact list, "he's a freaking jerk… but he just lost his mother. Anyway, I was just wondering, if you can watch over him this summer," she asks the student teacher.

The three boys stare at the skinny girl after she walks past them on her way towards the front of the room.

She pauses just inside the doorway and quickly spins around, catching the three boys still ogling her. "Why don't you just take a picture? It'll last longer!" she shouts back at the boys as she struts out of the room, snapping her little hips back and forth like America's Next Top Model.

"I believe she's got eyes in the back of her head," one of the boys said.

"Yeah, and horns growing out of the top," another boy adds.

The student teacher quickly glances through the contact list and pauses for a moment when he reaches the boy's name. He wonders what could possibly be going through the mind of a ten year old boy who just lost his mother. Images of his own late mother begin to race through his head.

The ten year old boy grabs James' arm squeezing it tight.

"Hey... what gives," James whispers.

"What's the deal with the freak in the back," the boy asks as they approach the tall teenager in the back of the room who's still sitting in the tiny chair with his long legs stuffed under the little table.

The two boys watch as the teen's eyes dart back and forth like a wild mouse on speed.

"What do you think he's looking at," James asks while waving his hand in front of the teen's pale white face.

"How the hell do I know," the boy replies as he claps his hands in front of the teen's blank stare. "Must have taken some kind of designer drug at lunch time, I guess."

The Professor stops next to the two boys and looks down at the Teen's face, his eyes stop darting and lock into a blank stare. Slowly his eyes well up with tears then the tears trickle down his ghostly face.

The Professor grabs both boys by their wrists pulling them toward the door. "I said class dismissed," he growls out. "That also means you two."

"But..."

"Out, now!" the Professor yells.

# Chapter 2

(7:00 AM Monday, June 28) Kevin O'Donnell pulled the hairdryer off the wall and within seconds his head was completely dry. He flipped on his thick black glasses then stepped back to admire his hair as he ran his fingers through it. "Not bad," he softly mumbled. "Not bad at all. And to think, my dad was completely bald when he hit the big 4-0... I guess all that money spent on those crazy, new and improved hair growth ointments really did pay off." Then he hurried down the steps and into the kitchen.

"Dad," Mark hollered down from inside his bedroom. "Are you going to my game tonight?"

Kevin shouted back up, "Have I ever missed a game?"

"No, but..."

"Besides, how else are you going to get there?" Kevin set down two pieces of toast with jelly and a tall glass of juice. "Now get down here and eat your breakfast!"

Mark rumbled down the steps and onto a bar stool in the kitchen. "Yeah Dad but, I mean are you staying 'til the end?"

"Mark, you know I can't make you that promise. I've got to go back to work about six o'clock. For you that's around the fourth inning, so I'll see most of the game."

"Dad? Are you chasing skirts again?"

"What?!?"

"I mean… Why are you the only father that has to leave in the middle of the game," Mark asked.

"Well, that's a great question Son." Kevin took a deep breath, wondering what it takes to trick a ten year old boy these days. "I'll tell you why I have to go back to work, if you tell me who said I was chasing skirts."

"Do you mean the last time I heard it?"

"Sure Mark, the last time," Kevin said in a frustrated voice.

Mark rolled his eyes up toward the ceiling as he paused for a moment to gather his thoughts. "Hmm, let me think. Last Tuesday, I overheard Jimmy's mom telling Stacy's mom what she heard from Jimmy's dad. But all the parents talk about it after every practice."

"It's nice to know I give those jackasses something to talk about," Kevin grumbled.

Mark looked up with a shocked expression, "Oh Dad, you swore!"

"Look Mark, my job has changed a lot in the last few years. We're both going to have to get used to me working long days and weekends. I've seen too many of my friends and colleagues get fired recently and at this point in my life I'm not sure I can handle looking for a new job."

"Don't worry Dad, I heard Jimmy's father talking and he said if you were to get the axe then he would hire you tomorrow. That way we won't lose our house."

"That's real nice of him to say in front of you," Kevin said in a dejected voice. "Look no one is losing their job, especially me. But even if I do, I won't be working for James."

"Why not, Dad?"

"It's not good policy to work for your best friend. Besides that, James is our neighbor and then there's the problem of you and Jimmy being best friends," Kevin explained.

"But Dad, why's there a problem with Jimmy and me being friends?"

"No, it's not a problem. But then, you also have Jimmy's mother who's adorable. And it's just not a good idea to work for people that you're friends with."

"What's adorable mean Dad?"

"Who said adorable?" Kevin asked.

"You did Dad, just now."

"No I didn't... I said abnormal! And that means she's a weirdo, a big weirdo."

"Well, Dad... I think she's cute."

"Where...?" Kevin begins rubbing the back of his upper neck trying to ward off the headache that was slowly creeping in. "I know I'm going to regret asking this, but here goes. Where did you come up with that "cute" crap?"

"You Dad... don't you remember last year? When Jimmy's dad had to drive you home because the police thought you shouldn't be driving? That's when you told Mr. M that you thought Mrs. M was cute."

"I've got to learn to keep my mouth shut when I drink. Either that or quit drinking," Kevin mumbled as he picked up his briefcase. "Alright, new subject... I've got to leave for work now. So let's go over your morning routine one more time before I go."

Mark looked up in frustration, "Dad, how many times do we have to go over this?"

"How about every morning until you get it right," Kevin said in a stern voice.

"Alright… Are you ready Dad," Mark held up a finger in the air. "One, finish breakfast and put my dishes in the sink. Two, lock our back door when I leave. Three, go through Jimmy's back door, grab two doggy treats, sit quietly on the couch and watch TV until Jimmy wakes up. Oh yeah, six, give Buttons his treats!"

"Good."

"What did I mess up yesterday Dad?"

"Yesterday?" Kevin paused a moment, "Let's see, you were fine when you grabbed Buttons his treats. But then instead of sitting on the couch, you decided to go upstairs to Jimmy's room; which wouldn't have been such a disaster if you hadn't gone into Jimmy's mother's bedroom by mistake. It was a mistake, wasn't it?"

"Yes, Dad," Mark responded in an irritated voice.

"Good, then give me a hug. I've really got to get moving now if I don't want to sit in bumper to bumper traffic for an hour."

# Chapter 3

**(8:00 AM Monday, June 28)** Diane Madison pulled the quilt up around her neck and rolled over to stare out the bedroom window of her waterfront condo. She closed her eyes and thought of Greg, his dark hair with just a hint of grey at the temples, his broad shoulders and strong arms, the scent of his perfectly tanned body lying on the beach next to her. It was all so familiar. Then the alarm sounded off again and she swatted at it with a closed fist while kicking at the covers until they fell to the floor.

"Damn it," she cried out. I hate Monday mornings and what kind of friend has their thirtieth birthday party on Sunday night anyway?!? This is going to be one hell of a brutal day she thought to herself as she rolled out of bed. And where is that awful smell coming from?

The combination of Big Azz margaritas and cheap Mexican food lingered on the rumpled outfit that she was still wearing from the night before. Diane held her breath while quickly pulling her stained blouse over her head then finally gasping for air as she threw it across the room. "Ewww... what is that dreadful smell?" She stumbled across the room while trying to strip off her skinny jeans on the way to the bathroom. She took a long hot shower, hoping to wash off some of the memories from the night before. I need to make a new rule she thought, any time I start dancing I need to stop drinking. I hate dancing! So, therefore, if I am dancing, then I've obviously had too much to drink.

She emerged from the shower, wrapped herself in a thick Turkish towel, and planted her behind on the stool in front of the vanity. She tried to focus her eyes on the destruction in mirror above the vanity. Oh Dear God, she thought, who stole that young girl that could get any man with just a smile or a nod? And why did they feel the need to replace her with this ugly bitch! Her hands shook as she lightly tapped moisturizer and concealer under her eyes. I'm almost thirty and have little or nothing to show for it, all those long days of ass kissing at the office and all those worthless men I've dated. No ring on my finger, no man in my bed, and no hope of finding one. Just one, she thought, as she stared into the mirror, that's all I want. "Is that too much to ask," she asked no one in particular.

She pulled out the mega jar of foundation then noticed a new wrinkle and groaned, "So this is what they mean by the terrible thirties." Staying smoking hot is just getting to be too much work. I'm not sure it's even worth it anymore! Whoever said 'It's what's on the inside that matters' is so full of shit! That's a phrase that old married people use to make themselves feel better. For me it's all about what's on the outside, now more than ever. She walked over and fell back down on her bed, "Shit!" I hope there are no incidents at work today. I'm not sure how much more I can take.

She thought back on her life and wondered what happened to all those nice guys she once knew. I wonder if I should have given in and just said "yes" when Rick asked me to marry him. Seventeen was probably too young, but the prospects of seeing myself in a white dress anytime in the near future are looking dimmer by the day.

She slipped on her patent leather peep-toe BCBG pumps then stood up to look into the full length mirror. Her long golden curly hair looked perfect as usual. The blouse showed off just enough cleavage without looking too slutty. Then she turned while taking a step back to check her butt and realized she had forgotten to put her skirt on. "Oh yeah!" That would have definitely gotten some second looks, and maybe even a standing ovation from the guys in accounting. Probably some freak... There's not one decent man that works in my office. I wish Greg worked there. Now that would be an entirely different story and I'd do anything to be a part in his book. "God..." There's nothing like a man in uniform, and Greg filed out that uniform in all the right places. She wondered what went wrong and if there was anything she could have done to prevent him from losing interest. She hadn't known him very long, but she had that feeling and that feeling was very rarely ever wrong. With a little luck and a nudge in the right direction, this guy had a chance to be the one. She stepped back again making her sexiest pose into the full length mirror. "Perfect, how can any man not want a piece of this?"

Diane stopped at the first red light on Route 28 and laughed softly to herself. Greg would have definitely appreciated the humor in that, he always loved seeing me with no pants on. And why wouldn't he? I should call and tell him what I almost did. Maybe he still loves me. Maybe he was just having a bad day last Thursday. I don't understand men! What the hell do they want from me?

The sharp sound of horn startled her so she looked up at the mirror and saw an older man in a pickup truck staring at her. "What? What the hell do you want," She yelled in response as she threw her hands up in the air. Then she took her foot off the brake and eased along with the flow of traffic. That does it! No more thinking 'til I get to the office.

Diane stepped out of the elevator and paused briefly; looking at all the cubicles filled with people she considers her friends as well as her colleagues. She glanced down the long hallway at her own office, took a deep breath and began walking toward it. Kevin poked his head out of one of the cubes, gesturing for Diane to stop.

"It's Monday, and once again, no sign of Lisa," Kevin mumbled while looking down as his feet.

Diane glared at Kevin for a moment with a look that would have made Satan proud. Then she turned on her heel and marched down the hall to her office slamming the door behind her. As Diane sat at her desk she couldn't seem to stop her mind from wandering back to

Greg. What sort of man takes a woman like me to Mexico one week, and things seem to be going so great, and... and then, nothing. Yeah, I may have only known him for a few weeks or so, but he was all that and then some. I bet he's thinking of me too.

The sound of the phone ringing startled Diane and she deliberated, maybe I should answer it and just bury my mind in work. That shouldn't be a problem considering the new management has everyone and everything in such disarray. As the phone rang for a third time, she considered letting it bounce back to her secretary. Isn't that Jan's job anyway? It can't be good news, not anymore. At some point in the very near future, my department is going to get sliced and diced; I'm going to be the bitch that gets stuck wielding the knife. These people are my friends, at least most of them. I hate to think of losing even one.

She thought back just three short years ago, when the talk of promotion was always on the table and every day was a battle, a race to see who the better man, or in her case who the better woman, was? Kevin was good at his job and a hard worker. But he's never been management material. You need to be well-liked by both upper management and your subordinates. The only person who likes Kevin is Kevin. The better *person* clearly won and the people working in this department are definitely better off now with me in charge.

As Diane checks her email, she notices the first three are from Kevin. What an idiot! I can't believe he's still writing these contracts. I hate to do this again but, she types "CONTRACT DENIED" and clicks "send".

Kevin sat at his desk tapping a pen on the side of his monitor, trying to match the beat of the last song he heard in his car. He sings softly, slightly off key, "Hey there Delilah, what's it like in New York City?" A small envelope appears in the bottom right hand corner of his screen notifying him of the arrival of a new email. It's from Diane. The inevitable has occurred and even though he can see it with his own eyes, he still cannot believe it. Kevin raced down the hall right past her secretary. Ignoring Jan's protests, he skids to a halt in the doorway of Diane's office. Caught somewhere between anger, doubt and uncertainty he stands there. Is this the end? He wonders, should I suck it up and keep mouth shut again, or do I throw it all on the table and force her hand? He looked in and saw her sitting at her desk staring down in silence. He sighs softly, I promised Mark… I guess its ass-kissing time again.

Diane looked up at Kevin, "What..? Well..? What the hell can I do for you?"

Kevin pauses for a moment, looking down at his shoes then back up at Diane who had a smug look on her face. "This is the fifth contract in a row of mine you've denied. You couldn't have spent more than five minutes looking over this one. Are you telling me, in your professional opinion, that not one of these deals is worthy of going in front of the board for a full vote?" As Kevin continued to plead his case his voice grew louder. "This one's a sure thing. I'm certain the board would agree with me on that. In two years, if everything goes right, this company will be turning a profit. And isn't that what we're here for, to help out local businesses? We deal with this corporation all the time!" Sweat began to ooze out of every pore of his body. "You yourself pushed through a number of contracts for them when you were in my position. Does my success really bother you that much? You just can't stand the fact that I'm the only one on this floor getting contracts signed. Oh that's it, isn't it? You Bitch! If just three of my contracts were approved this month, that would be more than the rest of the entire commercial department combined. And if that happened, then you wouldn't have a legitimate reason to fire me!"

Diane sat in her plush leather chair, slowly rocking forward and back. She checked her hair in the reflection of the window then slid her sun glasses off her face revealing her blood shot eyes. "Are you done yet," she inquired in a steely voice as she carefully slid her sunglasses back on. "That's it? That's all you've got? Because, in case you haven't noticed, I haven't sent anyone's proposals up for approval this month. Or are you too stupid to notice that?"

"I worked on this project for the better part of two months," Kevin shouted. "What am I supposed to do? Sit back and let all my clients go somewhere else? What the hell? I should just…"

"Just what, Kev?" She stood up and stared right through his pale white face, "Go ahead! Say it… Say it or get the hell out of my office!"

Kevin leaned over the desk and whispered in her ear, "I was going to say, I should just drag your skinny ass up to the balcony and throw you off. And no, there's no chance of me quitting." Kevin turned around and dropped his head as he walked toward her door. Then quickly lifted his head up and took a long whiff, "What is that perfume you're wearing? It smells amazing." He jumped, startled by the sound of something crashing against the door just as he closed it. He slowly walked down the hall trying not to make eye contact with any of his co-workers. But every cube he passed had a rubbernecker staring at the car wreck that is Kevin's life.

Diane sat back in her chair and took a deep breath as she thought about the brief skirmish with Kevin. There are two things I really hate about him. Number one, in a sad way he's right. It's not his fault this merger has everything at a standstill. Two, he's such an asshole. As soon as management lifts the freeze on laying off employees, that jackass is gone. I wonder if I could get a judgment against him for threatening my life. That's an excellent question, one that Greg would be qualified to answer. I should make the call right now while I'm thinking of him.

Kevin returned to his desk to see he missed three emails. The first two were junk, but the third was from Diane. He clicked on it with the hopes that she agreed with his argument and decided to change her mind. But it simply stated; 'Don't waste anymore of the bank's time or money by going on these business luncheons. I'm going to inform human resources to deny any more of your expense reports.'

Kevin looked over at the calendar on the wall, glaring at the one o'clock lunch meeting that was penciled in on today's date. He turned off his computer and slouched down in his old worn out chair, staring at the dirty white walls that outline his tiny cubicle. He pulled a small air freshener out of his drawer and placed it on his desk in hopes that it'll help cover up the stench from two hundred years of mold seeping out of every inch of this disgusting building. He wondered how much longer he'll have the privilege of working for this multi-billion dollar corporation that doesn't have a dollar to lend out.

Kevin drags himself up out of his chair and staggers to the break room. His mind begins racing in another direction altogether. Thank God my kid has a game tonight. I think we're playing Plum. We better kick their asses! There's nothing better than watching those parents squirm when their team is losing. They're all sons of bitches. Kevin glances at the clock on the wall and notices that it's almost one o'clock. I don't give a shit what was in that email. This meeting was scheduled more than two weeks ago. I'm not about to cancel it now!

# Chapter 4

(**1:35 PM Monday, June 28**) Tom and Steve are co-owners of Southside Development Corporation SDC and old friends of Kevin's. In this ever changing economy, a new problem arrives in the banking industry almost every quarter and like Pittsburgh Bank & Trust (PBT) most banks basically had no money to lend out. So Tom contacted Kevin with the hopes that he could pull a few strings and somehow get a loan approved. With the commerce industry collapsing right in front of their eyes, land and buildings were right there for the taking. All you needed was cash and you could walk away with these properties at half their previous market value or sometimes even less. Only one big problem, there's not one person on the board of directors who is likely to consider approving a loan with the current rate of defaults hitting a historic all-time high. That's where Kevin's talents come into play. He knows just what to say and who to say it to. And he knows exactly how to present these projects in precisely the right way to get guaranteed approval from the board.

Kevin handed out two small stacks of papers, one to each man. "If you can both sign your names where those tabs are sticking out I can get the process started as early as today," he said while handing out two pens.

"Kev, I'm still a little surprised you returned my phone call," one of the men commented. "I assumed your bank was going through the same financial difficulties as the rest of the industry."

"Look Gentlemen," Kevin responded in a confident tone. "If any one's going to worry about getting your money for you, it's going to be me. And I can assure you, I'm not worrying at all! We're still making loan approvals." He pulled his phone out and glanced and pretended to check his text messages before setting it down on the table. "In fact, I just received a text message while we were sitting here. Apparently Diane has already granted you preliminary approval and we're hopeful it'll go in front of the board for a vote later this week."

Tom and Steve provided their John Hancock's multiple times and Kevin quickly finished filling out his portion of the contract before downing his third shot. He slammed the glass onto the table and groaned as the whiskey burned its way down his throat. He sat there staring at the glass for a moment then took a deep breath before rising to shake hands with the gentlemen as they concluded their business.

Kevin picked up the black imitation leather portfolio containing the bill for lunch. He softly sighed at the sight of the one hundred thirty dollar check which included three shots of Jack Daniels and four beers. Thanks to Diane I'll probably never see a penny from HR for this lunch. Kevin quickly snatched up the three wrapped fortune cookies and tossed two at the men as they were on their way out. Then he peeled off the cellophane with a quick tear and snapped the cookie's crisp shell in two. Apparently his lucky numbers included seven and thirteen, and salt was pronounced "yan" in Chinese. This he could accept with little reservation, even the seemingly inconsistent seven and thirteen. The fortune, now that was another matter.

The blue print glared at him from the small rectangular strip of paper: 'Find a job you love and you will never work a day in your life.' "Bullshit," he grumbled. Somewhere between the friendly faces he would see scattered throughout the bank, to the stiff competition with a certain co-worker for the next promotion, maybe it was all that money, or how about the hot girls that work in my department; I did love this job once upon a time, Kevin thought to himself. Yeah, let's be honest, it's definitely the girls and money. Now, fifteen years after landing that coveted job at PBT, he should have been looking forward to getting that fifth week of paid vacation, plus the traditional bonuses, or maybe, just maybe, the coveted title of department head that Diane had stolen from him.  But instead, he's a forty-something single dad with a ten-year old son to worry about, and his employer unceremoniously announces that it has been bought out by a multinational conglomerate.  While many of the bank's employees received this news with the promise of promotions and new opportunities, Kevin now opened each paycheck with trepidation, wondering when the day would come that a pink slip accompanied his pay stub.  He just knew he was going to be laid-off, let go, fired; whatever you called it, the end result was the same.  Kevin obsessed about it.

His job was secure before the merger.  His work as the bank's primary commercial loan officer was solid, he knew that.  As solid as the traditional massive oak doors that mark the entrance of every branch of Pittsburgh's oldest banking institution.  Until only a few years ago, he was responsible for more than seventy-five percent of the loans that were passed through to the board.  Kevin worked at the main office which meant that he was given significant power, or control if you will, over all the loans that were sent up from the branch offices.  But with such power comes great responsibility and it was Diane's responsibility to watch over and control Kevin. While PBT may not have been the biggest financial player in town, the bank had the benefit of a history of steadfast dependability with a clientele that included some of the most privileged names east of the Ohio River.  And it treated its employees well.  However, like nearly every other banking institution in America, PBT had its share of bad debt.  Consequently, when the real estate market collapsed, the bank's rating was lowered making it a prime target for a takeover.  Unfortunately, for Kevin, the buy-out offer was too good for management to pass up.

While Kevin's meal ticket was spared for the present time, the merger meant that Kevin now spent his days working alongside Lisa Hartman who is ten years Kevin's junior, and in his eyes, half his IQ.  But God she played the ditzy blond so well, almost too well.  Even though Kevin hated her, he couldn't help appreciating how Lisa's short skirts hugged her toned and tanned thighs as she sashayed across the floor. With Lisa's stunning good looks it didn't take long for Kevin to lose a few of his clients to her. But with the suburban sprawl and new malls popping up all over the place, there was plenty of work for everyone, and they were all small time clients anyway.

Kevin looked back down at his shot glass and couldn't help thinking about Diane. *If that bitch turns this one down I might just have to really kill her. The bank will not only get most of its original thirty million back, but they have a chance to actually make money. This is a rare occurrence these days in the commercial banking industry.* Kevin crumbled the slip of paper and bit down on half of the cookie. He checked his phone as he reached for his wallet. He looked up and saw two elderly oriental women pointing at him from the foyer. *Oh hell, I need to get back to the office. Between the standard board meetings and the meetings with the new regime, there doesn't seem to be enough hours in the day.*

"Does either one of you speak any English," Kevin asked the two Oriental women. "English…? Can you put the meals and the drinks on two separate bills? Right here…" Kevin took a pen and circled the charges for the alcoholic beverages. "Separate this from the other… Separate… Oh screw it… Just put it all on this card!" Kevin stuffed the receipt in his wallet and headed for the door. *I remember when I would get reimbursed for the whole check, drinks and all,* Kevin thought. *Then I lost the drinks. Okay, that I can live with, but now they're taking away my lunch as well. Before you know it, I'll be forced to buy my clients their lunch and maybe even bring back lunch for all the board members. I don't know who's making all the decisions at the bank these days, but whoever it is sucks!*

Kevin shoved the door open and steamed out of the restaurant. "Have good day GI Joe," he heard one of the two women shout as he left. "You asshole," the other yelled when she noticed the skimpy gratuity.

# Chapter 5

(**12:30 PM Monday, June 28**) Lying on a pearl white sandy beach, with the blazing hot sun beating on her flawless spray-on tanned body, Lisa sat up long enough to check out her new boy toy. She watched as a single bead of sweat trickled down his perfectly sculpted body, it glimmered in the sun from the lotion she rubbed on earlier. She listened to the sound of waves crashing in the background as another breeze blew warm salty air across the beach.

She reached for her frozen margarita and spoke softly to herself. "It's one thing to be sitting here relaxing with the most gorgeous man I have ever laid eyes on," Lisa sighed. "It's quite another to be doing it in what is probably the most glorious resort in Mexico." Lisa took a long sip and licked her salty lips, "I've pinched myself so many times that I think I'm starting to turn black and blue. I still don't quite believe it. How do you get from no dating prospects at all, to lounging on the beach in paradise with the man of my dreams in such a short time? I can't wait to tell my mom, I think he's the one." She took another long sip, "I'm not sure why he had to fly to Mexico for work. He doesn't seem to do anything besides buy me jewelry and send those little men for drinks. I'm not sure what I've done to deserve such royal treatment. Yeah, I may be a ten… But he's at least an eight."

"You talking to me, Babe?"

"Nope, I'm just talking to my drink. Go back to sleep," Lisa replied. She closed her eyes as she sipped again while thinking; I've got to keep my friends updated on this situation. She pulled her cell phone out of her purse and quietly snapped a picture of Greg. They're not going to believe my good fortune. Lisa deftly types on her wall on Facebook,

"I'm sitting on the most beautiful beach somewhere in paradise. My perfectly pedicured toes are buried in the finest white sand and I have a margarita in my hand. There's a swim-up bar to my left and canopy beds scattered across the white sandy beach."

Then she uploads a picture of herself sitting under a thatched umbrella as proof. I wonder if any of my friends will get this from here, where ever the hell I am. A friendly young man stops by her chair to take away the empty glass and hands her a new margarita. She quickly begins slurping the new drink. It's hard to believe that you can be so far from reality in so little time. Let's see, a three and a half hour flight followed by a half hour taxi ride, destination Heaven. "Simply amazing…" Lisa snaps another photo of Greg as she considers his odd rule. The rule is simple, no pictures. "I hate rules, screw the rules," she mumbles to herself as she takes another long sip, then she types another comment.

"This guy buys me whatever I want. I'm plastered and this guy is freaking hot!!!"

Lisa finishes off her next margarita and types some more.

"Oh my! He's the one… I know it…"

She clicks "share" and another comment appears on her wall.

"You talking to your drink again," Greg says as he slowly opens his eyes.

"Shhh! Go back to sleep, Honey," Lisa whispers softly in Greg's ear. "You're going to need your energy for later." Lisa continues her daydreaming as another Margarita magically appears by her side. We've only know each other a few weeks, but he must feel the same way about me. Why else would he bring me with him to paradise?

Lisa polishes off another drink then lies back in her hammock with a white towel over her face to prevent the sun from burning it. "He hasn't even left the resort yet," she mumbles through the thick terry cloth. "If he's here for work, why hasn't he gone anywhere? Maybe he's spying on someone here at the resort. Someone right here on this beach with us... He's probably some kinda special agent police officer, so maybe he's here undercover."

Just then, Greg rolls over and nudges Lisa's arm. "Do you always talk to yourself, or are you just drunk?"

"I've only had one margarita..."

Greg picks up his Ray-Bans and carefully slides them on his slightly burned face. "One? Yeah, right... Well, come on Babe, we've got to go buy some stuff."

I love it when he calls me Babe, Lisa thought, almost as much as when he buys me things. Yeah, we're going to get along just fine, he's definitely the one.

Lisa pulls her watch out of her purse. "Oh shit! Is it really almost twelve o'clock? I have so much work to finish before noon! There were some delinquent payments due in on Friday. I had all weekend to check on this shit. Where's my damn laptop?" She grabs her purse and runs over to the cabana where she left her computer. "If I don't get this info sent to corporate before twelve o'clock I'm going to be on someone's shit list again," she cried while desperately typing as fast as she can. "We have an outstanding loan, due last month for millions. No one will refinance their loan because they're currently late paying us."

Greg stood beside her with an impatient look on his face.

"It's a small mall," Lisa continued to ramble on. "It's old and outdated. They've lost two of their anchor stores and will go belly up if they don't get some help soon. I know you don't give a shit, but I've got to get this done now!" She frantically typed while continually talking. "This was supposed to be one of that jackass Kevin's sweetheart deals, one of his "can't-miss" opportunities. But now that it's in the process of collapsing, I'm the one who's stuck trying to save the bank's interest in the loan."

"Babe, you're cute and all, but you do realize we're a full hour behind your office. It's almost one o'clock there."

Lisa closes up her computer as she realizes he's right. "I am so screwed."

They walked up through the gardens and open air lobby to the impressive front courtyard where guests wait for taxis to whisk them away on site-seeing tours or shopping expeditions. Lisa sits down on one of the marble benches, pulls out her laptop and begins typing again as they wait for their taxi to arrive.

**From:** Lisa Hartman

**Sent:** Monday, May 13, 2010 1:02 PM

**To:** Kevin.O'Donnell@PittsburghBankTrust.com

**Subject:** Kev, help please!

I need you to pull all info on the strip mall case and send it to corporate ASAP. My password is (bunny192) that should get you into my protected files. I owe you one. Thanks, Lisa

A taxi pulls up and a short heavy set man jumps out pleading with his hand open. "Five dollar… ride to town... five dollar." Lisa hits "send" and slides her small laptop into her oversized purse. Thank God for free Wi-Fi!

Greg handed the man a small roll of ones and within minutes the couple was seated at a seedy cantina, in what looked to be one of the poorest areas south of Cancun.

Lisa's eyes first scanned the back alley then the run-down shops across the street. "What the hell are we doing here? This place is nasty," she quietly asked.

Two locals approached from the alley behind Greg. Both were wearing worn out bell bottom jeans. One guy had on a pink tank top while the other man was carrying his shirt. Ewww, she thought, silently cringing on the inside.

Lisa tried to warn Greg but it was too late. The man that was holding his shirt wrapped it around Greg's eyes.

"Guess who, Amigo," the local Mexican chanted.

What the hell kind of criminals are these guys anyway, Lisa wonders?

Greg stood up to shake hands with both men. "We've got some business to attend Babe. If you're going shopping, don't leave this block. It gets kinda nasty back there. Oh, and by the way, don't eat the food. You'll be sick for at least four or five days."

A look of fear covered Lisa's white face. "You're not going to leave me here all by myself, are you?"

"You'll be fine Babe. This area's safe enough," Greg said with a reassuring smile.

"When it's light out," one of the locals snickered, followed by a sinister laugh.

"Besides, I'll be back in ten minutes or so," Greg added, "I just have to go with these men to buy something."

Lisa watched in disbelief as Greg walked off the patio and down the sidewalk toward the alley with the two men. They disappeared behind a grungy road-side shop. Lisa passed up uneasy on the fast track to panic.

"I can't believe he left me here by myself." She anxiously dug through her purse and pulled out her phone. Then she slouched down behind her menu and started typing.

"Holy crap! Greg speaks fluent Spanish. I think he's buying something, I hope it's for me. Or maybe we're here for his work. This looks like a great place for a drug bust, over and out."

She clicks "share" and just like that her latest update appears on Facebook. Lisa took a quick peek over the top of her menu and saw Greg walking back up the alley by himself.

"Hurry your ass up, I've got to pee something awful," Lisa yelled.

Greg fought his way back through the lunch crowd carrying a small brown bag.

"What's in the bag, Honey," Lisa asked. "And more importantly, is it for me?"

"Bag," Greg smiled and held it behind his back. "I don't see a bag!"

"Come on," Lisa pulled on his arm. "I can't wait another second or I'll explode!"

"It's a surprise Babe," Greg teased while holding the bag up over her head. "You'll have to wait until we get back to Pittsburgh for this one."

"You suck," Lisa whined while she stood fidgeting. "But I mean it; I really have to pee badly!"

Greg does a quick scan of the area and saw a group of unsavory looking locals scurrying about. Then he heard the sound of a kid screaming something derogatory about the sexy white girl in Spanish and saw a half dozen teenager boys staring at Lisa.

"Maybe we ought to wait 'til we get back to the resort Babe," Greg suggested. "I don't think this place is very safe."

# Chapter 6

**(3:45 PM Monday, June 28)** Kevin sat at his desk staring at the latest signed contract, one that the board of directors will never get the choice to approve or reject. As he slid it into the file folder and filed it in the file drawer with all the others, he heard the painful sound alerting him to the arrival of a new email. The clock on his computer slowly counted off every excruciating minute and with the touch of his index finger to the mouse he found a new list of foreclosures he'll need to start processing tomorrow. The days seem to drag on forever yet I never seem to get caught up with my work, how in the hell can this be?

Finally, the clock changed from three fifty-nine to four o'clock. It's about damn time. He rolled back from the desk and slowly dragged his ass out of the chair. He looked around wondering if this was going to be his last week inside this cubicle. Kevin shuffled his way down the hall toward the elevator. He hesitated every so often glancing into a few specific cubes. As he observed each of his so-called friends preparing to leave for the day he tried to bring to mind one good memory about each of them. I'm sure going to miss seeing Lauren every day, especially seeing her homemade cookies. And Jess, God I loved when she would stop by and give me a back massage, even if it only lasted a few minutes. But probably not Vic, he's always been a bit annoying and his freaking breath would drive away a skunk.

Strolling through the lobby, Kevin paused just long enough to admire the five hand-painted portraits of the bank's founders. I wonder how those men would feel about the greedy actions of their progeny.

Would they be proud or disapprove? Kevin turned around and high-tailed it out of there when he heard Diane's voice. "Uggg…" I'm pretty sure I won't miss that bitch, or Jack, and definitely not Dumb and Dumber over there. Each and every one of them has been a thorn up my ass at one time or another. Who am I kidding? They can all go screw themselves. I'm not going to miss any of these people, or the shit they put me through!

Kevin opened the door of his '03 Sonata, climbed in and considered his options as he backed out of the parking space. At some point they might be looking for volunteers for early retirement. They'll need to make room for the others. Maybe I should try going over Diane's head and talk to the Vice President. I'm sure I can make some kind of deal with him. I'm less than five years away from qualifying for something like that anyway.

Kevin raced up Route 28, knowing he doesn't have a lot of time to pick up Mark at the daycare and still make it to the field one hour before game time. He called Tom from SDC to bring him up to date on the progress of the loan. "This is Kevin. I just wanted to reassure you that everything is right on schedule and I will stay on this until it's voted on and passed by the board. Thanks Tom, I'll talk to you later." Fortunately no one picked up so he was able to leave a message in Tom's voice mail. Kevin shut off his phone thinking the best course of action might be to avoid answering any questions. Considering that it usually takes the board at least two weeks to decide in most cases, it would probably be best if Tom wasn't able to reach him. Kevin looked up at the sixth green light he'd hit in a row and blew his guardian angel a kiss of gratitude as he raced through the intersection.

Kevin picked Mark up from daycare and hurried to the field. He swung the Sonata into the crowded parking lot at Plum's baseball complex trying to avoid all the ten year old boys scurrying about. He snagged the baseball bag from the inside the trunk and swung it around Mark's shoulder and neck. As Mark began his race to the dugout, Kevin latched onto the bag and held it just long enough to give him a few words of encouragement.

"This team is going to try to intimidate you guys by throwing inside," Kevin explained. "So step in close to the plate... that way you can either get hit by the pitch or you can turn on the ball and drive it over the left field fence."

"Dad, what did you say intimidate means again?"

"They're just going to try to scare you," Kevin said while looking Mark in the eyes. "And you're not going to let them right?" Then he pointed in the direction of the visitor's dugout where Manager Ron was waiting and sent him on his way.

Kevin pulled a lawn chair and his cooler out of the trunk and began reviewing his early retirement options again. There's no way they're going to give me any special treatment. That's not how it worked when the other divisions got sliced up. I'm probably just fooling myself; I'm destined for the unemployment line. He drug his chair and cooler through the gravel parking lot, trying to dodge all the cars being driven by the frantic parents who knew they were running late. He passed the concession stand and saw it, his sanctuary, just beyond the centerfield wall. It's amazing how every bad thought temporarily fades away with just the simple smell of freshly cut grass, the sound of a little round ball slapping into a leather glove or the sight of ten year old boys throwing the ball to warm up their arms.

A smile comes to Kevin's face as he settles into his chair. Maybe it's the hot summer night, relaxing in my chair with my feet up on my cooler and a cold beverage in my hand; all of this with no one around to bother me and no thoughts of work. Either way, it's very therapeutic.

Kevin's reverie was shattered by the sharp sound of a familiar voice cutting through the sounds of cars crunching through the gravel parking lot.

"Come on Fourteen you need to catch the ball," James yelled from the concession stand area as he picked up the ball and threw it back to one of the ball players. "You boys are ten years old now. You have to catch the ball even while you're just warming up!"

"You might want to watch what you say to that particular player," Kevin whispered to James as soon as he got close enough. "Remember, his father is the manager this year!"

"Yeah, I know, and he's just as bad a ballplayer as his son," James grumbled. "And I'm sure he'll be batting at the top of the lineup, playing third base and pitching every fourth game!" James paused for a minute while set up his chair. "So that gives me every right to bitch!"

James McKnight, or should I say my best friend and neighbor James, has a couple of things going for him Kevin thought while watching his son Mark take batting practice. First of all, he never has to go to work again because he's a self-made millionaire. Second, his wavy black hair, his lean, muscular six foot four inch body and playful personality is apparently every woman's dream. Add to that he's a scratch golfer. Plus his wife is exceptionally hot and she has a great job as our local Magistrate. Alright, James has it all. Kevin watched as Mark took his last swing, driving the third ball in a row over the left field fence. No, he thought, James is missing just one thing, the most important thing. Kevin smirked as he laughed out loud. His son had the *second* most homeruns and the *second* highest batting average on the team last year.

James kicked Kevin's chair trying to get his attention. "What in the hell do you have to smile about," he asked.

Kevin's smile quickly evaporated as he mumbled in reply, "Yeah, you're right."

James handed Kevin two over-size travel coffee mugs. "Alright, let's hear it," he glanced over at Kevin who was currently whimpering like a lost puppy dog. "What did you do this time?"

Kevin pulled out a beer and carefully poured it into a mug. "Well, I really think I went too far this time. I shoved my foot so far in my mouth that I think I can taste my knee cap, and I'm not sure, but I think I might be looking for a new job this time tomorrow!"

James hesitated a moment, "Go on..."

"Honestly, I just don't understand what she's waiting for. Why the hell doesn't she just get it over with and fire me? She acts as if it's a big game to her, just sitting in her office all high and mighty. I can't stand the sight of that bitch! I know she's…"

"Hold on…" James threw his hands up. "Nice catch, Seven," he yelled out to his son who's playing centerfield. "Let me guess Kev, you drank too much at lunch and killed your boss."

"Close, maybe a little too close. Me killing Diane, hmmm…" Kevin pondered. "I like the sound of that. If there was ever someone I was capable of killing, it would be her."

"Shit, you kill someone? I don't think so," James stood up trying to get his son's attention. "Move up, Seven, this kid can't hit it that far!" He sat back down and continued, "What were we talking about? Oh yeah, if you do kill her, or kill anyone else for that matter, I don't what to know about it. Remember my wife's a judge."

"Nice stop Ten," Kevin yelled across the outfield as he watched his son throw the ball from short to first base. "Really? A judge? Yeah, right! She judges over the real hardened criminals, like the ones who run stop signs. Or what about those nasty kids who sneak out of school when no one's looking? A judge," Kevin laughed, "your wife is no different than my boss. They both get off by pushing men around. They're both man-haters!"

"It sounds to me like you have a thing for your boss," James suggested.

"The only thing I have for Diane is a burning desire to smash her face into the corner of my desk!"

"Oh yeah, you've got it bad," James continued trying to antagonize Kevin. "You know there's a fine line between love and hate, and you're all over it."

"I know that I hate you," Kevin took a long drink of his beer then handed the other mug to James. "This is what it's all about." He lifted the cup for a toast, "To the new tournament season, may every game end with a W."

"Here, here!" James took a drink. "Speaking of the new season, did you get a chance to go over the new schedule and the liberal crap your favorite manager spewed out in his latest email attachment?"

Kevin watched as Mark swung and missed a pitch thrown right over the middle of the plate. He jumped up against the fence with a look of frustration. "Come on Ten! Hit the fff... Hit the ball!"

"That's alright Honey," Kevin heard one of the mother's shout from the bleacher seats on the first base line. "Nice try Sweetie!"

"Listen to those women," Kevin groaned. "They're ten year old boys, not freaking babies!" He turned to James. "What did that Num-nut have in the email?"

"You know, if you'd use your BlackBerry for... oh, I don't know, maybe something other than keeping your son's stats," James said sarcastically, "then you might have a clue as to what's actually going on around here. This is just a scrimmage. You do realize that, don't you?"

Kevin pulled out his phone and wiped the dust off of it, "Am I sensing a little jealously in your voice?"

"Your son hit one more homerun than mine last year! And their batting averages were separated by less than ten points!"

"Just making sure you noticed, Dear James," Kevin scrolled down through his emails while drinking his beer. About half way down the page he saw an urgent email from Lisa. The subject read, 'Kev, help please!' He muttered to himself, "What did that moron do now?" Then he continued down through the list looking for the email containing the new baseball schedule. Eventually though his morbid curiosity got the better of him and he clicked on Lisa's email and began to read it.

"Shit... Holy Shit! What the...," Kevin searched for a rational thought. "Lisa, where in the hell are you? Why didn't you have this stuff all pulled and prepped for Corporate?" He took a long swig of beer, and then calmly started typing.

**From:** Kevin O'Donnell

**Sent:** Monday, May 13, 2010 6:23 PM

**To:** Lisa.Hartman@PittsburghBankTrust.com

**Subject:** RE: Kev, help please!

Lisa, fill me in on exactly what you did so far and what we need to do before the next meeting. I think they're having another merger meeting tomorrow. If this information isn't disclosed before the merger is finalized we could get sued. You've put yourself and everyone above you in jeopardy. Send me a list of what I need and who to pass it on to. I'll start pulling what files I can now and start preparing them. You're going to owe me big time. Kevin

Kevin moved the arrow above the send button. He sat there, staring at the email he'd just typed, his thumb poised to click... waiting... wondering...

"What the hell am I thinking," Kevin muttered as he carefully selected the option to delete.

James grabbed Kevin's arm to get a better view of his BlackBerry. "Did you get to it yet?"

Kevin jerked his arm away, "Quit that you jackass! I'm trying to get some work done. Something you'd know nothing about."

James raised his beer up in a victory salute, "Now who sounds jealous?"

"Come on Ten, hit it out here," Kevin hollered across the field to his son.

"Nice swing dear," the sound of a screechy voice cut its way from the dugout to the outfield. "Good job at fouling it off!"

"Can you tell which dumb ass lady is screaming that crap to my kid," Kevin asked.

"That would be our beloved manager, Coach Ron."

Oh yeah, Coach Ron's email, Kevin thought as he pulled out his BlackBerry again. Let's see, we've got a scrimmage tomorrow; nothing wrong with that. "Oh no, here it is! Why in the hell are we still rotating players? Doesn't he understand? This isn't in-house baseball, these games count," Kevin hollered back at James as he began pacing back and forth along the outfield fence. "Why in hell are the boys still splitting time?"

"Told you so," James snapped back sarcastically.

"These boys are ten now," Kevin groused. "The parents need to get used to the better kids playing more innings!"

"And in the more critical positions," James added.

"Ron's not capable of running a top-notch team like this one. His in-house teams are pathetic every year which proves he's incapable of evaluating talent, and equally incapable of managing a group of boys."

"All I'm saying is you'd better get used to it," James smirked. "I told you he thinks like a liberal. The next thing you know we'll all be paying extra to cover the kids whose parents can't afford the uniforms and the tournament entry fees. You know what they say about taking a village to raise our children!"

"Hey, watch what you say," Kevin barked out, "that might be my son soon."

"Well, the fact that you choose to donate all your extra money to the lovely and talented girls of Gloria's doesn't exactly mean you can't afford to pay," James replied. "You just need a good woman to keep you from wondering too far off the path."

"That reminds me... Can you take Mark back to your house after the game tonight," Kevin begged.

"Hillary was right," James said. "My village is already raising your child."

"I have a meeting, at the club. No skirt chasing, I swear."

"Yeah, I get it all right. A meeting," James sighed, "that's what they've been calling it since the caveman days!"

"I'm not going to hear the words 'chasing' or 'skirts' when I get back am I," Kevin questioned.

"Calm down. We'll take Mark back with us. Just be back by nine o'clock this time," James cautioned Kevin. "You know Kara's policy; you don't want to be on the wrong side of her bench again."

## Chapter 7

**(7:00 PM Monday, June 28)** What was once foremost in the minds of half the men in the Pittsburgh area is now the second or even third thoughts of just a few locals. Gloria's opened as one of the hottest new strip bars on Pittsburgh's Northside, but that was more than twenty years ago. These days, the smell of stale beer and sweat linger throughout every inch of this once fine establishment. Lost are the shattered hopes and dreams of every young girl that danced under the massive disco ball that hangs as a reminder of what once was.

Twenty years of abuse from drunks and druggies has turned Kevin's playhouse into a dump where now only the bravest souls will hang out. He wonders were twenty years worth of beautiful girls went and why he couldn't find one of them to call his own. Yes, Kevin could literally hide out from the rest of the world there. And sure, no one bothers him here, no one except maybe the occasional stripper looking for a quick twenty. Sometimes Kevin lets his mind drift into a fantasy world, a world where he races home from work every day to spend time with a loving wife, or at least *a* wife. Here at Gloria's, all he needs is a cold beer in his hand and a seat at his favorite corner table. There's something comforting about the soft music playing in the background with the occasional beautiful girl dancing across the old wooden stage. What would life be like with a wife? He's not so sure about that thought. Here, Kevin never has to worry about seeing someone he knows, or more importantly someone he doesn't like. If he were married, he would always see someone he knew, and then there's also the possibility of it being someone he didn't like.

Kevin took in the shabby exterior as he approached the building. This place has changed so much over the years, a lot of change, maybe even more than I have. Twenty years ago, I had to stand in line, just for the privilege of paying a cover fee so I could walk through those doors. Nineteen years and fifty weeks later you could just walk in and sit anywhere you damn well pleased. But now... Now I know what they mean by 'things going full circle' Kevin thought to himself as he once again found a parking lot completely filled with Harleys, the bike of choice for the new customer base that *She* has attracted to Gloria's.

"This is absolute bullshit!" Kevin yelled at the top of his lungs.

Feeling a bit frustrated, Kevin drove his Sonata around back onto the gravel parking lot. As he glances over at the clock in his car, he realizes that he'll only have one short hour with her. He rushed to the front door only to find out the bar was at its one hundred person capacity and thanks to the fire marshal he would have to wait in the front room until six people left.

Kevin glanced up at photos lining the walls of the small lobby and his mind wandered. As he mentally reviewed the last few years of his life, he wondered if there was anything new and exciting left for him in the future. It's sad to think it takes a miracle, or something close to it, just to surprise me anymore Kevin thought, as he stared down an empty flight of steps. The biggest bitch about surprises at my age is, when one finally occurs, very rarely is it a pleasant surprise like a new puppy dog. Those surprises are saved for cute little fifteen year old freckled-face girls. I get the ones set aside for forty-something year old men. You know, the ones like finding out you only have a hemorrhoid instead of colon cancer. It's probably a surprise worth drinking a beer over, as long as you're not sitting down.

Just two short weeks ago, I had a pretty strong feeling that these two new girls at Gloria's were something special, but I quickly learned that one brought with her a slice of hell. When you've spent nearly your entire adult life in a strip bar, pretty girls are a dime a dozen. But these two new girls were so different, in so many ways. The One is almost certainly an angel sent straight from heaven. From the way she looks into my eyes when we talk to the way she swings her hips when she's walking away, simply divine. The other, well let's just say she's a little more like hell. From the way she acts around the other men to the large following of riff-raff and low-lifes she brought along with her from that other club. It still amazes me how a couple of new girls can change the fortunes of a hole-in-the-wall place like this, seemingly overnight.

"Sir, you're good to go in now. Sir!" some twenty-something year old kid said as he pushed Kevin from behind.

Kevin rushed forward and slapped a five into the bouncer's hand.

"Whoa! It's ten now!" the tall, obese man shouted.

"Sorry!" Kevin yelled back as he turned to place the second five in the man's hand. Another reason to hate the new girl he thought.

A chill ran down Kevin spine when he reached the bottom step and gazed across the room, the room he still considered his sanctuary. Kevin stared at the mob of unruly men and wondered if he'll ever find the seat he wanted. He looked over by the bar and saw Dave, one of the bouncers working the floor tonight. Dave gave Kevin 'the nod' then pointed to her section. Kevin smiled back, nodding his head up and down like a love-sick school boy. As he began his attempt to cross the room he finds an empty chair at a table with two other guys.

Kevin grabbed the chair and swiftly scanned the room until he found an open spot in her section. He quickly hoisted it up over his head so as to not bump anyone while continuing on with the second half of his journey across the room.

A rowdy group of intoxicated men immediately began heckling him. "Down in front! You Dumb Ass!"

Kevin jerked the chair down slightly tapping a large bald head that was attached to a man dressed in black Harley Davison gear and tattoos covering both arms. "What the hell is wrong with you Pal?" Kevin heard as he quickly grabbed the back of the chair and began 'steering' it around the tables and people as if he were Jeff Gordon on a road course. He finally reached his destination on the other side of the room then slowly slid his chair forward between a table and the wall, all the way up against the stage. He turned to look at the open path left behind him. The perfect spot, he thought only one way in and one way out. Now it's just a matter of time.

A hostess stopped behind Kevin, tapping him on the shoulder. He quickly turned around in anticipation, but it wasn't Her. A dark-haired girl with creamy white skin wearing a gray Stetson and black leather knee-high stiletto boots with very little clothing in between crouched down next to him. She leaned in real close and tried to entice him into buying a Jell-O shooter or perhaps something special she could only show him in one of the private back rooms. Kevin politely declined and hastily waved her away. Then he turned back toward the stage, patiently waiting for the gates of heaven to open and release his new found angel.

She's the One. No other girl will ever do again. Kevin thought about her long flowing hair surrounding her lovely face with that million dollar smile, which magically appears every time he hands her a five. Oh yeah, and the way her perfectly rounded butt filled out those tight satin shorts. It's hard not to think about that all day.

Suddenly Kevin feels it, the gentle touch of a warm hand on his shoulder, a finger softly brushing against the side of his neck. Chills run throughout his entire body as his chest tightens up from the overwhelming rush of sizzling hot blood to his heart. Slowly he turns his head, trying to smile a perfect smile for her.

"You are such an asshole!" Kevin roared as he slapped Dave's hand away from his shoulder.

Dave threw both hands in the air as he stepped back laughing. "Sorry Kev, but you deserved that! I just came over to let you know she left early today. I tried to tell you but you were so focused on getting set up that you misread my hand signals."

Kevin stood up and tried to step around his chair. "You suck! You told me she'd be here tonight! I want my ten dollars back!"

"Just sit your ass down, Sunshine," Dave giggled as he shoved Kevin back toward the stage and into his seat. "I'm just screwing with you. She's here somewhere; I'll go see if I can find her."

Kevin stood back up on his toes searching for his special girl but all he could see was large groups of men surrounding each beautiful girl on the floor.

With no sign of his own personal angel Kevin reached into his jacket, pulled out his BlackBerry and then sat back down. With the stock market bouncing around like a super ball he decided to spend his spare time checking on his portfolio. Scrolling through the stock ticker symbols he saw that Pittsburgh Bank & Trust dropped another five percent so he quickly switched over to his Facebook page and began scanning his news feed. He quickly saw that Lisa had posted some new pictures. Hmmm, interesting Kevin thought. He clicked on the picture to open her new 'photo album'. The first one is of Lisa wearing a bright blue bikini, lying on a hammock, on what appears to be a gorgeous white sand beach. "Damn you girl!" Kevin hollered out as he clicked on the next picture and saw her dragon tattoo. The tail begins between her breasts, the main body of the dragon covers her tight abs and the head stops at her navel then the dragon's flames disappeared under her bikini bottom. Too bad the screen of his BlackBerry is so small.

"Okay Lisa, there ain't no beaches in Pittsburgh, so where in the hell are you?" Kevin asked no one in particular. He began scrolling through the photos until he found the perfect one. And there it was, the Holy Grail of Stupidity. It was a postcard worthy scene, the blue skies, the palm trees and the pearly white beach. But the highlight of this particular photo was Lisa rubbing sunscreen on the back of some hot new stud that was lying face down on a beach bed with a five star resort in the background, definitely somewhere in the Caribbean. Just uploaded via *Facebook for BlackBerry* this very morning, absolutely perfect he thought.

Kevin cringed when the crowd erupted into cheers and cat calls then his chair got shoved from behind by an overzealous drunk. So he scanned the room again to see what was causing all the commotion. His heart came to a complete stop when he caught a glimpse of her standing near the edge of the stage then she disappeared. Slowly she made her entrance from behind the curtain. Kevin shut down his BlackBerry and slid it back into his coat pocket. The crowd began chanting Roxy's name so loud he could barely hear himself think. She turned and walked straight toward Kevin, his heart beating out of control. The palms of his hands turned clammy while his shirt became wet with sweat.

Man, I love everything about this place Kevin thought. He watched as she vanished into the crowd and knew it would only be a matter of time. Kevin's eyes welled up with tears to the point he couldn't see the girls dancing on stage.

Just then, she leaned over next to Kevin, her soft lips nearly touching his ear lobe and the sweet scent of her perfume overtook the raunchy odor of cigarette smoke. He could feel her warm breath on the back of his neck.

"What can I get for you?" she whispered softly into his ear.

When Kevin turned around he found his lips mere inches from the lips of his dream girl. He tried to speak but his bottom jaw was seemingly locked in place and his tongue felt as if it had swollen to twice its normal size. So he held up two fingers as he tried to smile.

She crouched down alongside him with her left hand on his right shoulder then she leaned around him placing her right hand on his upper thigh. "Two? You want two of something?" she asked in a husky voice that was as sweet as it was erotic.

Kevin slowly bobbed his head up and down.

Okay. How about I get you... a double shot of Absolut Vodka? Does that sound good to you?"

Kevin slowly nodded his head yes while staring deeply into her chocolate brown eyes. Then he felt a little twitch, followed by another, and then another as his lips continued twitching until his face broke into an all-out smile, the perfect smile.

"You're just too cute," she whispered in his ear.

Kevin watched her walk away then slowly turned back around. Short of breath he desperately tried to swallow around the lump left in his throat. After what seemed like only one short minute, Roxy finished her act and the crowd started to quiet down and spread out. This may be my last chance to get this close to her tonight Kevin thought.

Coco placed her hand on his shoulder and softly tugged on it.

Kevin quickly turned around. "Dave you son of... Oh sorry Coco..."

"That'll be four dollars, Sir." Coco requested.

Kevin needed his fix, just one more time. So he looked up and leaned toward her with his hand next to his ear. "I'm sorry," he shrugged his shoulders. "How much is it?"

Coco placed the drink on the rail separating the seats from the stage with her right hand while wrapping her left arm around Kevin's back and whispered in his ear again.

Kevin took a long slow deep breath, the smell of her perfume was intoxicating and his mind began racing out of control. His hands began to tingle from the lack of blood flow as he clumsily attempted to pull out a five to hand it to her. He held it halfway out then said the same thing he always says. "Keep the change, Coco." As he watched her walk away only one thought filled his mind. God, there's nothing better than being cornered by a smoking hot girl.

Kevin saw Dave up by the bar, so he held up his shot in a silent toast to him then drank it in one long swallow. "Holy shit! What'd that crazy bitch bring me to drink?" he called out to Dave.

At just over six foot tall, packed with an abundance of muscle that's only partially disguised under a thin layer of fat, Dave Jones is one of Gloria's more intimidating bouncers. He hasn't worked here very long, but he already seems to know most everyone that walks through the doors. From the girls that beguile the men with their seductive moves to the johns that throw their hard earned paychecks at them, Dave knows them all. That's the life of a bouncer, knowing every little thing about every girl that works here, including their past history with men, all for the sake of helping him to protect them. It's easy to presume that Dave's dream job might have been to be a private investigator because he has a knack for finding things out about a person without them even knowing they're being interrogated. There's a rumor going around the bar that Dave used to be a CIA agent, but he was forced to resign because he had broken the unwritten rule by killing more than fifteen civilians in one year.

Dave walked over and sat in one of the many open chairs around Kevin. "Well Kev, was it a good night?"

"The best night ever," Kevin enthusiastically said as he turned his chair around so he's facing Dave. "So, come on, tell me everything."

Dave shrugged his shoulders. "What?"

"You can't hold back on me now," Kevin implored. "I'm finally getting somewhere with her. What kind of juicy info did you find out about My Girl?"

"Well Honey, her full name is Coco Chanel," Dave giggled as he trickled out the information. "She came over with Roxy from a strip bar called Omar's. I think it's located in the South Hills area. She's thirty-one and, most importantly, she's single. Did you ask her out yet?"

"No, not yet," Kevin snapped.

Dave shook his head he looked down at Kevin. "Well then, I'm sorry to say this Cowboy, but she's definitely not your girl."

"Yeah, she's not mine yet." Kevin thanked Dave by sliding a five across the table. "Sometimes, the way you talk just scares the crap out of me. If it wasn't for the fact that I've seen you with some pretty wild women, I would swear you were... you know. Not that there's anything wrong with that."

"What?"

"Ahhh, just forget it. You just creep me out sometimes." Kevin pulled out his phone, checked the time and then abruptly stood up. "It's already after eight. I've got to get out of here or I won't get to spend any time with my son tonight. Did you find out if Coco's working tomorrow?"

Dave stood up and followed Kevin toward the door. The soles of their shoes stuck as they walk across the beer-soaked floor. "Yep, she works from three to eight," Dave answered.

Kevin threw on his jacket. "In that case I'll see you tomorrow. Oh, and do me favor, try to find something that might help me get a date with her. Like maybe where she likes to eat, or how about a new movie she'd like to go see?" Kevin paused at the bottom of the steps then looked back at the decrepit bar still filled with dozens of old drunk men and thought... Man, I love this bar.

Driving home Kevin sent Mark a text message asking him to be waiting in the front yard in hopes he can avoid speaking with his neighbor Kara. But when he pulled into his driveway the whole group was sitting out on their front porch. Mark with a big smile, Kara with her arms folded and an irritated look on her face and James with a look of utter exhaustion.

"I give up," Kevin groaned to Kara as he hugged his son. "What did I do wrong now?"

Kara looked pointedly at the slender gold Rolex on her wrist. "Working late again Kevin?" Kara bitched. "It seems to me that entertaining clients at strip bars should be more of a thing of the past. I wonder if your bank still condones that type of barbaric behavior."

"It's only part of my job I still enjoy doing," Kevin replied calmly, trying to make a joke.

"Well, as your neighbor and president of the home owners association, it's part of my job to inform you that your lawn hasn't been cut in at least two weeks! That's a clear violation of rule number sixty-two. I should turn you in but I'm won't, not this time. I think your son has suffered enough embarrassment by seeing his father standing in front of a judge just last year. You do remember standing in my court room, don't you?"

"You never let me forget, Kara," Kevin responded in a dejected voice.

"Then cut your grass! Oh and here's another thought, maybe you could spend a little more time with your son? That would be something new!" Then she took her son's hand and stormed into her house.

James stood up and followed Kevin and Mark back to their house.

Kevin pulled out two beers and hand one to James. "You know, James, she's the poster-child for why some guys never get married."

"Don't let her get to you, Kev," James said as he returned his unopened to the refrigerator. "Any luck getting a date with the new girl?"

Kevin cracked open his beer. "No, not yet. These things take time, you know. You wouldn't understand because you've been married for over ten years."

"Yeah well, don't take too long," James suggested sarcastically. "Or someone else might sneak in and steal her away from you."

"We talked a lot... Well, we at least talked."

"Good night Kev."

"Hey! Did we score any more runs?"

"No, we lost by two," James moaned.

Kevin sat down at his breakfast bar replaying the past weeks' worth of conversations he had with Coco. It's funny how you can spend the entire afternoon with an old friend talking about anything and everything, yet later that day you can't recall a single word that was spoken. But when you meet someone new and exciting, you can talk with that person for what seems like hours, yet maybe it's only a few minutes of time. Weeks later you're still catching yourself reliving the moments, from every syllable spoken to the multitude of expressions that cross her endearing freckled face, from the silky sound of her voice to the sweet scent of her perfume. My friends contend that I'm just being obsessive. I'd like to think it's more about finally living.

# Chapter 8

**(6:40 AM Tuesday, June 29)** In this new and challenging world of finance where it seems that the banks' CEOs and upper management spend more time behind bars than their counter parts, the criminals that rob them, one has to wonder where it all went wrong. Kevin broods while sitting in bumper to bumper traffic on his way to work. I look around and all I see are people pointing fingers at me. The government wants to blame the loan officers for pushing bad loans through while the media censures the members of the board for turning a blind eye. And the foolish people, the general public, who believe the only reason banks exist is to give them fifty dollars when they're short on cash, claim there's a flaw in the system of checks and balances between the two. Well, that just wasn't the case at PBT. I helped develop the system we use today. This so called system wouldn't exist without me and it was damn near flawless. When implemented correctly there's only a three point eight percent chance of a loan failing. With about one hundred delinquent loans showing up in the fourth quarter and fears that our percentage might climb into double digits before the end of the year, we held off putting dozens of defaults on the books. We assumed the economy would come around and we'd find someplace to hide our mistakes the following year. Holy shit! Were we ever wrong! It now appears as if our failure rate this year might top twenty percent, a big difference in anyone's book. In the business world it's easy to blame everyone around you. Alright, in this case, there's absolutely some merit to that argument. Most of the people I work with at PBT are as dumb as rocks. So that does make them the easiest targets to blame.   But there's a rather large distinction between outright ignorance and simply closing your eyes while you fill your pockets, no, make that filling your briefcases with hundred dollar bills.  I could take the easy way out and blame myself, but that's not going to happen. There no way they can pin this all on me.   I did everything that was asked of me and then some.   I was told to write up as many loan contracts as I could and that's exactly what I did.  Her majesty, Diane, and the elitist board members were supposed to evaluate each and every loan that passed before them before giving their stamp of approval.

Kevin eased his Sonata into a particularly tight parking space and edged his front bumper up close to the convertible BMW that sat in the space in front of him.  He thought about Lisa and what a rookie business mistake she made.  Skipping out on work to extend the weekend is one thing, but doing it during the most crucial time of this merger is just a sign of her immaturity.  …And for what?  …An extra day on the beach.  The beach…  Man did she look sweet, that dark blue bikini contrasting her lightly tanned body and the way her short blond hair frames her baby face.  And that tattoo, oh dear God, Kevin sat there with his eyes glazed over staring straight through the Beamer as if it wasn't even there.  Diane's traveled to Mexico recently.  She sure would have looked good in that photo with Lisa, maybe rubbing some oil on Lisa's tight shoulders, and maybe she spills a little too much on her back as a single bead rolls ever so slowly down the center of her back, disappearing under the bottom half of that bikini.  But Diane can't leave it there.  So she slowly slides her hand between the swimsuit and Lisa's perfectly shaped bottom, rubbing ever so softly trying hard not to wake her up.  When Lisa does awaken she stays perfectly still in hopes that Diane doesn't stop.  She tries to contain her emotions but softly moans as she pulls her body closer to Diane's.  Slowly Lisa slides up arching her body ever so close to Diane's and with hands clasped tightly together their lips softly…

Kevin is shaken from his stupor when a horn began blowing somewhere close by.  He quickly scanned the parking lot and saw a tall thin man with long black hair and sunglasses stepping out of the BMW right in front of him.  The man pointed at Kevin with an angry look on his face so he quickly turned the key and held the power window button while hitting the lock button.

The huge man leaned down to look in the window of Kevin's car. "What the hell were you staring at?" The man began yelling at him through the glass. "And wipe that silly grin of your face!"

Kevin glanced up with a blank look on his face, paused for a moment and then uttered the first thing that came to mind. "Nothing Sir," Kevin chirped while blinking his eyes owlishly. "I'm legally blind." Then he slouched down into his seat and turned his head hoping the man would leave.

Kevin sat in his car wondering how soon he could expect to see Lisa's pretty little face at the office again and if he'll have enough time to implement his plan. He looked at the clock on his dashboard and realized he had a few more minutes of free time, so he went over the plan again in his head. Slowly he regained his composure and emerged from the car with a new sense of confidence. He strutted through the lobby laughing and saying hello to everyone he saw. He even stopped to speak with a few colleagues he disliked, shaking hands and telling them jokes. No more looking down at my shoes and mumbling for me he thought.

Kevin sat down at his desk and fired up his computer. He decided the first thing he needed to do was check to see if there were any new emails from Diane or Lisa. He opened Outlook and saw Lisa's name at the top of the list.

**From:** Lisa Hartman

**Sent:** Monday, May 13, 2010 6:23 PM

**To:** Kevin.O'Donnell@PittsburghBankTrust.com

**Subject:** Kevin… I'm still looking for help!

I hope you got the email I sent Monday. I'm a little concerned because I didn't hear from you. I also hope you were able to finish and hand in the paperwork on time. Thanks! See you Wednesday… XOXO Lisa

Then Kevin noticed a new email from Diane with the subject line 'Meeting'. Kevin smirked; maybe her majesty came to her senses and decided the contract was worthy enough to present to the board. *I did make some awesome points. And to think, I was worried that she may have mistaken my passion for insanity during my blow up yesterday.*

Kevin clicked on 'Meeting' only to find it was a reminder about the emergency board meeting that he needed to attend right now. He reached for his briefcase full of denied contracts, his mind racing. *Holy shit! Could this be my guardian angel looking out for me, or is it the devil playing his damn games with me again?*

Kevin rolled his chair back and stood up slowly. He picked up his jacket and shrugged into it. Exiting the cubicle, he paused to straighten his tie, glancing down the long hallway leading to the conference room. Before Kevin could take another step he spotted Diane talking to her secretary Jan so he stepped back into his cube. He waited a few minutes before sticking his head out of the opening to make certain the coast was clear. *Well, I guess it's time to start Operation Eliminate Lisa, there's no turning back now.*

On his way down the hall Kevin stopped to chat with Jan. "I know you're really busy, but I need to go over a few items with Lisa before we can finalize the foreclosure she was working on." Kevin asked. "If you can spare a few minutes, would you mind trying to find out where she's hiding? Maybe check her Facebook page; she tends to update it throughout the day."

Kevin knows Jan's personality quite well. She's the banks number one busybody which means she won't stop until she finds every little detail about Lisa's whereabouts. Fortunately, the way these meetings usually run she's probably got most of the morning.

Kevin opened the door and entered a conference room overflowing with Armani and Ann Taylor suits. He quietly surveyed the room then lowered his head. He quickly realized there were way too many people in attendance for the standard board meeting. As he walked towards his chair, he took another swift glance around and saw a lot of faces he didn't recognize. *I wasn't issued an agenda for this morning's meeting; maybe I won't even have an opportunity to implement my plan.* He took his seat to the left of Diane and wrote on a scrap paper 'I'm sorry about everything,' then slid it over in front of her. Diane grabbed it out of his hand to read it. She crinkled it up and stuffed it into Kevin's coat pocket then sat staring straight ahead without otherwise acknowledging his existence.

After the Chairman made a long-winded introduction of the new faces coupled with an explanation for their presence, he continued along as if it were just another boring meeting. Kevin began to alter his plan as the meeting persisted but had trouble focusing on the task at hand because of the intoxicating scent of Diane's perfume. *I wonder if she wears it just to distract me.* Just then her bare leg brushed up against his right hand. He pulled it out from under the table and leaned in close to Diane.

"I hate these large meetings," Kevin whispered in a seductive tone. "They take too long and I'm jammed in with you oh so tightly."

Diane stuck her middle finger out against the bottom edge of the table until Kevin looked down to see it.

Kevin smiled briefly and then refocused his thoughts. *If I chicken out now, I may never get a better opportunity.* His resolve wavered back and forth.

The moment of truth finally arrived when they got to the commercial department. Diane rose to give her brief report before retaking her seat next to Kevin.

The Chairman stood up and asked if there was any other pertinent information that needed to be added to her report.

Kevin sat there paralyzed by fear as conflicting thoughts racing through his mind. Which were the right thoughts? He took a deep breath as he slowly stood up. Ahhh, the sweet smell of... damn that perfume! Sweat trickled down both sides of his face, and his legs felt like Jell-O.

"Good morning, my name is Kevin O'Donnell," he mumbled as his right hand twitched out of control. "I work in the commercial loan department under Diane." He glanced up and saw everyone watching him so he quickly looked back down. "I used to be in charge of drafting commercial loans. Now, because of circumstances beyond our control, I spend the majority of my days checking on loan defaults. This morning, while reviewing my current list of defaults, I compared it with the list that was handed in at yesterday's merger meeting and noticed a forty-five million dollar discrepancy. There's a loan which is currently two months late that needed to be added to the list. Upon further review, I discovered that most of the businesses have left the strip mall. I'm concerned that this information probably should have been disclosed at the meeting yesterday." Kevin flinched briefly when he felt a sharp object puncture his right thigh muscle, then he looked up and continued. "I can go over everything with Diane and help her get it ready before the next merger meeting." He grasped his leg as he quietly sat down.

The Vice President stood up and stared directly at Diane. "I want that file on my desk in one hour. And Diane, I'm also going to need a full report on how this got missed by close of business today."

Kevin lifted his head and scanned the room. He wanted to see if there were any reactions from his new co-workers. Kevin saw a sweet looking older lady with short black hair smiling at him so he smiled back at her. Then he glanced to her right and noticed *him* standing directly behind the Vice President, in front of the large picture window, the huge man who had intimidated him in the parking garage. Kevin closed his eyes and slouched down in his chair.

When the meeting ended, Kevin made certain he was the first one out of the room. He raced back to hide in his cubicle until the halls cleared out. As soon as he was certain the coast was clear, Kevin made his way up to Diane's office. He furtively glanced in while swiftly walking past her door. Diane was standing with her back to the door looking out the window. Kevin couldn't help wondering if maybe he was pushing his plan a little too hard. He wandered down toward the elevator until he saw the large man from the garage who had threatened him. Kevin quickly turned and raced back up the hallway to Diane's office only to be stopped by Jan.

"Kevin," Jan whispered loudly, "Kevin, what do you need?"

"What?" Kevin whispered back.

"Now is probably not the best time to bother Diane." Jan hissed. "Didn't you get the email I sent out?"

"Thanks for the heads up Jan!" Kevin whispered back as he quickly walked back to his cube to check his email.

Jan digging deep enough to find some incriminating photos on Lisa was a no brainer Kevin thought, I practically gave her that much. However, she clearly went a step or two beyond my expectations copying and editing two dozen pictures of Lisa's escapades from this past weekend. Showing her in some of the most seductive positions with Greg even made my blood boil a little. I wonder if she realized that the man in those photos was Diane's latest ex-boyfriend. But Jan crossed the line and never looked back when she added captions under each picture before sending them out to almost everyone on our floor.

Kevin sat there paralyzed by the photo of Lisa and her dragon tattoo with Jan's witty caption 'Where there's smoke there's fire Lisa'. An instant classic Kevin thought… Suddenly he remembered the project he had to finish for the VP, so Kevin grabbed his notes and ran down to Diane's office.

Diane turned around with tears still in her eyes and makeup running down the sides of her face. She glared at Kevin with a look that would scare the hell out of even the devil.

"I don't have time for your petty bullshit," Diane shrieked. "Get the hell out!"

"I tried to stop him!" Jan shouted in from the hall.

Kevin held up both hands stopping Diane and Jan. "I'm not sure what's going on here. What I am sure of is this; if we don't get this work finished and handed in soon we'll all have a reason to be in tears."

"This was your contract originally," Diane said as she turned back toward the window. "You know what needs to be done. I shouldn't have to hold your hand, go do your job." Then she turned toward Jan. "When Lisa shows up, send her in to see me immediately. Oh, and if you see that piece of shit Greg, call security immediately and make sure you let them know he may be armed."

Kevin raced back to his cube and stood there typing.

**From:** Kevin O'Donnell

**Sent:** Tuesday, May, 14 2010 11:54 AM

**To:** Lisa.Hartman@PittsburghBankTrust.com

**Subject:** Just got your email…

I'm working to smooth things out. I don't know anything about the first email… We had a mandatory emergency meeting, you should have been there. It was something to see, all those so called gentlemen and ladies yelling across the table at each other.

Kevin grabbed every paper he felt he needed to give to the VP plus the latest contract he was trying to get shoved through and started down the hall. He reached the VP's secretary in less than a minute and stood there trying to catch his breath. "My name is Kevin…"

"Sir, they've been waiting for you."

Kevin stood outside the door opening. "They? Who the hell is they?" he muttered aloud to himself. "I didn't know I was meeting a they."

The secretary put his hand on Kevin's shoulder pushing him forward. "Please, you must go in now."

Kevin entered the exceedingly spacious room. After fifteen plus years at PBT this was his inaugural trip to the big man's room and from what he could see in this slightly dark room it was just how he imagined it, from the smell of the mahogany desk to the wrap around bar with the small red and green neon lights. Then his eyes became locked on the beautiful stained glass window where the silhouette of two oversize men stood. The bright sunshine shot through the clear panels directly behind the men making them appear as if they were almost angels. But he knew better, they were probably a lot more like devils, devils just waiting for me to make a mistake he thought.

Kevin walked slowly toward them, trying to find that air of confidence he had earlier. Then he nearly tripped over his own feet, just managing to catch himself by grabbing onto a large bronze statue of Terry Bradshaw. He approached the enormous U-shaped desk and placed the two bundles of papers on it. Kevin glanced up to see the Vice President standing alongside the man who threatened to kill him earlier in the garage. Kevin made the mistake of muttered the first thing that entered his mind. "Oh shit!"

"Kevin is it?" the VP asked as he approached his desk. "I'd like to introduce you to my son, Johnny. He's going to be working here all summer, possibly in your department."

"No, no I've never ever seen him," Kevin mumbled while he fought back the urge to tap his right hand against the side of his face. "It's really nice to meet you sir."

"Yeah, we met in the parking garage," Johnny said with confidence as he pulled Kevin's twitching hand away from his face. "Sorry to hear about the whole not being able to see thing."

"Yes, the not seeing thing. I'm sure it'll get better, thank you." Kevin rested his right hand on the large stack of papers. "I have all the information you requested earlier from my department. I'm surprised that Lisa Hartman missed getting this info to Diane. I guess Lisa should've cut her trip short."

"Your bold move earlier today may have saved our bank from a very embarrassing situation." the VP suggested.

"Yes," Kevin said while looking down at his feet. "Thank you Sir." Kevin began tapping on the little bundle of papers. "I also have here copies of the latest contract I've been working on. I was hoping, if you have the time… Maybe we can try to get the board's approval, if they have a chance to review it."

"I like that idea, Kevin, is it?" The VP picked up the small bundle of papers and handed it to Johnny. "I think my son and I can work on this project together."

"This Lisa, she works in your department?" Johnny asked. "Has she been a problem in the past?"

"Lisa? Yes." Kevin said as he awkwardly executed a half-bow, half-wave maneuver while walking backwards out of the office. "Thank you, Sir."

Kevin slipped back to his cubicle, trying not to make eye contact with anyone. His goal was to lay low for the last three hours of the day, hoping that his plan will continue its destruction on Lisa's reputation.

# Chapter 9

**(5:00 PM Tuesday, June 29)** There are two types of wealthy people in this world. You have James who has more money than his family could ever spend in three life times, but he lives as if he's just another one of us white collar workers trying to survive in this unstable economy. Then there's the ass-hole who buys the last phase in our freaking plan, twenty-three lots at roughly a hundred thousand a lot, then he builds a house big enough for three families to live in simultaneously while still not seeing one another. But that's not enough for him. Then he rubs it in your face every chance he gets. Yeah, that guy is Ron Grassman. Or should I say Manager Ron? At five and a half feet tall, he stands just an inch or two above the tallest ten year old on the team. As a manager of one of FC's baseball teams, Ron is required to dress in full uniform. When the team lines up for the national anthem, he not only looks like one of the boys, but with his high-pitched voice he sounds just like one of the smaller kids.

Kevin drove the short distance from his house, through to the end of the plan where Ron's driveway began. He parked in the cul-de-sac knowing he'll need to sneak out partway through the party. He and Mark tried to enjoy the view of the flowering Rhododendrons and petite Alberta spruces that lined either side of the beautifully stamped concrete driveway as they trudged the distance to Ron's house. Fifteen minutes later they finally made it to the wrought iron gate that lead to the sidewalk; Kevin paused for a moment to catch his breath.

"Thank God," Kevin groaned. "I can finally see the house!"

"Bye Dad," Mark yelled back as he ran to the house.

The sound of music and screaming kids continued to grow louder as Kevin circled toward the back of the house. He peeked through the gate before opening it. The sight of beautiful women scattered across the concrete patio in their bikinis drowned out the obnoxious noise from the kids who were splashing around in the Olympic size pool.

Kevin groaned as he fell into an Adirondack chair next to James. "You know we're in the heart of baseball season when in-house is over and Ron has his party to kick off the tournament season." Kevin sat up and slipped on his mirrored sunglasses. He cracked open his beer and raised it for a toast. "Here's to…" He looked over at James. "How many tournaments are we signed up for again?"

"Seven!"

"Well then, here's to seven first place trophies," Kevin shouted out as the rest of the men raised their beers in camaraderie.

Kevin's attention was quickly diverted by the sight of a tiny satin pink bikini covered with white polka dots and the gorgeous body it's tightly strapped around. His eyes slowly worked their way down from her small shoulders past her firm abs then down her long slender legs until he noticed the woman was spilling her drink all over her feet. Kevin slowly slouched back down next to James when he realized the woman was Kara.

"There's something great about seeing all the baseball moms half-naked and drunk." Kevin pulled out his phone and began taking random pictures of everyone at the party. "You never know when I'll need to download one of these images from my brain, or download them from my phone."

"How do you live with yourself?" one of the men asked in disgust.

"Look, I'm doing everyone a favor by taking these pictures." Kevin mumbled while reviewing some of the new photos.

"How's that?"

"Simple, you know one of these sweet little ladies will say something stupid to piss me off during the season. And when she does, I can just smile while I'm looking at a picture of her in an awkward pose in her little swimsuit." Kevin took a drink of his beer while still snapping photos. "Or if I'm desperate enough, I can always use one to blackmail an out of control mother."

"Do you have any good pictures of my wife," one of the men hollered. "I'm always looking for new ideas on how to get the upper hand in my marriage."

"Oh, you'd be shocked at some of the precarious positions I've found the women in at these parties over the years!" Kevin yelled back. "And I've caught it all on my phone… It's all about that one night out of the year when these very conservative mothers let their guards down."

James shook his head. "Just don't aim that phone toward my wife!"

"I'm especially look forward to seeing a lot more of your wife and a lot less of her black robe." Kevin laughed as he continued to snap photos as fast as he could. "Tell me the truth. Does she wearing anything under that robe when she's at work? Forget I asked. Don't tell me. It's probably better if I just use my imagination."

"Alright that's enough of that!" James interrupted. "Save the personal questions until I have a couple more beers." James noticed Kevin raising his phone up and shifted his eyes over and saw his wife bent over while facing the other way. "Give me that you jackass!" He ripped the phone out of Kevin's hand. "This is that one day of the year when all of the other parents embarrass themselves by drinking and carrying on in the same way you do the rest of the year."

"Oh, speaking of hot women with very little clothes on..." Kevin grabbed his phone out of James hand and began scrolling through his pictures. "I got one hell of an email today. Apparently it wasn't enough that Lisa didn't show up for work the last two days. No, she decided to post on her Facebook some awesome pictures of not only herself, but with Diane's ex-boyfriend." He passed his phone back to James. "It's amazing how fast something like that gets around. All I needed to do was drop a few hints into the right person's ear and everyone else in the office finished the job for me. It was almost as if someone was looking out for me. Oh, maybe I've got a guardian angel on my side."

"An angel, huh? Seriously? Do you ever think about what you're saying before you say it?" James mused as he shook his head in disbelief. "You just destroyed a young lady's life, and in the process humiliated your boss. You did all this in an attempt to save your lousy job, a job that if I'm not mistaken, you hate!" James shouted out in frustration. "Tomorrow morning, Lisa's probably going to find out she's unemployed. And poor Diane, who didn't even do anything to you, is going to be the butt of all the jokes 'round the water cooler for at least the next couple of weeks or so. Do you want to know the really sad part?"

"What did I do wrong this time?" Kevin asked in a rueful voice.

"That's the sad part." James snapped, "You don't even think you've done anything wrong. Oh, and you think there's an angel somewhere watching over you?" He pointed down. "It sounds to me as if it was the work of someone else."

"Holy Shit!" Kevin began to rub his forehead with both hands, "When you say it like that..." Then he started laughing out loud. "Diane did seem a little bothered by the sight of her ex-beau shacking up with her subordinate." Kevin took his beer and began pouring it into his frosted mug then paused for a moment at the sight of new flesh. "Oh my..." A petite, thin woman with her hair tied up on the top of her head began stripping off her jeans and blouse to reveal a little bright red one piece swimsuit.

James kicked Kevin's leg. "Kev, you're missing your mug."

"Oops." Kevin gradually gathered his thoughts. "Who's the new hot momma?"

"That's Stacy's mother, Jules," James said while trying to wave her over.

Kevin grabbed his arm pulling him back down. "Stop, you ass! She's at the perfect distance, close enough to see, but not so close that it's uncomfortable to stare."

"I'm sorry," James said. "I guess I never realized, but apparently there's a set distance for ogling a woman."

"You do know you're talking to a seasoned pro," Kevin replied sardonically. "Now tell me all about her and please tell me she like a widow or at least divorced."

"You should know who she is." James sat back down. "She's Tony's wife, I introduced you to him yesterday. The tall, skinny guy with the big frizzed-out hair, dressed in those hideous blue and white checkered pants."

"You mean that moron choking on the cheap cigar," Kevin asked.

"That's him."

Kevin slid down in his chair a little more and thought to himself. Stacy, what kind of father names his son Stacy? He opened his phone and noticed it was almost six thirty. "Is there any chance you guys can cover for me for an hour or so? Oh, and maybe you can keep your comments about me chasing skirts to yourselves tonight."

Kevin snuck out the front door so none of the wives would see him leaving. Then he ran down the long sidewalk. His run slowed down to a jog by the time he reached the gate, and then the jog quickly turned into a fast walk. By the time he got to his car, Kevin had sweat oozing out of every inch of his body. He turned the air conditioner on high and sprayed approximately a half a can of Tag on himself. Then he raced his way through the plan of homes and down Route 28. He arrived at Gloria's in record time.

Kevin stopped at the edge of the parking lot and began looking for a spot which would afford him a quick getaway. "I'm getting a little sick of all these freaking people!" He grumbled loudly as he continued his way through the back lot with a dust storm trailing behind him engulfing the entire parking lot. Kevin looked at the clock on his dash as he was climbing out and saw his precious time slipping away. So he sprinted toward the front door trying to fan a path through the dust cloud. Kevin stumbled down the steps choking while trying to catch his breath. He stopped near the bottom and did a quick sweep of the room. With no sign of Coco in sight, Kevin hastily moved to his backup plan, Dave. He fought his way through the mob of men straight across the floor to the surveillance room. He walked in on Dave who was sitting on a stool slouched over one of the security monitors getting his neck and back rubbed by one of the girls who is currently going to school to be a massage therapist. Kevin snuck in and slowly slipped his hands between the girl's hands and Dave's shoulders and began rubbing. He quickly worked his way up to Dave's thick neck and then dug his fingers in trying to choke him.

"Honey, can you give us a minute alone?" Dave asked while patting the stripper's little bottom. "Don't stop rubbing Kev... right there." Dave pointed to a spot below his shoulder blade. "Start rubbing or I'm not talking."

"You know, if I would have touched her butt, even by accident, you would have kicked my ass out of this place," Kevin griped while working on Dave's back muscles. "And where the hell is Coco?"

"Yeah, I love the fringe benefits around here," Dave said with a groan. "Ahhh, way to hit that spot."

"Coco, is she here tonight?" Kevin grumbled.

"Coco? Yeah… no, sorry Chump, but you just missed her."

"You told me she'd be here," Kevin complained as he pulled his hands off of Dave's neck.

"Don't stop Kev. You're a natural."

"I've gotta go." Kevin griped as he turned to leave.

"Wait, I did some kick-ass recon work for you." Dave exclaimed, grabbing Kevin's hand trying to place it back on his shoulder.

"Make it quick. What have you got?" Kevin impatiently asked.

"I think you'll want to hear this juicy info." Dave stuck his hand out with a silly grin. "Come on, Sugar, don't leave me hanging."

Kevin pulled a five out of his wallet and waved it in Dave's face. "You know, I'm beginning to question your so-called talents as a private investigator." Kevin pulled out a second five. "All I can say is, this better be worth ten!"

"Well, let's see… Oh yeah, you might not like this one, she's got a four year old child." Dave said with a sickly expression on his face.

Kevin gave Dave the first five. "That's a good thing."

"I think the kid's a girl."

Kevin pulled the second five away from Dave. "Alright that sucked!" he yelled back as he stepped out of the room.

"I've got more!" Dave tried to shout over the crowd noise. "I know this because she had to leave a few minutes ago. She may have said the kid was sick. But I told her, 'Sweetie, all kids are sick.'"

"I'm sorry, but that's not worth five!" Kevin said in a frustrated voice.

"One more thing Kev, you wanted to know something about where Coco likes to eat, I think she said something about Chinese food."

Kevin happily passed Dave the second five. "P.F. Chang's, perfect," He shouted back as he maneuvered his way through the mob of unruly men. "I guess I'll see you tomorrow Dave, maybe around seven!"

Kevin walked out the back door wondering why his guardian angel failed him at his most critical time.

"Kev?"

Kevin stood frozen like the statue of Willie Stargell on the coldest day in January. Then he heard her call out again, the sound of an angelic voice coming from the far side of the gravel parking lot.

"Hey, Kevin… over here!" Coco hollered.

Kevin stepped up on the running board of a SUV parked beside his car then hoisted himself up until he was able to spy Coco waving to him.

"Kev!" The sound of her voice shot like a lightning bolt across the parking lot piercing through his chest and into his heart.

Kevin stood on the running board watching Coco slowly back out of the parking space then loop around through the parking lot. His feet and hands began to tingle from the rush of blood to his heart. He quickly lost all feeling in his hand as it slipped loose from the roof rack and he tumbled down onto the gravel below. Kevin stood up gently dusting the dirt off his pants then looked up when he heard her voice again. His eyes met hers as she continued driving toward him. She stuck her head out the window and smiled. Once again Kevin was dumbstruck by her million-dollar smile, her perfectly straight white teeth, her sweet dimples and peachy freckles, and finally her gorgeous, auburn hair blowing ever so gently in the breeze.

"Leaving early today?" Coco softly asked.

Kevin stepped forward trying to think up something witty to say. Tears welled up in his eyes as he realized he will finally get that chance to talk to her alone. A lump appeared in his throat so large that an industrial size plunger couldn't flush it out. As he approached the car he thought, I'll just be honest with her.

"The girl, the person I wanted to see, she wasn't here today." Kevin replied in a nervous voice.

"I didn't know you had a favorite," Coco said while continuing to edge her car forward. "So who's the lucky girl?"

Kevin walked along the car as she slowly drifted through the parking lot. "I probably shouldn't say and I'm not sure you would know her anyway."

"Oh, a mystery man, I like a guy with deep dark secrets," Coco said in a flirtatious voice while running her fingers through her auburn hair. "But I think I know all of the girls here now."

Kevin continued walking as fast as he could, trying to keep up with Coco's car. "I wouldn't want anyone to get jealous or anything!"

"You're a smart man, but I was just trying to help you out," Coco said. "You seem like a nice guy, who probably deserves better. Either way I need to get home, my mom called and said my daughter's sick."

"If you... one of these days..." Kevin stammered through his thoughts, "would you like to go out for Chinese sometime?" he asked.

Coco hollered out the window, "I hate Chinese food!" Then she sped off leaving Kevin standing there in a cloud of dust.

Kevin stood there watching Coco's car disappear over the crest of the hill then he dropped his head in disbelief. "You've got to be shitting me!" He screamed aloud to no one. "I finally did it. I finally reach out and put my heart there for her to see. Then I stood there, watching as she ran it over, smashing it like a boy smashes a bug!"

Just then he heard the sound of an air horn blowing off in a distance. Kevin looked around and saw he was standing in the middle of a four lane road, he turned his head and his eyes quickly focused on a large truck barreling down the hill straight at him. So he darted across two lanes then leapt over a guardrail hitting his head on a small tree and tumbling down through some briars. Kevin pulled himself up, looked over at Gloria's and screamed. "Dave... you asshole! I want my money back!" He leaned on the guardrail to catch his breath. He stared at Gloria's thinking, I need to do a better job of verifying the info Dave gives me, at least before I use it.

Kevin made his way back to Ron's party only to find Kara sitting in his seat.

"What the hell happened to you?" Kara asked with a sinister grin on her face.

"I was at work." Kevin softly mumbled. "Why?"

James pulled a towel out from under his head then tossed it up to Kevin. "I could be wrong, but I think she might be asking about the blood that's oozing out of your forehead."

"That's right, the blood, the dirty face and the scratches on your arm," Kara laughed as she stood up. "Let me guess you got a little to fresh with one of your stripper girls and a bouncer was forced to give you a correcting impulse!"

"Well, you're right about the bouncer being a problem," Kevin said while wiping off his face and arms.

"Just don't get kicked out of there for good 'cause you're not holding one of your sleazy strip parties in our neighborhood." Kara said as she watched Kevin fall into the open seat. "I'm just a little curious though. What do naked women and banks giving out loans have to do with each other?"

"Real classy, Kara," Kevin replied in a snippety tone.

"I'm going to call your boss and find out if your bank condones this type of barbaric behavior from their loan officers." Kara stated before walking back to rejoin the group of mothers on the other side of the pool.

"You really know how to kick a man when he's down, Kara." Kevin hissed at her retreating back.

"I don't want to see you standing in my courthouse again." Kara hollered back across the pool full of children. "Just because you can't control your shameless antics." she added.

"I don't know what you see in that woman of yours," Kevin said to James as he shook his head. "Alright, I get what you see on the outside. Anyone can see that, but one does have to wonder just what the hell is going on in that little pea-brain head of hers."

Just then Ron ran past James and Kevin, shrieking like a little girl, chasing one of the little boys.

"Okay, can we change the subject?" James suggested. "Like maybe what in the hell are we going to do about Manager Ron?"

"I don't understand where the vice president of baseball gets the authority to appoint this year's manager," one of the other men said. "I think we should've gotten a chance to at least voice are opinions on the matter!"

"That jackass couldn't manage a ten year old girls' softball team," another man added.

"No, that's not true." Kevin laughed out. "Anyone can do that! Trust me, my brother-in-law manages one. Anyway, Ron throws and hits like a girl, so he would fit right in with them."

"We've got to get rid of him," James said. "Does anyone have a suggestion?"

One of the other fathers leaned over and whispered to the small group of men. "What do you think about poisoning him? Not enough to kill him or anything. I'm thinking; just make him sick enough that he has to step down."

James looked around at the men sitting in their circle. "Every father here is more qualified than Ron to run this team. Do we all agree?"

Kevin pulled James aside and began whispering to him. "And you said there was something wrong with me. Are you actually going to consider his dumb ass suggestion? Half-kill Ron? You guys want to kill someone for the sole purpose of winning more games? Look, I'm not saying winning isn't everything but..."

Kevin watched as Ron picked up one of the skinny little boys then threw him through the air into the deep side of the pool. Then he picked up the next child in line, with his left hand he would grab their arm just above the elbow, then slid his right hand up their leg grabbing them high on the thigh. He slowly lifted them out of the water, catapulting them ten feet through the air and back into the water. Kevin eyes shifted over to the cabana, where a small group of mothers including Kara and Jules were sipping their tropical drinks while involved in their typical gossip gathering.

"This is going to be easier than taking candy from a baby." Kevin reached his hand out in front of James. "Let me see your BlackBerry."

James pulled out his phone then hesitated for a moment before reluctantly placing it into Kevin's hand.

Kevin scrolled through the list of contacts until he found Jules' name, then he typed a short text.

**You didn't hear this from me. But I heard a rumor that Ron was arrested for being a pedophile just a few short years ago.**

Kevin hit "send" and tossed the phone back to James with an ominous smirk on his face. "Gentlemen, sit back and observe as your lovely and, for a couple of you, sexy, wives do all the dirty work for us."

The four men sat back in their chairs drinking beer and laughing it up as they watch the small group of women pointing at Ron. One by one they wave over the other six mothers as the unfounded rumor spread like a wild fire on a dry and windy day. And as each woman passed the story along they found it necessary to embellish it just a touch. Within five minutes all the women stood in solidarity, with the exception of one. Ron's wife Dee was inside the house berating her wait staff for not having more hors d'oeuvres and Cosmos ready to serve.

The mothers all watched in horror as Ron fondled their children, but not one of them knew exactly what to do. That was until Jules noticed that her child, Stacy, was next in line.

Jules ran across the deck shrieking, "Don't you dare touch my little baby!" Then she grabbed Tony by the arm, insisting it was time to go home. All the other wives quickly followed her lead and one by one the families began to flee the scene. Most of the husbands left shaking their heads in confusion, while the mothers hugged their ten year old babies. The kids did what they do best, complained that they wanted to play in the pool just a little longer.

James looked over at Kevin in disbelief. "What, or how, did you just do that?" He pulled up the text message Kevin sent to Jules and read it. "I don't understand. What was Ron doing that was so wrong?"

"More often than not, the eyes see what the mind tells them to look for," Kevin explained. "As soon as I placed the idea into their heads, especially such a disturbing idea, the women had no other choice. They were bound to see something that bothered them, it's simply human nature."

"You've got a sick and twisted mind," James said. "Someday you'll have to teach me your ways."

Kevin said just three little words. "It's a gift." Then he gave Mark the international sign for let's get the hell out of here, his index finger pointing toward the car. "I'm sorry, but no one can teach a gift. You've either got it or you don't!"

"A gift, my ass," James whined. "You'll need to explain or I'll rat you out, you sick bastard!"

"If it was as easy as simply explaining, I would hold a seminar and charge people."

"Alright, let's start with this. Why Jules?" James probed.

"Oh to be so young and naïve," Kevin said as he mocked James. "In your case, just naïve... Okay, first of all, she's a stay at home mom."

"So she cares more about her child?" James cut in.

"Shut the hell up or I'm not going to explain anything to you." Kevin growled. "No, that doesn't make her a better parent. On the contrary, it merely means that she's a better target. You see, spending all day at home with Stacy, and having only one kid, that makes her more dependent on her child."

"That's it, I'm sure I could have figured that out."

"However, the primary reason I chose Jules is because she's new," Kevin expounded. "She doesn't really know anyone here yet, so she doesn't know who she can trust. But more importantly, she'll probably never see most of the parents here when the season's over. Therefore she'll feel more comfortable saying and doing whatever she feels necessary to protect her family."

James began clapping. "I'm stunned, how do you know so much about her and her family?"

"Easy, you can learn a lot about a gorgeous woman by watching how she interacts with her young child," Kevin said with an elitist tone. "If you combined that with simple human nature… Plus, she's the only one who had her phone in her hand."

"Okay Sensei, what if you don't know the person at all? And you don't have the opportunity to stare at her crystal butt for two hours?"

"Rookie," Kevin said taunting James. "Three questions, that's all it takes. You might want to get your BlackBerry out and start taking notes right about now!" Kevin held up his index finger. "First, ask him a question you both are sure to know the answer to. Second, ask a question that he has no chance of ever knowing the answer to. Third, ask him a question that's so stupid neither one of you should care what the answer is. His actual answers doesn't matter all that much, it's how he reacts to each question… That will tell you all you need to know about the person."

"You're a sick bastard. You know that, right?"

Sick? That's your opinion right now. We'll see who's sick after tomorrow's game." Kevin suggested as he began the long walk back to the cars with James. "If everything goes according to plan, it should prove to be one hell of an interesting evening. That is, if Ron even survives the night as manager." Kevin hollered back to Mark who's just climbing out of the pool. "Come on Ten! Let's go!"

# Chapter 10

**(7:30 AM Wednesday, June 30)** Kevin sat in his car watching his hand shake uncontrollably as he reached for the keys. He wondered was it all the alcohol from the night before or the three strong cups of coffee he drank this morning. Just as he was ready to get out of his car Kevin saw Lisa's peach colored Honda Civic pull in and park two rows in front of him. Fashionably late he thought. But today there seems to be a change in her typical routine. Lisa isn't doing her standard, 'hot chick sprinting to the front door' thing. She just sat there calmly in her car, carefully applying her lip gloss. He decided to wait her out for a few minutes. I guess Diane didn't fire her. Was it a poor plan? Or maybe it was just poor execution he surmised. "Damn I'm an idiot." I was alone with the vice president, he thought, I had his ear. I should have drug her name through the dirt a little longer. Kevin thoughts are interrupted by the sound of screeching tires. His eyes shifted over to a red Corvette flying into the parking lot and not slowing down until it reached the space next to Lisa. Kevin watched as Lisa slowly slid out of her car then smoothed her skirt down her hips. She climbed into the driver's side of the red 'Vette facing toward the back and wrapping her body all around Greg who was still in the driver's seat. Kevin turned his key in the ignition to check the time and his head lights flashed on hitting Greg right in the eyes. Kevin hastily jumped out of his car and darted across the back of the parking lot hoping that neither Lisa nor Greg realized that he had been spying on them.

By the time he arrived by his cubicle Kevin was certain he was in the middle of a full blown heart attack. His heart was fluttering out of control, his hands and feet were tingling, but the conclusive evidence of the heart attack was the knife-sharp pain in the center of his back. Slowly he wandered from one cube to the next pleading with his co-workers for just a little sympathy. Most of them questioned whether or not he actually had a heart, yet he still managed to pick up a few suggestions. One of his colleagues recommended taking two aspirin. That was something he had heard before so Kevin continued toward the break room where the aspirin were kept in the first aid cabinet. Another co-worker, Jess, suggested massaging his heart. Not really a viable option, not to mention scary... Damn, that girl has got some real issues.

En route to get his aspirin Kevin passed Diane's office and noticed her calmly typing so, of course, he was compelled to stop.

"Diane, do you know anything about heart attacks," Kevin asked in a timid voice.

Diane glanced up over her computer screen. "What's the matter Kev... you don't grab enough of those poor women at your "club" that now you need to do it at the office as well?"

Kevin quickly slid his hand out from under his shirt. "How can you joke around at a time like this? I could have a serious problem."

Diane looked back down at her computer while shaking her head. "Oh, and now you want me to play nursemaid to you... Will the pain from working with you never end?"

Kevin watched her for a few seconds. She is way too calm he thought. "Time to try plan B... 'The Hail Mary'," he mumbled under his breath.

"I'm sorry Kev, are you still here?" Diane asked sarcastically. "Because I thought looking down at my computer and ignoring you was the international sign for get the hell outta here!"

Kevin sprinted back to his cubicle and typed up a quick email to Diane.

"Wasn't this your latest boy toy?  :)"

Then he attached the sexist, most provocative photo of Lisa and Greg at the beach and clicked send.

Kevin began working on his next sets of foreclosure notices while continually checking for new emails from either Diane or Lisa. With no new developments after fifteen minutes, Kevin began to panic and quickly moved from plan B to plan C. He decided to email the VP.

"I just want to make certain that all the paper work I dropped off yesterday was to your satisfaction. I'm also concerned that when I mentioned Lisa's name at the meeting that I may have somehow put her in jeopardy of getting reprimanded or fired."

Send.

Kevin continued splitting his time between the new list of emails he received and the list of foreclosures until he heard the light sound of finger nails tapping on the side of his cubicle. Kevin looked up and saw Lisa's head poking in the opening.

"Is it safe to come in?" Lisa whispered.

Not sure what to do, Kevin said the first thing that came to mind. "Ummm… sure, it's safe. C'mon in…"

Lisa slid her way around the corner and sidestepped out of the door opening. "What'd I miss while I was… away?" she asked in her soft seductive voice.

The smell of four days' worth of coconut oil swamped Kevin's cube and the image of Lisa in one of her more provocative swimsuit occupied Kevin's mind. Her glistening silky skin and that perfectly perky top, all stuffed into that tiny French cut bikini… just one of the many unforgettable photos she uploaded to her facebook page just two days earlier. "What... what do you... what?"

Lisa stuck her head out into the hallway and looked both ways before stepping back in. "I mean... well, I heard I missed a mandatory meeting with members from the new bank yesterday. What else did I miss?"

Kevin stared at the back of Lisa's perfectly tanned, long luscious legs. "I'm sorry... were you talking to me?"

Lisa crouched down next to Kevin's desk and began whispering again. "Should I expect any repercussions? You know, from not sending in the updated list of loan defaults on time? Or did you manage to... Was Diane given the information in time to present it to the board?"

"Ummm," a lump developed in Kevin's throat so tight he couldn't swallow.

"Kev, I have no idea how you manage to hold on to this job as long as you have. You never seem to have the slightest clue about anything," she whispered a little louder.

"No... I'mmm..." Kevin continued stumbling along.

Lisa stood up and stuck her head out the door again. "Jan's at her desk now... I'll ask her. She is like the queen of office gossip."

"Lisa..."

Lisa leaned over Kevin's desk placing an elbow on either side of a five by seven photo of Mark. "What's up, Kev?"

Kevin glared down at the photo. "Do you like surprises?" he asked as his eyes slowly drifted back up, getting lost somewhere deep in Lisa's cleavage.

She reached across the desk running her fingers partly through his hair, mussing it up. "What kinda girl would I be if I didn't?"

"Good." Kevin said with a deep exhale.

They both looked up when they heard the sound of a soft cough coming from the door opining.

Kevin screamed, "Yeah."

But Johnny only hears Lisa's response. "Well, hello. Come on in Big Boy!"

Johnny stepped in next to Lisa. "Hey Kevin! Man, that stuff we talked about yesterday? It was perfect!"

"Perfect!" Kevin looked over at Lisa then up to Johnny then back to Lisa. "I mean… we should probably discuss it later."

Lisa looked down at Kevin. "Who the hell's the bean pole? And what's so perfect?"

Johnny stepped back to address both Kevin and Lisa. "Well, for starters, I remember hearing him say something about the new board being formed. And that he's going to be on it… And rumor has it; they should be set to begin approving loans again next week, once all the board positions are finalized."

Lisa sighed, "New loans? That's great news. Huh, Kev?"

"Yeah… And those stacks of papers you left on his desk," Johnny added. "I think that stuff was damn good stuff!" Then he left as quickly as he had appeared to return to his own office.

"Damn good…" Kevin mumbled. "Perfect… That's great, I guess."

Lisa gave Kevin a quick wink. "You're such a Dear, Kev. Was that my paperwork you..?"

Kevin and Lisa looked back to the opening when they heard Johnny clearing his throat again. "Oh, and I did exactly what you wanted."

"What... did I want?" Kevin cautiously asked.

"You know, that Lisa chick... you wanted her fired." Johnny threw his thumb up in the air as if he was a first base umpire at a Pirate game. "She's out of here!"

Lisa snatched up a hand full of pens. "Freeze, you son of a bitch!" she screamed back at Johnny.

First she looked down at Kevin who was holding his arms straight up in the air like he's about to be robbed at gunpoint.

"I'm unarmed." Kevin shouted.

Johnny turned and stuck his head out the door opening, screaming down the hall. "Help... someone call security!" Then he was pelted in the back of the head by a scattered shot of pens.

Lisa looked down at Kevin then pointed back at Johnny who was on his knees picking up the pens. "Who in the hell is this jackass?"

Johnny stepped between them with his back to her. Then he glared down at Kevin with a devilish grin. "I'm still struggling with this whole mind reading thing, Kev... You did want her fired, right?" Then he turned and handed Lisa a dozen pens before scurrying through the door and down the hall.

Lisa stepped towards Kevin with her arm cocked back grasping the new round of pens. "Is he my replacement?" she yelled. Then she went storming out the door with tears streaming down her face. "Go ahead and run... You sniveling coward!" she screamed at Johnny as he jogged towards the elevators.

Kevin followed Lisa out the door, trying to calm her down, but she continued her virulent string of profanity until Johnny disappeared into the elevator. Then she turned back to Kevin. "Oh... and thanks for all your help Kevin! And to think I actually touched your hair... eeyeuuw!"

"That was the VP's son," Kevin replied calmly as he attempted to nudge Lisa back into her cube. "I guess no one introduced the two of you. And as far as helping you…"

"I'm going to kill you Kevin!" Lisa growled as she viciously shoved him away.

They both froze and looked at each other.

"Oh shit," Lisa muttered when she noticed the security guards standing close by.

"I don't think you should have said that," Kevin whispered. Then he stepped back and watched quietly as two men dressed in pseudo police uniforms grabbed her arms and escorted her from the loan department, kicking and screaming like a Tasmanian she-devil.

The sound of Lisa's screeching eventually faded away as Kevin surveyed the damages. From where he was standing he could see at least three broken plastic windows and a number of odd items lying on the floor.

Kevin couldn't help but wonder if getting fired was all part of some elaborate scheme Lisa had cooked up. He kicked Lisa's stapler over into a pile of debris which included her smashed trashcan. Maybe she knows something that no one else in this office knows. Maybe she figured if she left now she'd be eligible to collect unemployment while she got a head start on the rest of us at exploring new job opportunities. Or maybe it's nothing more than Lisa being a young foolish bitch.

Kevin continued down the hallway, trying to repair the havoc wrought by Lisa's tantrum when he glanced up to see Diane reaching up to pull something off her office wall. Oh dear God, what an incredible butt!

"Kevin… how'd that heart attack work out for you today?" Diane asked as she carefully packed some of her personal items in a box.

"Ummm… I think I'm okay now."

"Was that you screaming like a little school girl earlier?" Diane inquired calmly.

"No, I'm thinking that was Lisa you heard." Kevin mused.

"Management canned her?" Diane asked.

"Yeah, they sent the VP's son down." Kevin replied.

"Bummer… I was actually hoping I would have the opportunity to kick her ass out of here." Diane said matter-of-factly.

Kevin hurried back to his cube and decided that keeping a low profile just might be in his best interests right now.

# Chapter 11

**(3:50 PM Wednesday, June 30)** In every office, no matter what type of business you're in, there's always that one smart ass, or perhaps I should say dumb ass, who suggests the following: 'the busier you are at work, the faster the day goes by.' There may have been a point in my life when I would have agreed with that philosophy, Kevin pondered. That is, until now... Now I spend my days either filing foreclosure papers on clients whom I had once considered to be good friends as well as associates. Or, if they're lucky, I merely threaten them with the grim prospect of foreclosure. All the while, I'm hoping that they'll find a way to bring their accounts up to date so I won't have to follow through with my threats. No matter how busy I may be at work, time seems to stand completely still. It's almost as if I'm nothing more than one of those useless portraits that line the hallways of this filthy building. On the other hand, when I'm sitting on my ass in a lawn chair just beyond the outfield fence, literally doing nothing but watching my son play baseball, two hours seems to fly by at mach speed. If only I was some kind of superhero... I would somehow find a way to alter the way time appears in my mind.

Just then Kevin sees the new envelope icon appear in the task tray indicating the arrival of a new email. It's from Diane... the subject line reads,

"Must be finished by the end of the week!!!"

Kevin reluctantly clicked on it only to find a list of new delinquent clients for whom he'll need to draft foreclosures notifications. His eyes glazed over about halfway through the long list so he slowly shifted them over to the lower right hand corner and noticed it was almost four, close enough to slip out. There's nothing better than four o'clock on a Friday... Too bad it's only three fifty on a Wednesday.

Kevin poked his head out of the cube, scanning both hallways looking for a sign on which way to make his escape. The main hall to the elevator was clear... I need to take my chance now he thought. He quickly power-walked his way, almost jogging at times, down the hall until he arrived in front of the elevator. He pushed the down arrow then ducked into the break room to wait.

Kevin stood there considering his evening plans while continuing to check the hallways for Diane. The decision would have been a lot easier had there been a game scheduled tonight. I should probably just lay low, maybe go home and cut my grass. I hear it hasn't been cut in two weeks. When the elevator doors opened he found Diane standing on the other side. She stepped out with a blank look on her face but it quickly turned sour when she spotted her secretary marching out of conference room with two of the biggest sleaze bags that work in the building.

"Jan," Diane shrieked, "I'm still waiting for the name of the SOB who sent those pictures out, especially the unflattering one of me versus Lisa in our bikinis!"

"I voted for you," Jan enthusiastically exclaimed in support.

"Yeah thanks... But that particular picture was taken before I started working out; my body is a lot firmer now!" Diane struck a sexy pose for Jan. "Look at this butt now!"

"I must say, Miss Diane, it is spectacular!"

Kevin slid his finger between two slats of the blinds pulling down ever so slowly, revealing Diane partially bent over with one hand pulling up the bottom edge of her jacket while the other is lightly patting her bum. Yeah, she does have some kind of sweet ass.

"But I think that could be a consideration under the new sexual harassment rules," Diane stated in a shrill tone. "That means I can fire Kevin on the spot... I mean... whoever the coward was that posted them anonymously!"

"I'm sure I can trace it back to Kevin, Miss Diane," Jan suggested in a low voice. "That is, if that's what you want me to do?"

"Well, yeah," Diane began to snicker as they strolled down the hall together. "But only if it actually was him... I guess."

Screw that, Kevin thought, as he heard the two women's voices fade down the hallway. Doing yard work around the house means Kara gets her way and I really have to draw a line in the sand someday. As president of the home owners' association, one of her duties is to inform any and all members of their rules violations and she has no problem performing that job. It's bad enough when that high and mighty bitch sits on her throne at work, looking down her nose at all the innocent people placed before her by an out of control police force. But she stomps all over the line when she brings that elitist attitude back to our plan of homes, treating all of our neighbors, including myself, like we're nothing more than common criminals. Just because I haven't cut my lawn in two weeks, or someone else may have missed shoveling their sidewalk the day after a snowstorm, that shouldn't give her the right to play judge and jury over us in our own back yards, or our front yards for that matter.

Kevin looked back down the hall and with no Diane in sight he cut across the hall and ran down the steps. Screw it! I'm going to at least stop in to Gloria's and say, "Hi."

Kevin carefully pushed open the door at the bottom of the steps. You know it really shouldn't be this hard to leave work. I feel like I'm an inmate sneaking out of a psych ward. He quietly surveyed the lobby. There was the usual crowd of bank tellers and a few customers milling about. With no sign of the beast, Kevin high-tailed it across the room dodging an elderly couple entering the building before slicing his way through the closing doors. "Free at last, free at last..." he muttered to himself.

Johnny sprung out from behind one of the large pillars supporting the front balcony. "Hey, Old Man, I've been hiding out here for more than an hour waiting for you. Where are we going tonight?"

Kevin stood there looking down at Johnny, as if the devil himself stood between him and the chains that bind him to this sucky job. "I get it... No, actually I don't." Kevin walked down the steps and stood in front of Johnny. Only now he was looking up at him. "What the hell do you want from me?"

"A good time..."

"Sorry kid, but this door doesn't swing that way," Kevin cut him off sarcastically.

"No, you don't understand. I've been away at school and haven't lived in the Pittsburgh area for more than five years now." Johnny explained. "I really don't have any old friends that I can call." He stood there watching Kevin walk right past as if he wasn't standing there talking to him. "So where are you going tonight? I'm just looking for something to..."

Kevin stopped abruptly and glared up at Johnny. "Screw you! You've been working here for how long? And you're already firing people... Screw you!"

"Sorry,' Johnny said as he circled around, trying to stay in front of Kevin. "I really did think... that... that was what you wanted."

"Well, it was but..."

Johnny followed Kevin into the parking garage and over to his car. "Kevin, I think we can help each other out. Just listen to me for one minute."

"You're going to help me?" Kevin snorted. "This ought to be precious!"

"If I can't convince you I'll... Look Kevin, you don't know me, but sometimes that's the best person to talk to... I don't know..." Johnny stumbled to find just the right words.

Kevin slid down into driver's seat. "Johnny, or whatever your freaking name is, I'm sure you're a smart kid... probably went to the best college and all that. And I have no doubt you mean well, but when you go back to college in three short months, you probably won't even remember my name. And if you were ever to come back to work at PBT you're likely to find that I'm no longer employed here. So why in the hell should I help you out? If I'm lucky enough to still be working here you'll probably end up being my boss."

Johnny jammed his foot inside the car to stop Kevin from closing the door. "You're not much for understanding who people are, are you? I can assure you..."

"I've spent my entire life judging and profiling people," Kevin barged in. "Getting to know a person in an instant is how I know what to say and when to say it. It's the whole reason that I've been able to build such a large and profitable client list."

"You think you know me," Johnny smirked. "You're so far off."

Kevin sat there for a moment then leaned over and opened the passenger door. "Well, I guess if you're going to be my boss in two years then I best start kissing your ass now. Go ahead, jump in!"

"Yeah, I don't trust you." Johnny stood there with his foot still lodged in the door opening. "Get out and we'll go in my car."

"What?"

"Besides, I can't be seen in a four door sedan," Johnny explained. "I'm trying to build up my reputation!"

Kevin reached across the center console and pulled the passenger door shut. He hit the lock button as he stepped out. "Okay, what now?"

"Now," Johnny pointed at his Beemer, "jump in and let's see how fast we can get this beast going!"

Kevin hesitated for a moment then slid in the passenger seat and quickly strapped his seat belt on. "This is great," Kevin groaned. "Did you have something in mind? 'Cause I really wanted to go home and cut my grass tonight."

"Watching you cut the grass? Hmmm, that's funny because I was told you're the man to talk to if I'm looking to score with the ladies." Johnny slowly drove through the parking lot, stopping at the steps leading to the front door of the bank. Then he began revving up the engine.

Kevin turned to his left. "What... something wrong with your fancy sports car, Johnny?" Then he turned to his right as he heard a familiar voice calling his name and saw Diane standing by the entrance of the bank with her arms folded and a stern look on her face.

"Kevin," Diane hollered down from the top step. "You need to..."

"What the hell are you doing," Kevin whispered. "Let's go." Then he slowly slouched down as low as he could in the seat as if he could hide from the beast.

Johnny looked over at Kevin and smiled. "The man said... Let's go!" Then he jammed the gas pedal down to the floor and the tires began to screech as they flew across the last two hundred feet of the parking lot. Johnny didn't slow down until he approached the first red light.

"I would think at your age, you've learned all the hot spots in Pittsburgh to party," Johnny suggested.

"I've gone to the same old bar for some twenty-plus years," Kevin replied without pretention. "I don't consider it a hot spot, but if I'm going to get stuck babysitting you, then it's as safe as any other place to go."

"If it's good enough to entice you into going there for, well basically my entire life, then it must be an awesome place. Just point me the way, Old Man." Johnny raced from one stop light to the next. "So, who in the hell was the bitch that went all crazy on me this morning?"

"Lisa?"

"Yeah, maybe you can hook me up with her sometime," Johnny asked.

"I'm not so sure that's a good idea!" Kevin tried to holler over the sounded of the engine revving, the loud radio and the wind blowing through the open windows. "For starters, you just fired her ass. You're probably the last person she'll want to see. Also, I imagine the company's sexual harassment policy wouldn't permit it!"

"Yeah," Johnny screamed as he locked up the brakes at the next red light. "But I'm all for that type of passionate women."

"I'll help you find someone at Gloria's," Kevin shouted. "I'm thinking... five minutes alone with Roxy and I'll guarantee that's all you'll be dreaming about for the next two months!"

"Gloria's? This isn't... Wait a second," Johnny hesitated. "Please don't tell me you're...?"

"No... Hell no! You'll see, this place is full of hot-looking girls... women." Kevin groaned. "Females, all females," he shouted out while trying to send a text to James explaining the situation he found himself in and begging him to watch Mark for a few hours. "So was I right about the whole college thing?" he asked. "Are you in training to become my boss?"

"Yes and no… I'm going to college, but I'd like to be a writer." Johnny explained while continuing to race from stop light to stop light until they reach the turn to Gloria's. "But I might get stuck being a teacher, and I'm not so sure that's going to work out either."

"No?" Kevin asked as he pointed to the next turn.

"No, and I don't understand why there's a need to make the classes so difficult," Johnny cried out in frustration. "I mean, do you really need to know how to spell these days? Isn't that the whole reason you have spell check on your computer? And why in the hell do I even have to take a math class? It doesn't make sense… Anyway, I'll probably flunk out!"

"Well, maybe it's for the best. Teachers don't make shit. And I don't think people even read books any more. Pull in here," Kevin said as he gestured to a small asphalt parking lot off to the right. "TV, or the movies, that's where it's at." he added.

Johnny pulled into a nearly empty parking lot at Gloria's and parked in the space nearest the exit. "You told me this was a happening bar, a great place for picking up hot girls. I knew you were full of it!"

"They'll be here!" Kevin jumped out of the car. "Trust me, they'll be here!" Then he made a mad dash through the front door and down to his regular table.

Johnny looked up as he reluctantly stepped out of his car. "Oh dear God," he mumbled to himself while staring up at the faded lime green building with the name *Gloria's* hand-painted in fuchsia across awning covering the front veranda. "But there's no one else here in the parking lot." Johnny continued his in-depth conversation with himself as he stumbled toward the front door. He paused at the entrance then slowly turned around; the building was completely surrounded by old run-down, abandoned mom 'n' pop stores.

Johnny quickly darted into Gloria's open door before coming to an abrupt stop at the top of the steps. "Kevin?" he called out softly, staring down the steps toward the poorly lit room below. "Kevin?" Johnny whispered as loudly as he could. "Where the hell did you go?" With the ceiling clearance being less than seven foot at the highest point, Johnny found himself having to lean back while lowering his head as he slowly tip-toed down the steps. When he grabbed a hold of the rust-pitted handrail, it wobbled to the point he was worried he might pull it off the wall. "Kevin, this isn't funny," Johnny mumbled again. He paused at the bottom step and stared. All he could see was three dim lights shining down onto an old dilapidated bar. "If you snuck out the back and left me here, I swear, I'll have my dad fire your ass in the morning!"

"Johnny! Over here, Johnny!" Kevin stood up and waved his arms above his head as if he was an air traffic controller trying to direct in a jumbo jet.

Johnny shuffled his feet along the floor of the dark room until he hit a sticky spot and stumbled. "Come on. Let's get out of here while we still can." He whispered fervently as he caught himself by grabbing a couple of chairs. He deftly spun one around so he could sit down next to Kevin. "I'd hate to be around when one of the local mobsters shows up and wants to slash our throats for invading his territory."

Johnny turned to scan the dark room when he heard the sound of grunting and groaning. "That's real classy," he said sarcastically. "Apparently they don't provide a back room for sexual intercourse."

Suddenly, a gigantic black man stepped out of the darkness with a half barrel of beer resting on his broad shoulder. "Holy shit!" Johnny cried out as he slid himself and his chair behind Kevin.

"What now?" Kevin turned around to see what all the commotion was about. "What? That thing..? It's just Dave." Kevin stuck his leg out in a false attempt at tripping him.

"Sweetie, if I fall, I'm landing on you..." Dave said as he kicked Kevin's foot out of the way, almost knocking him off his chair. "And that's one lap dance you'll never forget." Then he hollered across the room as he slid the barrel down to the floor. "Kev, I think you made quite an impression on our lovely Coco yesterday!"

Kevin looked around to see if she was in the room as he hurried over, "Why? What'd she say about me?"

"Let me think... Hmmm, what did she say?" Dave paused for a moment with his hand out. "Nothing, just like my empty hand... she said nothing. But I'm here to tell you, she's looking a little extra special tonight!"

Johnny followed Kevin to the bar and pulled on Kevin's arm. "Okay, I'm beginning to get the picture here. This is all about a woman for you."

Johnny began to get a better look at the entire room when Dave flipped on a few of the stage lights. The raunchy smell he noticed when he first entered the main room may have been coming from the cigarette butts smashed into nearly every crack and crevice on the floor, or maybe it's the mold growing out from around them. The walls that first appeared as modern art now look as if they're nothing more than stain marks left by beer and mixed drinks, splattered by overzealous drunks. "But, this place, it just doesn't seem at all safe."

"What are you a chicken shit or what?" Kevin smirked as the two men took their seats facing the stage. "What are you six and a half feet tall? And probably go around two hundred pounds? Who's going to mess with you? I'm sure if someone's going to get knifed in the parking lot later, it's going to be little old me they target, not enormous young you."

"That's a real comforting thought," Johnny said as he noticed small groups of grungy men beginning to file in. He nervously scanned the room again, scouting the locations of the nearest exits. "Alright, so tell me, what's the deal with Coco?" he asked as he continued searching the room. This time he had hopes of seeing what the girls actually look like. "I'm assuming you have a thing for her... Oh! Oh no!" Johnny started laughing. "Please tell me it's a girl and not some kind of dog that does tricks on stage!"

"Funny."

"And what happened to the girl you promised me," Johnny questioned.

"Coco's our waitress, so I'm sure you'll meet her in a few minutes. As for your girl, there'll be five or six to choose from, but I recommend the one named Roxy." Kevin suggested. "If she's not the sweetest thing you've ever laid eyes on then..."

"There ain't nothing sweet coming out of this place," Johnny said while looking around in utter disgust. "And there's no way in hell that I'm touching anything that works in this dump!" Johnny covered up his mouth, hoping no one heard him. He lowered his voice and continued. "Do you have any idea what kind of diseases are passed around in this cesspool? I wouldn't feel safe taking a leak in the men's room here!"

Kevin gave Johnny the glare. "Don't tell me you're one of those germophobes!"

The men continued to argue about which is worse, the men's room at the bar or the one that never seems to get cleaned at the office. Suddenly Johnny realized that almost every table was occupied.

"I give up, we've been sitting here for at least fifteen minutes, and I haven't seen one girl yet." Johnny asked, "What's the draw?"

Just then Coco snuck up behind the two men. She pulled out a chair, slid it backwards between them and sat down. She slowly leaned over close to Kevin and whispered into his ear. "Hi Boys, what can I get for you this wonderful evening?"

Kevin turned and briefly met Coco's eyes before quickly turning away, struggling to find his voice. He cleared his throat and tried again, turning to face her. But he was too slow. Johnny smoothly made the request for two beers and a blonde stripper with long legs. Then he handed her a short note wrapped in a hundred that read, 'He's going to ask you out on a date tonight, if you're not interested in him then send the drinks back with a different waitress.'

Both men watched Coco's little ass, as she sashayed across the floor, disappearing into the crowd of unruly men on her way back toward the bar.

"Please don't tell me," Johnny turned to Kevin and began laughing uncontrollably. "Oh yeah, Old Man, you are so screwed!"

"What?"

"What? That girl is way out of your league, definitely too young and way too hot for you. I mean, you two, you're not even playing in the same sport. She's a…"

"Yeah? Well, screw you too," Kevin growled.

"Calm down, little man," Johnny said, lightly elbowing Kevin. "I come bearing great advice for you. Because I feel so… so very sorry for you and your dismal life, I'm going to help you land that hot sexy fish."

Johnny started out with a brief lesson on how to earn the love and respect of a good woman. Then there was the lesson on what to say and, most importantly, what not to say. So when Coco returned with the cold beers Kevin felt a budding sense of confidence.

Kevin stood up and took a deep breath. Looking deep into her eyes he smiled and calmly asked Coco about her daughter June… like how old she was and if she was feeling any better. After she answered,

Kevin told her about his son Mark... like how he loves to play baseball and writing being his favorite class. Within a few minutes Kevin had a date set up for the next evening. They scheduled it sometime between baseball and putting Mark to bed and Coco getting off work and putting June to bed. They found there was about twenty minutes of free time to date.

Coco smiled and gave Johnny a wink then spun her chair around to the next table and began taking the next costumer's order.

"Alright Kev, now that I helped you with your pathetic problems," Johnny said, "it's your turn to... well, return the favor. I need to know everyone's function in the loan department. That's the only way I'm going to get a grasp on what I'm supposed to be doing there. Let's start with the contract you asked me to help you get approval on. Then I'd like to know what Diane's role is within this process. Oh yeah, and last, I don't care about any sexual harassment rules. I need to know everything there is to know about that crazy bitch we battled with this morning."

Kevin took a long drink of his beer and began to explain the process. "Well, I started working on that particular loan about two or three months ago. The company is stable and we've dealt with them many times in the past. Generally speaking, what I do is meet with potential clients on new or existing commercial properties. They start out giving me their best sales pitch on how it will make enough money to not only pay back their loan, but pay it back with interest. If I think it's a solid investment, I'll write up a contract and have the client sign it, and then it gets passed on to Diane. She basically does the same thing as me... Which in my mind makes her worthless, but the bank insists on having two points of view on each project no matter how small it might be. I guess it's one of those "cover your ass at any cost" deals that apparently doesn't always work. She does background checks on both the owner and anyone who may be leasing the property. That's if she feels it's worth presenting to the board."

"Okay, stop right there," Johnny abruptly cut in. "That sounds like a lot of bullshit!"

"Yeah, it is, but obviously with bankruptcy filings and loan defaults at an all-time high, there apparently wasn't quite enough bullshit in the past several years."

"But what if Diane shuts down the loan?" Johnny continued to probe. "I mean… do you still get paid if the loan is denied?"

"Getting paid… the almighty dollar…" Kevin stood up and looked for Coco. He scanned the entire room. "I don't see her anywhere. Let's go, we have to get the hell out of here now!"

Johnny stood up and began chasing after Kevin. "Wait… What about the girl I was supposed to meet? You suck!"

Kevin ran up the steps, yelling back over his shoulder. "You said you wouldn't touch a thing that came out of this dump! Those were your exact words!"

Johnny followed Kevin as they both stepped out the front door. "What about your job at the bank?"

"Wait until we get in the car, then I'll explain what I do at the bank!" Kevin demanded in a frantic voice. "Now unlock your doors so we can get out of here!"

"When I asked what about your job at the bank," Johnny drawled as he pushed the unlock button. "I meant, I'm going to have your ass fired if you don't show me this supposedly hot girl now!"

"Tomorrow… I promise," Kevin said as he jumped in, slamming the door and securing his seat belt in one hurried motion. "I'll introduce you to her tomorrow. I'll even put in a good word in for you. Now drive!"

Johnny raced out of the parking lot. "I don't understand… If the bar was so safe, then what's the big hurry? Did you see someone you owe money to or something?"

"Sorry Johnny, I just didn't want to give Coco a chance to change her mind about the date with me."

"Just a little insecure, are we Kev?"

"Alright, you asked me about my pay," Kevin continued his earlier explanation. "Let's start with the fact that I get a base salary of about fifty thousand. Additionally, except for the last two years, I've always gotten an annual bonus of anywhere from five to as much as ten thousand. But the real money comes from the commissions."

"Commissions..? So you're telling me, the more loans the bank approves for you the more money you make? How much are we talking about? Just give me a ballpark figure… like ten grand per loan?"

The two men continued their discussion as Johnny raced down Route 28.

"It doesn't work exactly like that." Kevin said while watching the telephone poles zip by faster and faster. "You've got to slow down. The speed limit is only forty-five mph here, you're doing seventy."

"I just want to know, what's in it for me?" Johnny asked. "What if I can help push through all your loans? How much are we talking?"

"I like the way you think, Kid. It's all about the money." Kevin tightened his seat belt nervously. "Let's try to get the first one through; then we'll talk numbers. Now, for the love of God, could you please slow down!?!"

But Johnny continued hitting the lights just as they turned yellow, so he kept weaving in and around the traffic.

"Slow down!" Kevin shouted as he turned around to see a blue and red bubble light flashing on the plain white sedan close behind them. "I thought I heard the sound of a siren mixed in with this trashy music."

The officer sat in the undercover car for what seemed like an eternity. He finally stepped out and lingered behind Johnny's car, first looking down at the license plate then typing something into what appeared to be a phone.

"Oh, this is freaking great." Kevin groaned.

"What did you do?" Johnny barked out.

"What did I do? Seriously? I told you to slow down," Kevin whispered. "I know this cop... he's an arrogant jackass! On top of that, he's Diane's ex-boyfriend... and for two weeks he helped her torment me."

Kevin cringed as he watched Greg approach in the side view mirror. He quickly turned towards the passenger window and slid down in his seat trying to disappear. He picked up a folder from work and held it in front of his face as if he was reading it.

"Can I see your driver's license and registration, please?" Greg requested in a low steady voice.

Johnny pulled a stack of papers out of the glove compartment and began fumbling through them.

"Do you know why I pulled you over, Son?" Greg asked.

"My name is Johnny, not Son. And no, I'm actually clueless as to why you would take time out of your busy day to harass me."

"Did you know both of your tail lights are smashed out, Son?" Greg asked in a stern voice.

"Here's the thing, Pops... I don't think they are," Johnny responded with quite a bit of attitude.

"No? Well, they could be... Son," Greg suggested with a sinister grin on his face.

Johnny turned toward Kevin. "Yeah, you called it, Kev. This cop has got a clear case of over-bloated ego syndrome."

Kevin slapped his hand over Johnny's mouth then whispered forcefully. "Settle down before you get us both hauled off to jail!"

Johnny pushed Kevin's hand out of his face and turned back towards the officer. "I'm certain I'm not your son, so if you could show a little respect and call me by my first name, which by the way, happens to be Johnny."

"I'm going to have to ask you step out of the car, *Son*. Or should I call for back up and a tow truck, so I can take you both down to the station? Where we'll likely spend the better part of the night doing paper work?" Greg looked in at Kevin. "How does that sound to you in there, Sir?" He saw Kevin holding a folder with Pittsburgh Bank & Trust written across the top. "Hey, I know someone who works at that bank. Do you know either Lisa Hartman or Diane Madison?"

Johnny held out his license to Greg then stepped out of the car slamming the door shut behind him. "Yeah, Diane's our boss. And yeah, I know all about you and Diane tormenting my new friend Kevin... and we're not taking any of your shit tonight!"

Greg glanced down at Johnny's driver's license. "Have you been drinking? Mr... Johnny Meyer? Because, I think I smell a touch of alcohol on your breath." Greg held up the license. "And I know you're only twenty years old, so that means we're all going to take a little ride in my squad car. So if you would be a dear, and turn around and put your hands behind your back, then I can place these shiny new hand cuffs on you."

Kevin leaned out the driver's side door as Greg was putting Johnny in the back of the police car. "Would it be okay if I just drive his car back to the bank for him?"

Greg walked back over to Johnny's car. "It depends, would you like to spend the night in jail for resisting arrest?"

Kevin stepped out of the car and assumed the position. Greg pulled out a second set of handcuffs, snapped them on and then stuffed Kevin in the back seat of the cruiser next to Johnny.

"So Johnny... Is this what you had in mind when you talked me into taking you out for a drink?"

"We only had one..."

"You're not twenty-one yet," Kevin whispered in anger. "What the hell were you thinking? This cop is a psycho and your father is going to fire me!"

"No one's getting fired, I'll make sure of that," Johnny barged in. "And as for the underage thing... Are you going to sit there and tell me you never done one stupid thing, something you might even regret?"

They both turned around when they heard the sound of glass shattering and saw Greg swinging his night stick into the second tail light of the Beemer.

"You were right about one thing. This dude has got some real anger management problems!" Johnny said with a smile, while shaking his head. "I'm sure I can help him, assuming he wants help."

"Of course I'm right! He's the one that should be locked up, not us." Kevin whispered.

"So this mind reading shit, can you teach me?" Johnny asked.

"Johnny, you've done nothing but torment me since I've met you... Sure I can teach you, but I'm won't."

"And why not," Johnny asked in a solemn voice.

"Simple... it'll take me all summer just to teach you how to act like an adult." Kevin explained, "Besides mind reading isn't done the way it's portrayed in the movies. It's a little bit more complex than that."

"Well, can you at least give me something to start with," Johnny pleaded. "It's the one special gift I haven't been able to master."

Kevin took a deep breath then thought back over his day and how Johnny helped him find solutions to a variety of problems. "Sure, okay, I'll try... You probably do some variation of this every day and just don't realize it. It starts with knowing what you're looking for. You seem to know a lot about picking up girls, so we'll use that as our example. You're at a bar and you see a girl you're interested in. What do you do?"

Johnny smiled. "Easy... Pull out a wad of hundred dollar bills and buy her a drink with one."

"Are you picking up a hooker or trying to get laid for free?" Kevin asked mockingly. Then he paused for a moment to think. "Okay, the first thing a smart guy does, you know, a guy who doesn't have a wad of hundreds... is watch her until she looks at you. What she does next is very important. If she smiles at you, drops her head, turns to talk to her friend or maybe she looks back at you to see if you're still looking her way. This is all about starting the process of reading this particular girl's mind."

"It seems easy enough."

"Sure, but the idea now is all about controlling the situation you're in. You're sitting, talking and she's getting comfortable with you. Maybe she's smiling and gazing into your eyes, that's when you hit her."

"What?" Johnny recoiled. "I'm not hitting a girl, not even an ugly one!"

Kevin shook his head. "No, you dumb ass, you tell her you're broke... You have no money, no job and no hope of ever having anything."

"Yeah," Johnny interjected, "this is getting stupider by the minute."

"Listen, it gets a little better," Kevin continued. "Then it's all about reaction and response. If she cringes and turns away, if she so much as blinks one eye, then you need to run like a skunk is ready to piss all over you. Because that girl is either looking for love or money. On the other hand, if she's still gazing into your eyes and smiling as if she didn't hear a word you said... Well, then, I'd say you've found yourself a real winner."

Johnny's smile disappeared altogether as he mumbled to himself, "Yeah, I can see you're going to be a real project."

Kevin shrugged his shoulders. "What? You didn't like that?"

"No... It was actually kinda awesome. It almost sounds like your trying to manipulate the situation to come up with the result you want."

"Yeah! You're close!" Kevin barked out, "But the best is yet to come."

Yeah, the best... This guy is a real moron Johnny thought to himself. He noticed a Rolex hanging from the rear view mirror of the squad car and wondered how much of his short life he'll need to spend on this fool and his childish problems. His eyes glaze over as he sits impatiently watching as precious time slips away and slowly his mind begins to drift off in a parallel direction.

I know rule five clearly stats never ask why, but this time I do have to question their motives. This dufus appears to be nothing more than the typical forty year old man-child who just doesn't get it, and probably never will. Maybe I'll start with that, maybe that's the whole job... Teaching Kevin what most he's missing in life... *It.* "It" is an easy concept to explain, at least to a person of average intelligence. It may not be a simple concept for a ten year old boy, but for a guy in his forties, it should be understandable. On the other hand, it would clearly be more effective if he could figure "it" out on his own. Either way, I can't believe my talents are being wasting on this buffoon… I can only assume that God has specific plans already set aside for him. Holy shit! My time is way too important to be wasted on this jackass.

Johnny was suddenly awakened from his thoughts by the sound of a tow truck pulling in.

"So Kev, you didn't answer me." Johnny said while watching the truck hook up to the front of his car. "Do you or do you not have any regrets? Like perhaps taking me out to your favorite bar? Before you answer, remember you have a date with the lovely and talented Coco… That probably doesn't happen if I'm not your wingman."

"Regrets?" Kevin thought for a moment. "That's a hell of a word."

"So tell me about your biggest."

"Well, I'm not sure how this night's going to end yet." Kevin answered. "But as long as I don't end up in front of the magistrate tomorrow, then no, I don't have any regrets including going out and drinking with you."

"Nothing," Johnny drops his head in frustration. "What if you get fired?"

"You said I didn't have to worry about that," Kevin softly moaned. "I look at it this way… I was probably going to get fired sooner or later anyway."

"So you never regretted anything… ever?"

"Look Johnny… Sure, almost everybody has some kind of list. Mine's probably longer and more embarrassing than most. But if you don't have a list before your forty, then you probably didn't live a full life."

Johnny perked back up. "Alright you've got my attention. "Let's hear it, give me your number one."

"What would you do if you found out that the woman you loved, the mother of your son, killed someone?" Kevin asked. "And... and there was no chance the police would ever come up with the evidence to convict her, unless you give it to them. What would you do?"

"You're so full of shit! You never turned your girlfriend in to the police?"

"I may be full of shit!" Kevin tried to hit Johnny then realizes he still has his handcuffs on. "But I'm full of shit with no regrets. Sure I've done my share of foolish things, but I don't regret a single one! That's what makes me who I am."

"Kevin... You do realize you're hated?" Johnny asked in a serious tone. "By almost everyone you've ever met?"

"Yeah, but if I'm disliked by a group of jerk-offs." Kevin replied in a serious tone. "Does that make me the sleazy person? Or them?"

"They all think you're an asshole at the office." Johnny expounds sardonically. "Your whole department can't be wrong. Remember, I said hated, not merely disliked. I'm just saying, maybe you should think about regretting at least one stupid thing you've done. Because it's made you who you are and it appears as though most people think you are an asshole... You do the math!"

"Ha!" Kevin laughed. "You're the one in the back of a police car with me!"

"You seem to have a real problem with seeing things that are sitting right in front of you." Johnny added. "I know I've made plenty of decisions I'd like to go back and change, if I could.

"Shit… Your dad's a millionaire. Why would you even care about your decisions and how they've turned out?"

"We're done talking about me," Johnny ground out in frustration. "Tell me about our boss, Diane. Were you two a thing at one time?"

"Hell no," Kevin shouted, "never!"

"Well, there's got to be something going on between you two," Johnny suggested. "Why else would she have sent me out to spy on you tonight?"

"You were sent to spy," Kevin gave Johnny a dirty look. "And to think I was starting to get comfortable hanging out with you. This was the first time I went out with anyone from the office, ever."

"Thanks, I guess," Johnny said. "I think that was the creepiest compliment I think I've ever received."

When the three men entered the lobby of the police station, Kevin glanced over at the directory and noticed that the honorable Kara McKnight, District Magistrate, was in Room #5.

"You're not going to make me see the Magistrate, are you," Kevin asked.

"Nope, you're free to go," Greg said as he took off both men's handcuffs. Then he directed Johnny to the first open office for processing.

Kevin found a chair tucked in the back corner of the lobby and hid there. After twenty long minutes he saw Johnny's dad enter the lobby and walk straight back to the Sergeant's office, so Kevin did the prudent thing and made a mad dash out the front door.

# Chapter 12

**(8:29 AM Thursday, July 1)** Kevin arrived at the office at eight twenty-nine and ran straight to his cube trying to avoid eye contact with everyone on his floor. As Kevin settled in behind this desk, a comforting, almost safe feeling enveloped him. The job may suck, but no matter what's going wrong out there, it's always safe here inside these hard plastic walls. He logged on to his computer and opened Outlook.

"Twenty-nine new messages... holy shit," Kevin cursed under his breath. The first half dozen were either junk emails or, even worse, work related. So Kevin began his day in the usual manner, by either answering his emails or simply deleting them all together, until he saw it... the one from Diane. So he slid the arrow over on the words 'Dumb Ass' and clicked on it.

SUBJECT: 'Dumb Ass.' It has a cartoon picture of a women's ass falling off, with a caption that reads, 'I'm laughing my ass off at you.' "Great job getting the VPs son arrested, Kev."

Kevin read the first thee lines of Diane's email, and then glanced through subject lines of the remaining emails only to find they were all related to his evening escapades with Johnny. So he highlighted all the new emails including Diane's and clicked on the delete button. Minutes later the sound of a new email rang out and before he could check on it two more sounded off. Kevin found himself being inundated by emails from co-workers in different divisions as well as those outside the main branch, some in support and some trashing him for his stupidity.

Jan stopped outside of Kevin's office and noticed him violently tapping on his delete button. She watched as his face turned a bright red with veins bulging from the top of his forehead all the way down his neck, until they disappeared under his shirt collar. Jan lifted up the hard cover book she was holding and dropped it to the floor.

Kevin sprung back from his desk. "What the hell was that?" he shrieked.

"I was just trying to get your attention." Jan replied. "One of those emails you were deleting with such rage was from Diane. She wants you 'in her office now.' That's a direct quote."

Kevin slid out from behind his desk as Jan picked up her book. The two slowly walked side by side down the hall until Kevin came to an abrupt halt.

"Now means now Kev." Jan said in a firm yet comforting voice. "One word of advice… Before she has a chance to start screaming at you, just asks her if she's been working out. Or tell her you think her butt looks spectacular. For some reason she thinks it does." Then she reached out grabbing Kevin by the wrist, trying to pull him along. "If you ask me she has no butt, I personally prefer a little more meat on the bone."

Jan stopped Kevin outside of Diane's closed door. She softly tapped on the glass with her finger nail then opened it.

"The moron, umm I mean, Kevin is here." Jan whispered as she stuck her head in Diane's office.

Jan shoved the door open with her left hand while pulling on Kevin's hand with her right. Suddenly, Kevin felt the grip of a large hand on his bicep pulling in the other direction.

"My father would like you to stop down at his office." Johnny said. "He didn't say immediately, but I think it might have something to do with... well, last night's trip to the police station."

Kevin leaned in through Diane's door opening, "I'm going down to say 'Hi' to the Vice President." He smiled and raised one eye brow. "Do you think he wants to discuss a promotion?" Then his smile turned into a frown as he dropped his head and followed Johnny down the hall.

"So, how you feeling about regrets right now?" Johnny asked in a hushed tone.

"Freaking great," Kevin snapped as he nervously tapped his ear with his index finger, "because when I'm finished with that arrogant cop, he'll be the one that's regretting crossing paths with me... with me and you."

Johnny rolled his eyes towards the ceiling in frustration. Maybe I wasn't sent here to get that Lisa chick fired he thought... maybe he wants me to destroy that police officer's reputation. This guy has a real problem with authority. First there's Diane, his boss... and obviously, he has issues with marriage... then there's that police officer.... I'm thinking that poor cop probably pulled over the wrong two guys yesterday.

Then Johnny turned toward Kevin with a forced smile. "Yeah, you were right. I didn't like his attitude at all." Johnny whispered trying to calm Kevin down.

Kevin grabbed Johnny's arm stopping him. "Don't worry. We'll get even with that cop." he said with a firm voice before continuing down the hallway. "I'll just wait until he makes a mistake. Everyone has flaws... everyone!" Kevin shook his head. "I just have to figure out what his weakness is, and then simply use it against him."

"Are you alright?" Johnny asked. "Are we still alright? I mean, what's with the self-mutilation of your ear?"

"Sure, we're great, if I can just somehow manage to keep my job." Kevin sneered. "But you're going to owe big time, and you can start by finding a way to get that loan approved for me."

"And the ear thing," Johnny questioned.

Kevin lowered his hand from the side of his head. "That's just a little trick my dad taught me. It's supposed to remind me to listen before I speak. It works every time."

Kevin stood at the threshold of the office of the Vice President rehearsing his thoughts for a moment while watching Johnny make one final attempt to smooth things over with his dad. Silently Kevin entered the room with an uneasy feeling. He froze at the sound of the two men trying to argue quietly. There is no way in hell I'm going to survive this mess he thought. Then he closed his eyes and slowly did the sign of the cross while taking a deep breath. This room smells amazing. Is that lavender? No, I think its vanilla. Why can't my office smell this sweet? His eyes flashed open when he heard the muffled sound of a man's deep voice. He looked up to see Johnny standing all alone in the back corner. Kevin scanned the room nervously but couldn't find the VP anywhere.

"I said, would you please shut the door," the VP grumbled. "Why can't I get one person to listen to me around here?"

Kevin heard the man's voice but couldn't make out where he was standing or what he was saying so he continued stepping forward leaving the doors open. "Here we go... I think this is it," he mumbled to himself.

Kevin lunged forward when he was startled by the cracking sound of a door being slammed behind him. Slowly the man's voice became more and more in-focus until he was able to finally distinguish part of a heart-felt apology.

"My son's a bit of a knucklehead," the VP said. "He has had some problems dealing with the transition between being a teenager and becoming an adult. He's a good kid and all. I hope there's no..."

Kevin quickly interrupted, "I understand just what you're going through, Sir." Kevin stepped over to shake his hand with a concerned look on his face. 'I've had similar problems with my own son. Please, I'm sure it's at least in some small way... partially my fault."

"My hope is that this incident can be contained right here and right now," the VP stated in a determined voice.

"I think the best thing to do is just forget this ever happened," Kevin suggested as he turned to leave. He rolled his eyes up towards the heavens and breathed a deep sigh of relief as he quickly exited the enormous office.

On the way back to his cube, Kevin passed by Diane's office and paused just outside her door opening. He wondered if it made sense to waste his time by honoring Diane's request for a meeting. He slowly peeked in the room and saw her staring out the window while talking on the phone, then he quickly shifted back behind the wall. Kevin looked down both empty hallways, at Jan's empty desk and then back into Diane's private domain. Her personal items were still neatly decorating every inch of her spacious office. Her pictures and diplomas were still hanging on the walls, right where she placed them back when she was awarded the big promotion. He slid back behind the wall, took a deep breath and then leaned forward again... his eyes quickly shifted to the dark window where Diane stands looking out. His gaze locks on her long golden curly hair that leads to her soft shoulders. His eyes get lost when they slide down the back of this beautiful women hiding out in a dark bulky business suit. He wonders what her body really looks like under all those clothes and what drives her to wear that sexless style of clothes in the first place. God she's got the sexiest head of hair I've ever seen in my life Kevin thought. I'd love to march over there right now and run my fingers through it. His mind drifts back to the first time he met her, and the time when he had a little crush on her, just a few short years ago. She always wore the raciest clothes in the office. Damn Sam, she set that bar quite high. I thought that bar would never be reached. And then along came Lisa, now I wonder who's going to fill that void.

Diane noticed Kevin's reflection in the window and smiled for a short second before quickly spinning around with her hand cupped over the phone. "What in the hell are you staring at," she whispered in a harsh voice. She watched as Kevin quietly slithered out the door. "This isn't one of your ten dollar peeping-tom shows," she yelled at his retreating back.

Kevin turned and poked his head back through the door opening for one more look.

"What," she cried out.

"Jan told me to compliment you on your firm ass," Kevin whispered loudly. "I'm not sure why, I don't see anything special." Then he continued on the journey back to his cube but couldn't stop wondering why wasn't she packing up her things yesterday? What the hell is going on in this building?

# Chapter 13

**(5:30 PM Thursday, July 1)**  Kevin flew through the parking lot knowing he was already late.  He immediately checked the scoreboard and saw that the visitors were up by one run in the top of the second inning.  That's the way to start off a game, Kevin thought, as he raced over to the chain link fence that parallels the third base line.  He paused for a moment when he noticed a runner standing on second base.  Then, out of the corner of his eye, Kevin's attention was captured by the moves of the next batter as he approached the plate.  Most ten year old boys that play tournament baseball are roughly about the same height and build.  If not for the bright bold numbers on their backs most of the parents wouldn't recognize their own children from a distance.  But in just an instant Kevin knew who the new batter was.  It's his own son, Mark.  He has that one distinct difference that separates him from all the other kids and that's the patented Willie Stargell cranking motion.  Kevin watched in anticipation as his boy prepared to swing.  One crank, followed by a pause, then a second crank quickly followed by a third; exactly the way his idol did it so many years ago.

Every spring before the baseball season starts, Mark religiously watches an old video tape of Pop's.  Then he runs up the steps and emulates the motion in front of his mirror, practicing until he gets it just right.  Kevin heard that sweet sound of an aluminum bat striking a Wilson baseball and watched joyously as the ball soared over the third basemen's head.  Mark rounded first digging for second, while Kevin jogged down the third base fence line following the baseball and the left fielder into the corner, all the while screaming, "Go Mark, go!"

Kevin stood there, leaning against the fence, trying to catch his breath. He lifted his head and saw Mark standing on third base as if he just won an easy game of king of the hill.

I wonder if any of the other parents get it, Kevin thought, as he proudly strutted out to his favorite spot to sit. Yeah, James has his multimillion dollar company and sure Ron has his palace at the end of the street, but I have something that all their money combined can't buy... a son batting over six hundred.

Like most self-made millionaires, James is a bit of an overachiever at times. Like the fact that he religiously fills out an official score book at every game, keeping notes in the margins on all the little nuances of the game. Such as the double Stacy hit before Mark's triple or the fact that Mark was pitching a no-hitter, but before James could finish his own personal version of ESPN's highlight reel Kevin butted in.

"Okay, that's great news! Now give me all the gory details, and don't leave anything out." Kevin clasped his hands together as if he was praying. "Did itty-bitty Ronny weep like a little girl when he was removed as manager," he asked in a baby voice.

"Oh, that..." James paused. "Sorry, my friend, both you and your son struck out once today!"

"What?"

"Yeah," James screamed out while watching his son hit a double that drove Mark in from third base. "Do you believe it? Ron is still the manager. I guess you're just not quite as good as you think you are."

"Hmmm... Try to have a little patience my old and filthy rich friend, I'm just getting started!" Kevin threw his hands behind his head and leaned back, resting his feet up against the outfield fence. "I've got all summer to torment Ron. Although truthfully, I am a bit shocked. And, frankly, I'm more than a little disappointed in the lack of concern these mothers are showing toward their so-called babies."

James made the patented "L" with his thumb and finger plastered to his forehead, while taunting, "Loser!"

"No...! If I thought for even one moment," Kevin whined, "that what I texted to Jules was true, I would never have let Mark play for Coach Ron again. I'm telling you, I've really lost what little respect I had for those so-called mothers!"

Twelve outs and forty-five minutes later, Kevin looked at his phone and saw that he was out of time. So he folded up his chair and waved goodbye to Mark as he ran to his car. I hate missing even one minute of a game, he thought. But tonight does have the potential of being a special night.

Kevin arrived at Gloria's with just a few minutes to spare and Dave gave him the nod as he sat up at the bar.

"Brother, I don't know what you said to that girl yesterday," Dave giggled. "But hot damn... she's fully charged and ready to go."

Kevin began frantically chugging his beer, hoping to take the edge off of his nervousness, but also knowing he will barely have enough time to finish one.

"What the hell does that even mean Dave," Kevin questioned. "What's fully charged... and what's ready to go?"

Dave grabbed the beer out of Kevin's hand spilling it on the counter between them. "Calm down Sunshine, I'm just screwing with you."

Just then Coco stepped out of the dancers' dressing room and noticed Kevin arguing with Dave. "Stay away from that big ol' teddy bear," she exclaimed as she grabbed Kevin's arm pulling him away from Dave. "He's nothing but trouble."

Kevin's eyes rolled to the back of his head as Coco began to softly rub his back. Slowly he slid his right hand under the back of her shirt running a single finger up then down, delicately stroking her lower back.

Coco slowly leaned in closer to him. Her warm breath ran chills down his spine. "Stop that," she whispered sharply. "That freaking tickles… besides, there are rules around here. I can touch you all I want. If you touch me Dave has to throw you out."

Kevin dropped his head. "Sorry."

"Plus, I'm not allowed to date the patrons," Coco explained, "and you know I can't afford to get fired."

"Maybe we should just head over to get that cup of coffee now," Kevin said sheepishly.

"Good idea," Coco softly replied as dimples dotted both sides of her gorgeous smile. "They have a corner booth in the back." Then she winked to him.

The two new friends took the short walk across the street and down the road one block to Starbucks. Like any true gentleman Kevin opened the door for Coco. As she took one step inside, she swiftly spun around and stepped right back out the door.

"Ummm… we can't go in there tonight," Coco murmured in a disappointed tone.

Kevin stood there with a confounded look on his face.

"It's nothing, Kev. It's just… there's someone I know in there." She grabbed his hand and began pulling him back out the door. "I'm sorry. It might be best if we just go back to the bar."

Kevin held tight to the door trying to stand his ground. "Could that someone be a guy you once dated?"

Knowing her ex-boyfriend and his nasty personality, Coco continued tugging on Kevin's hand. "He's very possessive… he'll make your life a living hell." Then she let go of his hand and began walking down the sidewalk toward Gloria's.

Kevin cautiously looked around as he entered the restaurant. The first thing that caught his eye was a pair of older men sitting at a table, playing cards. I hope like hell she didn't date one of those two old geezers. He continued methodically scanning the room as if he were casing the joint. His eyes shifted slowly from one table to the other until he spotted the next group, two teens sipping their Grande Frappuccinos and playing games on their iPhones. Next, he saw a younger man with short black hair sitting at a corner table with a slightly gray-haired man, both facing the other way… bingo he thought. His eyes caught sight of two navy blue ball caps hanging on the coat hooks on the end of the half wall separating him from the men. Kevin slowly tip-toed over while continually watching the back of the men's heads… then he spun one of the hats so he could get a better look at it. "You've got to be shitting me," he muttered under his breath as he flipped the hat back on the rack. He watched in horror as it spun on the rack before falling to the floor.

"Hey Son, where are you going in such a hurry," one of the men hollered at Kevin's retreating back.

Kevin stopped, turned around and found himself standing face to face with Greg.

"Hey, it's that dumb ass that I pulled over yesterday," Greg yelled back to his partner who was picking up his hat off of the floor.

Kevin's face turned beet red as he hurried out the door. He began jogging down the sidewalk, anxiously looking for Coco, until he noticed her car pulling out of Gloria's parking lot. Kevin slowed to a walk and decided it was probably a good time to call it a night and drive home also.

As he swung his car into the driveway he saw James standing in his yard.

"Ladies and gentlemen," James proclaimed as if he were a herald in the royal court. "It is my privilege to introduce to you to the amazing Kevin!  I am not worthy," he said while bowing down deeply before Kevin.

Kevin looked up with a big smile on his face. "One question… why can't I get the ladies to say those words to me," he asked while climbing out of his car.

James grudgingly pulled a hundred dollar bill out of his wallet. Then he crinkled it up and threw it across the yard at Kevin.

He picked up the crumpled bill, smoothed it out and stuck it in his back pocket. "What… I won the bet… already?"

"Well, now, that depends on what your definition of winning is," James gave Kevin a look of disgust.  "If you think going from a manager that throws like a girl to one that looks like a girl is a good thing… then yeah, you won."

"What the hell does that mean," Kevin asked.

"Apparently while the game was going on," James explained, "the women had their own little meeting up in the bleachers between themselves.  They called the vice president of Fox Chapel Baseball Association and he decided that it was best for the team, not to mention the entire baseball organization, for Ron to step down from his position as manager.  At least until the matter of his criminal background can be reviewed at the next FCBA meeting…  Then because Dee was the team mom, handled all the paper work and regularly attended all the meetings, they decide to appoint her as acting manager."

Kevin began rubbing his temples.  "Who the hell is Dee again… and why would anyone pick a woman to be the manager?"

"Dee is Ron's wife. You know, the mother who collects all the money, emails out the tournament schedules and all the changes… the team mother. Don't you pay attention to anything that goes on around here?"

"Whatever… Anyway, it's all about winning, and I won the bet," Kevin rolled his eyes and shrugged his shoulders, "You never know, she might be a better manager than Ron… She can't be any worse. I have no doubt she can throw faster and hit further than him. And she's got to be better looking than him… right? Please tell me she's better looking than him."

"A woman manager…" James groaned. "We're going to be the laughing stock of all Little League baseball." James sat down on Kevin's front porch and cracked open a beer. "Speaking of better looking women… and your fantasy world… How did your date go with the stripper?"

"The date? Hmmm…" Kevin sat there thinking over the short time he spent with Coco. "I think it started out okay."

"The kiss… Please describe the good night kiss. Did she just give you a little peck on the cheek," James spoke in baby talk. "Or was it on the lips? Ooh, or was there tongue involved?" He shouted in an enthusiastic voice. "The more tongues the better."

"No, I'm certain I'd remember if there was a tongue involved," Kevin slowly shook his head in disappointment. "I've got to be honest with you. I don't believe there were any kisses."

"There had to be a kiss good night."

"No," Kevin continued shaking his head, "I think something might have gone wrong. I'm not sure… I'll have to call her tomorrow to find out." Kevin looked over at James who's staring out into the dark of the night. "Hello? Are you listening to me?"

"Yeah, I heard you... no kiss," James mumbled his response and then he paused for a moment to think. "Did she at least show up wearing pasties and a G-string?"

"Are you sure this is my fantasy girl and not yours," Kevin snapped back. "Because last time I checked she wasn't a stripper, so quit trying to imagine her that way. That's my job."

The two men passed the next hour or so drinking beer on Kevin's porch until Kevin's cell phone beeped once signaling a new text. He saw it was from Dave so he anxiously opened it in anticipation of getting a message from him about Coco.

**"I have 2 of your friends here & they're PLASTERED!!! Come remove them immediately!!!"**

**"WHAT-- I'm a taxi driver now?"** Kevin hits send.

The phone beeped again. **"If I call a cab to this address, the cops & media will beat them here looking 4 another incident!"**

**"Neither one of us wants that to happen & they're looking 4 a reason 2 close Gloria's. I'll B there soon!"**

Kevin hit send, and then tried to talk James into going along with him. He struck out with James, so he found himself driving back to Gloria's all alone to try to rescue his two buddies. He began his search by sifting through the small crowd of men who were gathered on the steps by Gloria's front door. Kevin worked his way through and when he finally reached the bottom he saw a mob swarming near the close end of the bar. He reluctantly shoved his way through outside layer of guys only to find himself standing in the middle of some fool's bachelor party where two overzealous dancers were busy fighting for every dollar the men had to offer. Kevin quickly glanced over to the far end of the bar and saw Dave twitching his head to the right, gesturing in the direction where his friends were located. Kevin scanned the back corner leading up to the stage only to see a half dozen screaming girls with their hands held high, waving dollar bills.

Dave reached in and pulled Kevin out of the tight group of men then pointed up past the screaming girls to the stage.

"Oh no, my eyes," Kevin yelled out as he looked up on the stage to see Ron and Tony already stripped down to their t-shirts and underwear. "Is there any worse sight on the face of this earth, than two out of shape forty-something year old men, stripped down and trying to dance?"

"I don't know which one of your friends I find more repulsive… the one in plain tighty-whities wearing the gray sweater, or the short guy wearing white boxers with pink ducks all over them who sounds like a girl." Dave complained. "Or are those pink flamingos?"

"I find the fact that you're looking at them that closely the most revolting," Kevin suggested while partially shielding his eyes.

"Hey, it could be worse. What about…?"

"No," Kevin hollered, "don't say it! I can't take any more of those disturbing images in my head… Ahhh crap, it's too late! Let's just get them off the stage before the image in my mind turns in to reality, because it's one hell of a disturbing picture."

"Ewww gross! That's not a freaking sweater," Kevin shuddered as he and Dave dragged Tony off the stage.

Then the two men went back for Ron. The girls continued stuffing dollar bills in his shorts as they pulled Ron down off the stage. They sat the two drunks down at a small table near the stage.

"Well, I was going to ask which one of you…" Kevin stepped back to get a better look at the two men, "which one of you two stud muffins is too drunk to drive home? But I think we all know the answer to that stupid question!"

They both begin laughing hysterically and pointing at each other.

"Did you hear the great newsssss," Ron stood up and spoke in an exaggerated whisper, slurring heavily, "The mothers fff...fired my assss!" Ron began swaying back and forth waving a handful of dollar bills in the air. "Woohoo!"

"That's real nice," Kevin replied in an irritated voice. "I give these girls my hard earned money, and they pass it on to you two fools." Kevin tried to shove Ron back down in his seat. "Please lower your voice a little, there's people here trying to enjoy the strippers in peace and quiet. And, for God's sake, put that money away. The last thing we need right now is a bunch of those vultures over here!"

"I think she'sss going to leave me," Ron said before downing his next shot. "But I'm...mm... okay...? I think."

"Jeez!" Kevin waved Dave over to the table. "Could you possibly quit sending shots over to our table?"

"Sorry Kev," Dave said. "The short one bought a bottle when he came in, so I have to keep pouring as long as they keep asking or until the finish the bottle... whichever comes first."

"But I thought our plan was to avoid an incident if at all possible," Kevin asked.

"It is how we make money here, Sweetie, by selling drinks," Dave responded in a sarcastic tone. "Don't panic, Kev... They were pounding them pretty damn quick, they should be finished soon."

Ron slouched down in his chair, staring at his shot glass. "What should I dooooo?"

"I'll tell you what you shouldn't do..." Kevin said while counting the empty glasses on the table. "Let's start with this... Quit talking to your shot glass like it's a crystal ball."

"I've got... It..." Tony muttered. "I think... No make that I know..."

"Whatever you have, keep it to yourself," Kevin quickly snapped. "We don't want it all over us!"

"No... I mean...nn it... This is... going to be good." Tony explained while constantly glancing over at a four foot tall girl dressed in a sexy white lace diaper and baby bonnet. "When my clients ask me if they should sell a certain stock in their portfolio, I tell them... to ask them... self... would I... they... buy stock in that company now? Therein lies... the most pertinent question!"

The three men watched as the petite girl danced over next to them. Slowly she pulled the Velcro loose and removed the diaper to reveal a tiny white lace thong which appeared to be held together by rhinestone-studded diaper pins. Then she placed the diaper on Ron's head as she rubbed her breasts sensuously into the back of Tony's head.

"I'mmm sorry... but... are youuu a real baby?" Ron asked the miniature stripper.

"What the hell are you babbling about Tony?" Kevin stood up and grabbed the two men's jackets. "Put your pants on so we can get the hell out of here!"

"No... Hold on... I think I know what you're sssaying!" Ron shouted across the table at Tony while still wearing a diaper on the top of his head. "I should... go home... March right into my bedroom... and ask my wife... if she knew everything about me... Before us ggg...got... Would she still have married me anyway...? I like that idea!"

"Yeah... great idea! You're almost as wise as Confucius over there," Kevin latched onto Ron's arm pulling him up out of his chair. "Oh, and Ron, if you want your wife to take you seriously, you'll want to take the diaper off your head. And Tony, unless you're planning to walk home, you better get your Confucius ass in my car!"

# Chapter 14

(5:30 PM Friday, July 2) Kevin was scrambling to try to get his chair set up before the first pitch was thrown. He zigzagged his way along the fence line trying to avoid the puddles which were scattered on the path that circled the field. Then he felt a strong gust of wind blow across the back of his neck. He turned around to gaze up at the dark sky when the next gust brought with it a light mist that slapped him across the face.

"I hope we get this game in today," Kevin said as he quickly unfolded his chair between James and Tony.

Tony raised his coffee mug full of beer in salute. "Congrats Kevin, that's a job well done."

Kevin glanced over at James. "I'm guessing you filled him in on 'Operation Eliminate Manager Ron'."

Tony slapped Kevin's shoulder. "Hell yeah, he told me... and I must say I'm pretty impressed. Maybe next time you can perform some real magic and install a man as the mannnnnager? Get it! It's in the freaking word... m-a-n-ager."

"Got it," Kevin moaned. "Obviously I'm not proud of the end results of this particular operation. I mean... having a woman managing our kids isn't quite what I had in mind." Kevin turned to James. "Did you tell him about 'Operation Eliminate Co-Worker'?" Then he looked over at Tony. "If you think getting Ron removed as the team's manager was something, you should have spent the last week at my office. You would've shit yourself... It was truly a thing of beauty. I was about to…"

James stopped Kevin as soon as he started. "I've already filled him in on your sleazy ways." Then he heard Ron's voice coming from the third base line and getting louder. "New subject, here comes Ron."

Ron stopped next to Tony and began setting up what appeared to be some type of tent. James offered his condolences to Ron for losing his manager's position and the other two guys quickly added their sympathies as well.

"I don't get it," Ron grumbled. "They told me that incident would be expunged from my record."

"I blame the internet," one of the men quickly cut in.

"How did you know," Ron asked in a shocked voice. "I hosted my brother-in-law's bachelor party at my house and one of his jerky friends downloaded kiddie porn onto my computer…"

"Too much information," Kevin cried as he covered his ears with both hands.

"But I was innocent… you guys gotta believe me," Ron pleaded.

"Alright, please make him stop," Kevin cried out, "I'm feeling just a little uncomfortable."

"I wonder how in the hell someone else found out," Ron asked.

Suddenly the soft mist turned into a slight drizzle.

"I don't know about you two, but I'm ready for a new subject," Kevin sighed.

"I've got a subject for you, Kev," Ron barked. "How about... We need to find a way to get rid of my wife as the team manager."

"Speaking of your loving wife Dee..." Kevin hollered over to Ron. "Did you decide to recite Tony's words of wisdom last night?"

"Yes and no..." Ron moaned. "I tried, but I think in my drunken state I may have mixed up the order of the words a little. And now I think there's a possibility I might have made things a bit worse."

"Now how could anything possible go wrong," Kevin asked sarcastically. "Tony spelled out every step for you. It seemed almost fool-proof."

James raised his hand. "I'm guessing 'fool' was the key word there!"

"All I remember for sure is..." Ron said. "When I was done explaining she said she wasn't really thinking about a trial separation, but if that's what I was suggesting, she was willing to give it a try!"

"Who would've ever thought I'd be handing out relationship advice," Kevin said mockingly. "But here goes... Never, under any circumstance, should you take marriage advice from a drunken man... especially when you're plastered yourself. It's just not a good policy!"

"Bad subject..." Ron complained. "Got anything else to talk about?"

Kevin watched as Stacy deftly stepped to the right to backhand a hard-hit ground ball behind the second base bag before turning to make a strong throw to first base.

"How about this one," Kevin asked. "Tony, what kind of father names his boy Stacy? That sounds more like a girl's name."

The three men paused while setting up the tent and shouted out at the same exact time. "She IS a girl! You Dumb Ass!"

"Damn Sam…" She's better than most of the boys, Kevin thought, this could really get embarrassing for some of the parents.

A couple of innings later, the four men huddled under Ron's tent and watched as the rain began to fall a little harder and a little harder, until the inevitable finally happened… a flash of lighting followed by the roar of thunder.

"The good news is, we're winning. And we've played enough innings," Kevin stated, "so if they call the game, we'll get our first victory!"

"Sorry Ron," James said, "I'm sure it's just a coincidence."

They watched as the kids raced through the brown soupy infield and into the dugout. Then with a wave of the umpire's hand the game was called and the four men began packing up their things. Tony pulled Kevin aside and quietly asked him if he could hang around to talk for a few minutes after everyone leaves.

Kevin ran from his car to Tony's and jumped into the front seat. "You're not mad about the whole girl thing, are you?" Kevin jokingly asked. "Because I was just kidding, I knew Stacy was a girl." They watched as their two kids chased each other in the wet sloppy outfield, slipping and sliding, until Stacy finally pushed Mark over into the slop. "She's not only fast but also strong… Are you sure she's a girl? Because she's pretty tough and a damn good ball player."

"Yeah, she's a girl… And yeah, she's a good ballplayer, but that's not why I asked you to stay." Tony began to explain exactly what he does for a living as an investment advisor. "With the economy still so sluggish and the residual fear of investing, things are getting really bad for my business."

"I'm sorry," Kevin said interrupting Tony, "but I already have a financial advisor. I'd like to help you out… I can't imagine what you're going through, but I don't have much money. What little I do have, I've invested it with my cousin, Joe Nicholson. I hope you can understand."

Tony patiently waited for Kevin to finish then laughed. "No, that's not it at all. I'd never try to give you a sales pitch, especially not out here."

"What? My money's not good enough for you," Kevin asked in an indignant voice.

"Nothing... What? Look Kev, the help I'm asking for is... Well, I'm not sure how to say this without me sounding like an asshole, but here goes... I just lost one of my bigger clients to a competitor and now she's trying to convince two of my biggest clients into making the switch to her new advisor. If they go with her, they'll take with them about twenty-five percent of my business. But that's not even the worst part... No one wants to stay with a sinking ship. When word gets out, I'll lose everything... Everything my dad built up over the last forty years will be gone in a few days."

"What do you want me to do," Kevin reluctantly asked.

"We need to somehow convince them into staying," Tony explained. "Think it over this evening... Try to come up with a few strategies and we'll discuss them tomorrow. If you think up something worth trying, I'll give you a thousand dollars just to implement the plan." Tony handed Kevin an envelope before continuing. "Here's a hundred for your time tonight... All I'm looking for right now is to save one client. That's all I need. I'll give you two thousand more, if you can accomplish that much."

"Aaaah..." Kevin sat there stuttering with his eyes glued to the envelope.

"Well, what do you say Kev?"

"Shit... you're damn right I'll do it," Kevin grabbed the envelope out of Tony's hand. "What do you think I'm crazy? I'd do it for free." Then he got his BlackBerry out and started taking notes.

"Okay, give me as much information about the two clients as you can," he enthusiastically asked. "I'm thinking maybe we can sort of blackmail them, maybe just a little… Perhaps we can convince them that leaving is the wrong thing to do, without pissing them off to the point that they do leave. Don't mind me I'm just thinking out loud. I'm sure there's a fine line, I'll just have to walk it. Give me their names and…" Kevin paused to think. "I'm sure phone numbers are out of the question… emailing them won't work either. I need some way to send them something anonymously… Hot Damn! This has the potential of being fun."

"Oh, one more thing…" Kevin added, "if they're thinking of leaving you, do we know where they're moving the investments to? I mean, do they have a new advisor already set up?"

Tony took a deep breath then sat there in silence.

"What? Did I say something wrong," Kevin asked.

"I was afraid you were going to ask me that. I'm almost certain they're both following the first person… and…"

"And…" Kevin prompted him to continue.

"And… she has already moved her investments to your cousin, Joe's firm."

Kevin began softly laughing as he considered Tony's dilemma. "You're kidding right?" He looked over at Tony who sat simply staring at the dash board. "Oh shit, you're serious!"

"I'll understand if…"

"Oh no, you don't… Give me a day, let me think," Kevin looked out the window at Mark who was completely covered in mud. "Let me ask you this… What's the very worst thing you can do in your profession? I mean something you'd lose your license over?"

"The worst," Tony thought for a second. "I guess... embezzling money."

"Alright," Kevin paused a moment, "but this has to be something he's done... Plus we'd have to prove it. Maybe we should start by telling me why your clients are considering leaving you?"

"I invested their money in tech stocks back in the late nineties," Tony promptly answered. "As you could imagine, that didn't go over very well. So as we made some of the money back, of course, I went the safe route and moved their money into bank stocks and real estate."

"Hmmm, I'm guessing that didn't go over too well either."

"Nope, they've lost a lot of money," Tony looked out the window and saw Stacy making mud angels in the infield. "Joe's known in the investment circles as a true risk taker. All we need to do is send a ninety year old widow over to him, and after he throws her money into a risky stock investment..."

"Hold up," Kevin butted in. "Are you looking for results while we're both still alive? Maybe I should just think it over tonight. We'll talk again tomorrow"

On the way home Kevin thought about what Tony said and decided he might need some help with this new project. At first Johnny's name came to mind, he's a sinister kid with both money and connections. But who better to get advice from than The Master, his own flesh and blood, Joe.

When you finally make the decision to take someone down, Kevin thought, usually the best, most effective course of action is to pray on their greatest weaknesses. Joe is not only a conniving son of a bitch, but I've never met another human being who's fuller of himself. I bet he'll have some great ideas for me.

Like any good small business man who works with the public, Joe has a variety of ways that he can be reached. First Kevin tried the traditional phone call. He started by calling Joe's office in town, then he tried the home office followed by the cell phone. After striking out on the phone calls, he decided to try the new feature on his phone and sent Joe an email, but Joe was playing hard to get... Finally, Kevin had one last hope. No one can resist the 'text', not even Joe. Within seconds, Kevin received a reply and clicked on Joe's text to open it.

**"I'm trying to avoid talking to you, Dumb Shit."**

So Kevin texted back, **"It's an emergency... Call me now!"**

Joe's a typical man who loves to hear bad news about anyone other than himself. But there's nothing better than hearing bad news from a distant relative, especially when your own life is in a free fall.

Kevin picked up his vibrating phone and heard Joe's deep voice on the other end. "Alright... What did you do now, you Dumb Ass?"

"I need to meet with you tomorrow," Kevin answered in a panicked voice.

"Out of the question, Kev," Joe replied forcefully.

There's only one thing Joe likes better than hearing about my miserable life. That's when he's given an opportunity to share his wisdom with me on how I can patch it back together Kevin thought.

"Joe, I need to go over my portfolio," Kevin began begging. "I know this doesn't make sense to you now, but I'll explain my problem to you tomorrow over a beer. Please, you're the only one I can count on."

"Fine," Joe groused. "As you know, I have a very busy schedule, so I'll grant you ten minutes. Be here at six... And you better be in a lot of trouble! I want to hear that you're going to prison or something worse."

## Chapter 15

**(6:00 PM Saturday, July 3)** Kevin slowly drove through Joe's neighborhood looking at all the houses. Each one appeared to be bigger and more beautiful than the last. *Geez, I can't believe there are enough doctors, lawyers and CPA's in the Pittsburgh area to fill this development. I bet some of these houses are owned by drug dealers or something he thought.* He pulled his Sonata onto Joe's stamped concrete driveway and sat for a moment staring at the flawlessly landscaped yard that surrounded a house that appeared to be modeled after Cinderella's castle. As he meandered up the flagstone sidewalk past topiaries that would have made Walt Disney proud he couldn't help wondering how Joe made enough money to afford all this. *Shit, now I know where all my invested money went... I should take a couple of these stones or maybe a small shrub with me when I leave.*

Joe met him partway down the sidewalk, "So, whatcha think of mi new casa? It's fantastico, eh?"

"I don't understand... How did you..." Kevin muttered while pointing at the turrets and the spires rising out of roofline of Joe's new house.

"If I'm still in a good mood when we're done exploring your problem, then maybe I'll give you a tour," Joe said in an elitist voice.

"Didn't we have a stock market crash in two thousand and hasn't the market gone up and down since then like a yo-yo?"

Joe looked down at Kevin and shrugged his shoulders, "What?"

Kevin pointed up at Joe's house and across his front yard. "What do you mean what? Where did you get the money for all of this?"

Joe began walking towards the left side of the house. "C'mon, my office is around the side now. We'll talk there."

Kevin followed Joe along the beautiful flagstone walkway that meandered through the gardens surrounding the two and a half story Victorian style house. He stopped in the middle of a small arched bridge that crossed over one of the two ornamental koi ponds and gawked at all the concrete statuary mixed in with the shrubs flanking each pond. Kevin couldn't help but think to himself that no one deserves to live a life in this fantasy land.

As they entered the octagon room, Joe pointed out the vaulted ceiling and the eight foot high doors. "My builder suggested I have them installed so I wouldn't feel as if I was always walking around in a cave."

Kevin sat down across the desk from Joe. As he sat there staring at Joe's huge body, he couldn't help but think to himself there is no way I'm related to this freak of a giant. His father must have sprinkled HGH (human growth hormone) on his Wheaties or something. Joe pulled out a remote control and pushed one of the buttons. Slowly the blinds inside the windows opened revealing a built-in swimming pool with a pool house that wrapped half-way around the far right side. At the far left side, there is a thirty foot waterfall that cascades down into the pool.

Joe stuffed the remote back in the top drawer of his desk and pulled out his laptop. He opened up Kevin's file and spun the laptop around to show Kevin his so-called portfolio. It was nothing more than a one page report detailing his three different investment accounts.

"Okay, Kev, what's the big emergency," Joe impatiently asked. "Why did we have to meet on a Saturday evening… just to go over this?"

"It's not my portfolio that I'm worried about," Kevin answered. "I'm more concerned…"

Joe stood up and leaned over the desk. "I didn't think so," he glared down at Kevin. "I figured you were here to steal free advice from the Genius… I want to know who sent you," he demanded arrogantly.

"I don't need any free advice," Kevin snapped back. "Well, I do… But not stock advice per se. I just met this guy. He's one of the fathers from Mark's baseball team. You might know him, Tony Carlino. He's in the same line of work as you."

"Shit… is he trying…? If he's trying to steal you away from me… if he is, he can have you," Joe laughed. "Of course, it is your duty to at least fill him in on the fact that you don't have two nickels to rub together?"

"Can we forget about Tony for a moment and get back to my concerns," Kevin ground out in frustration. "Tell me all about how this investing stuff… how does it all work? Why does it seem like everyone's jumping out of the market when it's down and then they wait until it goes up to get back in?"

"Well, here's the thing Kev… You can't go by what those jabones say on TV," Joe explained. "By the time they report something it's already old news. What I'm trying to say is… you just have to trust me to take care of your, well, your small portfolio. And don't worry… I won't steer you in the wrong direction. Besides I'm doing great. Except for the tech bubble in two thousand and the drop after the terrorist attacks, I'm up considerably. Not only that, but I'm in the process of pulling off one hell of a coup. While that moron is so busy trying to steal you from me, he's blind to the fact that I'm about to steal his two biggest clients."

"How big is that," Kevin asked.

"If I can land just one of the two, I'll snatch up another cool twenty to thirty grand more per year. Things looking bad," Joe smirked. "Thanks, but you don't have to worry about me."

"Yeah, right…" Kevin snorted. "But my friend…"

Joe snapped his head up from his lap top, "Your amico? Come see me when you what to discuss your neighbor James and his finances."

"Ummm…"

"Is that who we're talking about," Joe paused for a moment. "It is, isn't it? You dog! Why didn't you say so?"

"Is that good…?"

"Good? Kev, I swear, you're so naïve," Joe sighed. "That's why you're never going… Forget it… Kev, you get me a chance at his money and I'll make it so worth your while."

"Yeah, I don't know… it sounds shady," Kevin paused as he tried to think of a way to work this situation into his new plan.

"Kev, forget how it sounds! It sounds like a boat load of freaking cash for me… I mean, for both of us, Kev."

Kevin sat there nervously tapping his car keys against his ear. "Give me a day or two to figure out how to approach James with the idea."

"How about we make him an offer he can't refuse," Joe said in his best mobster's voice.

"Is this legal, you giving me a kickback?"

"Kev, my friend, let's just keep this between us… capisce?"

Kevin cracked a quick smile then sat there stone-faced for several seconds. "I've got a great idea. I'm going to meet some friends at a bar down the street from my house. Why don't you tag along and I'll try to talk James into stopping by... At the very least you can give me some talking points on how to first approach him about making the transition to your firm."

"Kev, I like the way you think... that's why you're my favorite cousin," Joe took off his thick black glasses. "Are there going to be women at this place? I've gotta go throw my contacts in if we're chasing skirts."

"Aren't you married," Kevin asked, surprised.

"Divorced... and sober for two long years now," Joe proudly proclaimed. "And I haven't really been out since then either."

Kevin picked up the glasses and handed them back to Joe. "Put these back on and grab a hand full of small bills... I've got the perfect place for you!" Kevin flashed him a wicked smile. "Young and desperate women as far as the eye can see... That's the good news. The bad news is your buying, 'cause I'm broke again."

The two men made the short drive to Gloria's, Kevin in his Sonata followed by Joe in his Hummer. Kevin led Joe to his favorite table in the corner. At first Joe was being relatively conservative, drinking club soda and just enjoying the scenery. But Kevin made sure Joe's favorite drink, Jack Daniel's and Diet Coke, was always on the table within easy reach and there was always a girl on his lap. At least until he loosened up a little. After three hours, Joe had downed approximately thirteen mixed drinks. Kevin began to realize his original simple plan was morphing into a much more complex plan... and he was going to need some professional help soon.

Kevin knew it was time to set the wheels of his new plan in motion when he observed Joe slurping his fourth shot of straight Jack directly off the belly of a stripper who was lying across the bar top in front of them.

Joe slid off the bar stool then staggered his way to the men's room for a final pit stop before calling it a night. While his cousin struggled to remain upright at the urinal in the men's room, Kevin quietly approached Dave at the bar and asked him to call his connection at the police station.

Dave called the dispatcher and explained to her that he had a customer who was clearly too drunk to drive. Yes, he tried to get the keys off him, but unfortunately the customer refused to comply.

Kevin sat back and watched as his cousin staggered up the steps leading to the front door. Then he stood up and high-fived Dave. "Tonight we win one for Tony!" They cheered as they raced up to the back door to see the show. The two men covertly poked their heads out, watching until Joe was past the back exit and standing out by his car.

Joe managed to open his car door before dropping his keys on the ground. While he was bent over trying to pick them up he was startled by the sound of sirens. Within seconds, three police cars swarmed in surrounding the Hummer. Joe panicked and did the worst thing imaginable; he stood up and began running. One cop hit him high as another one hit him low. Joe went down like a soft running back, smashing his face into the gravel parking lot. By the time the police were finished with Joe, he was tasered twice, smacked in the back of the legs with a nightstick, cuffed and stuffed into one of the squad cars. Kevin followed behind the cops, catching all the action on his BlackBerry by using the video camera feature.

Dave walked over to talk with one of the cops just as Coco stepped out to see what all the commotion was about. "What'd I miss," she asked Kevin while leaning on the rail next to him.

Kevin shrugged his shoulders, "Nothing, I guess."

"Kev, isn't that your friend getting hauled away?"

Kevin slowly nodded his head, "Yeah... Yeah I believe your right."

"Well, I guess the only bright spot is I don't see the news media," Coco observed with a smile.

"Yeah, we can't afford to have this end up on the six o'clock news," Kevin replied sarcastically as he rolled his eyes.

Coco took the blue ribbon out of her hair then ran her fingers through it fluffing it out. "What do you think?" she paused and pointed at the police all gathered around the one squad car. "Why are the cops hauling him out?"

"I'm not exactly sure what happened... But the good news is... I mean... I just might be four grand richer." Kevin said in an upbeat voice as he forwarded the video to a couple of his friends in the media business. The two stood there on the back patio of Gloria's bar watching as the excitement wound down. Suddenly they noticed that one of the officers was Greg, so they both turned to rush inside at the same time, running into each other.

Kevin quickly pushed Coco back into the bar and decided the timing couldn't be more perfect to pop the question.

"I couldn't help but notice that you're trying to avoid being seen by that one particular cop. Is there something I should know about you two?"

Coco smiled while running her fingers through her hair. "Is that the sound of jealousy rearing its ugly head?" Then she slowly put her hair back up and retied the blue ribbon.

"Seriously... I want to hear it all," Kevin repeated his request.

"Hmm, let's see... There's not a lot to tell," Coco replied softly. "Up until a few weeks ago I worked at Omar's bar in the South Hills. Just about every Saturday night Greg would show up late with his out of town buddies. Everyone who hangs at Omar's has money, but theses dudes had tons of cash. The girls loved it when Greg showed up with his friends. And why not? He treated us all like princesses. When I first met him, I didn't realize he was a police officer." Coco's smile slowly disappeared. "Most of the time Greg acts like a nice normal guy. You know, like someone you'd like to have a beer with, fun to be around. Although, I swear... one time, I think I walked in on them while they were snorting cocaine. Anyway, long story short, we went out a few times, then we broke up and I took the job here at Gloria's. Other than that, I'm not sure there's anything else I can tell you."

"How about his so-called friends, where were they from," Kevin continued to probe.

"Hmmm... I'd say for the most part, they were different men from different areas. There was one guy who was with him almost every time though. Oh! How 'bout this?" Coco pointed into Kevin's face. "Some of them didn't even speak English."

"That's a start," Kevin said trying to encourage her to give a more detailed explanation. "Do you remember anything they talked about?"

"No... I don't know." Coco shook her head. "I have no idea what they would discuss. There was one guy that would show up with Greg maybe once a month. I don't think I ever heard his name, but that guy really gave me the creeps!"

Kevin gave her his best surprised look. "You work in a strip bar; every guy should give you the creeps." Then he shook his head. "What the hell? If I didn't know myself, I would tell you never to talk to me!"

"Yeah... well, he was different. He would grab me as if I was *his* girlfriend. But that wasn't the worst part; he did this right in front of Greg. He knew we were a couple and that we were vacationing together at the time. It didn't seem to matter to this creep... he did whatever he wanted. Greg would just sit there and act as if nothing had happened. Eventually, I learned to just stay away when he would show up."

Kevin laughed, "Well, at least, you had a little common sense."

"Look Kevin," Coco explained, "you've got it easy. Being a single mom with a four year old, I don't get out of the house very often. Work tends to be my only time away from reality and I almost never date anyone who frequents strip bars, but Greg seemed different. So I eventually gave in and we dated for a while. Maybe after a few weeks, he asked me if I wanted to go with him on a business trip to Mexico. He was only going there for a couple of days. I'd never traveled outside of Pittsburgh. So I thought, why the hell not? Like I said, he seemed like a nice guy... maybe just a little over-protective. Anyway, after that trip, we went there three more times. But don't worry; it's been over between us for months now."

Kevin dropped his head. "Shit... is that it," he muttered as he slouched down in his seat. "I think I'm going to need another beer."

Dave sat down next to Kevin while Coco ran for the beer. After a brief celebration for a job well done, both men sat back and watched as a tall brunette with chestnut colored skin stripped down from a Native American Indian outfit.

"I think I'm gonna go over to Omar's tomorrow," Kevin said, "This trip is long overdue. I'm a bit curious to see where Coco worked. I might need some back up... Any chance you'd like to tag along?"

The girl shimmied out of her buckskin wrap dress revealing a short turquoise lace skirt with matching balconet demi bra. She sashayed over to their table and draped the wrap around Dave's broad shoulders.

Dave smiled, "Now that depends... you buying Kev?"

"Sure, why not?"

"Two guys... out on the town... together!" Dave's smile turned into an all-out giggle. "I've been dying to see what all the hoopla is about! I'm off at five. We'll call it a guy's night out... We don't need the women to have fun, right?"

Kevin closed his eyes and shook his head. "Yeah… I don't know. Please, just don't talk while we're there… okay?"

When the song was over, the only items remaining on the body of the five foot ten inch dark skinned girl was a head full of feathers and a rhinestone studded thong.

"You know, if they were dressed like that back in the Wild West days, there would have been a lot less fighting with the cowboys," Kevin observed.

"Yeah… There's really not very many places to hide a hatchet in that outfit," Dave added.

# Chapter 16

**(7:30 AM Sunday, July 4)**   Kevin tapped on Mark's door letting him know it was time to wake up before making his way down the steps and into the kitchen.  He poured himself a cup of coffee and stared at the clear glass cup as the cream slowly mixed with the dark coffee.

Kevin wondered if he was really doing the right thing by helping his friends, especially considering the way that he *helps*.  With the world in such disarray, what makes them so much more important than everyone else?  He no sooner finished the thought when the answer popped into his head... they're *his* friends.  That's what makes them so damn special.

Just then, the phone rang startling Kevin out of his daydream.  He promptly checked the caller ID and a phone number he didn't recognize appeared on the screen with no name above it.  He picked up his coffee and took a slow sip, contemplating whether or not he should answer the unnamed caller.  It could be one of the new parents on the baseball phone tree, he thought, the games times and locations seem to change almost every day.  If I miss just one game because of a change in the tournament schedule it'll piss me off for the rest of the year.  The phone rang for the fourth time and Kevin groused as he reluctantly picked it up.  Before he had a chance to say hello, Kevin heard the sound of a man's voice rambling out of control.

"When James suggested that I talk to you about helping me, I thought he was crazy! And when I decided to give you a chance, it was more to humor him than anything else!" Tony was all but shouting into the phone. "I thought it might be a long shot to get even one… two would be way out of the question! I really expected maybe in a week or two we would just give up. I can't believe you can do so much destruction in one freaking day!"

"Ummm… what the hell are you talking about," Kevin inquired. "Oh… And who the hell is this!?!"

"I've already received a call from one of the clients assuring me of his intention to stick with my firm," Tony continued his babbling, "But that's only the half of it! The best part is he's trying to convince his friend into dropping Joe and switching back to me! Which is very ironic seeing as his friend was trying to talk my client into making the switch to use Joe's services. If this works out right, I might be giving you a bonus."

"I'm sorry," Kevin interrupted, "am I crazy? Or did I miss your name again?"

"This is Tony, you Dumb Ass! Didn't you look at the paper or watch the news this morning? I don't know how you did it, but…"

Kevin looked out the window and spied the Post Gazette, encased in a red plastic bag, lying at the end of his driveway. He dropped the phone and ran for the entry door. He turned his head and hollered good-bye as he crossed the porch and charged down the sidewalk. Kevin paused for a second as he arrived at the edge of the road where his newspaper sat staring back at him. Then he picked the red bag, slipped the paper out and hastily began eliminating sections as he sprinted back towards the house. By the time he made it back to the kitchen, most of the paper had been discarded, leaving only the Local News section. Kevin stood there gasping for air, practically drooling all over the paper. He opened it to page two, revealing a six by eight picture of Joe right below the headline, which proclaimed 'Nuisance bar at it again' in dark bold letters. On the third page there was another grainy picture of Joe in handcuffs. The caption read, 'Prominent business man caught up in strip bar escapades!' The article was even more devastating, describing the incident in excruciating detail. 'It took two shots with a stun gun to bring this large man down.' Kevin laughed out loud as he read the dramatic account. It's almost as if the reporter had been there taking notes while the arrest was in progress. Then he glanced around to see the Sunday paper scattered across the floor, down the hall and out the door.

Kevin was busy retrieving all the scattered sections of newspaper when his telephone rang again. He hurried back inside to find his phone ringing and vibrating across the floor.

"Did you see it? Oh my God! Please tell me you had something to do with this! Oh yeah, this is Tony again. Well... what do you think?"

"You don't know the worst of it," Kevin said as he stuffed the shredded remain of his newspaper in the trash can. "Joe bought me drinks and lap dances all night. Well, that is... until his altercation with the police."

"You might want to have a talk with your doctor. I think he has you on the wrong medication," Tony jokingly suggested. "I'm not kidding. You are one sick son of a bitch! I'd love to go to your next family reunion... I would think you might have a few new things to talk about with your coz Joe!"

"Yeah, real funny..." Kevin replied sardonically with a fake laugh. "You'll be the first person I call... if I get an invitation."

Tony stopped to take a deep breath. "Anyway, believe it or not, I actually called for another reason. I have this friend I'd like you to meet. He has a special problem that you may want to consider helping him with. I thought I should probably speak with you first... you know, before I recommend you're... uh... services."

Kevin walked into the dining room and opened the doors to his china closet. "Well, I have no idea what the hell you're talking about…" he said, "But, why not? If the price is right, I'd consider doing just about anything… for anyone." He pulled out three baseballs and began juggling them while holding the phone between his ear and his shoulder. "Although, I wouldn't mind hearing a little bit about his situation before I talk to him."

"I'll bring what I have on him to the game today," Tony said. "Show up about fifteen minutes early and we'll go over it."

Kevin placed the three autographed balls back on their stands, first Willie, then Barry and last Mark. His gaze shifted to Mark's baseball trophy case, six first place trophies and four seconds, not bad for three years of work. His carefully continued his visual tour of the trophy case as well as the surrounding walls, pausing briefly on each photo before moving on to the next, remembering every hit, every catch, every dirty, dusty slide into home.

"Regrets," Kevin softly mumbled. "Who doesn't have them? I wouldn't have all these memories scattered throughout this room if I wasted my time worrying about regrets."

# Chapter 17

**(4:30 PM Sunday, July 4)** Kevin slowly pulled into the gravel parking lot, carefully edging his Sonata in right next to Tony's Mercedes. The two men climbed out of their respective vehicles while their kids, Mark and Stacy, raced down the fence line and headed out to the grassy outfield to start warming up. Kevin slings his chair strap over his shoulder and grabs his cooler out his trunk while Tony snags his chair in one hand and a manila folder stuffed with papers in the other. The two men begin their conversation to the sweet cracking sound of a ball slapping leather. The distant purr of a lawn mower grew louder as a man began dragging the infield. A dust storm quickly engulfed the area making it impossible for the guys to talk without choking so the two men walked out to their favorite spot beyond the outfield fence.

"So enlighten me," Kevin inquired, "if you can… With the market going down year after year and people losing money hand over fist, how do you justify making money off them?"

Tony pulled a Cuban cigar out of his shirt pocket and tapped it on the palm of his hand. "Well, it's actually a very complex system of numbers and percentages… The average mind can't comprehend the markets idiosyncrasies. But I'll try to explain it in a way even you can understand. You seem to know baseball, right!"

"Yeah… but…"

"If you compare my track record to the Pittsburgh Pirates' record, you'll notice that I finished above even at least once this decade. That's one more than you can say about them." Tony pointed his cigar into Kevin's face. "You know... and they still get paid... a ton of money, every year... each and every one of them."

"That makes some sense... I guess," Kevin slouched down in his chair. "Alright, so tell me about your friend. What does he need from me? And how can I go about getting it done? Oh yeah... and let's not forget the money."

"Before we get into that, I feel like I need to thank you again for handling my potential problem so quickly. Also, I don't have any commitments yet but I should know in a week or so if I'm going to lose anyone." Tony said, "In the meantime, a little bird told me that Joe's clients are already jumping ship and that's leaving me with a large list of promising new clients, thanks to you. If this pans out, I'll give you a cut. Please keep in mind that this is all off the books. Some people might even say it's unethical."

Kevin sat up abruptly. "What kind of money are we talking about?"

"Well, if someone comes in with one million dollars, I invest ninety-nine percent of it in a variety of companies. You know... stocks, bonds and smaller amounts just go into mutual funds. Then I retain the remaining one percent. That's ten thousand dollars for those of you that can't do the math. So I'll give you, let's say, ten percent of that. Just keep in mind that most of my clients are in the hundred thousand dollar range rather than the million." Tony sat down and lit his cigar. "So now you can see why just two of my wealthier clients can make such a big difference." Then he slid down in his chair and put his feet up on the outfield fence. "Now the friend that I was telling you about... That's a completely different story." He mumbled while still puffing on the cigar. "My friend, he's got a shit load of money, and he sort of works in conjunction with Senator Michael Stanton. I'm assuming you know who he is, right?"

"Yeah, I know him… go on."

"Well, it looked as if the good Senator will be granted another six years," Tony explained. "However, with the economy as shaky as it is, there are no guarantees these days. This guy that he's running against has his hands into a variety of businesses in the Pittsburgh area. So I've been thinking… In your line of work, you should have no problem digging into this guy's financials as well as his partners' and maybe find something we can use on him."

Kevin felt a vibration in his pants pocket and he jumped up. "Oh shit!" He pulled out his phone and looked at the number on the caller ID. "Shit! I'm supposed to meet Dave tonight." Then he looked down at Tony.

"Not a problem, I'll gladly take Mark home after the game. He can hang out with Stacey and maybe keep her out of my hair." Tony handed Kevin the folder. "Here Kev, look this stuff over tonight and tomorrow we'll compare notes."

Kevin grabbed the folder and sprinted to his car.

Dave sat on a bar stool, impatiently tapping his thick fingers to the beat of the song playing in the background, while staring at the tiny clock in the middle of the wall of booze behind the bar. Six o'clock, he thought to himself, that jackass stood me up again. "Damn him," he muttered as he swung off the stool. I really wanted to go to Omar's just to see how the big dogs roll. He grabbed his jacket from the surveillance room before poking his head into the changing room to say goodnight to the girls. He saw three incredibly gorgeous, scantily clad women sitting in front of the mirrors applying makeup.

"Knock them dead tonight girls," Dave rumbled in his soft deep voice. "Oh… and be safe too." He heard a trio of good nights as he turned to leave. Just outside the door, he paused for a moment to think. There's not a lot of men in this world who can open up the door to a girls' dressing room and stand there chatting with them while they're practically nude, and not only do the girls thank me, but the owner pays me to do it… I love this country.

When Dave stepped outside he saw Kevin's car parked beside his. As he approached he noticed Kevin looking down into his lap.

"Are you still planning to go to Omar's tonight," Dave yelled as he opened his car door to get in. "Or are you going to sit in your car… playing with yourself all night?"

"Sorry," Kevin shouted back. "But I think we've got a new job. Tony gave me this folder full of names and photos… I can't seem to make heads or tails out of this bullshit!" Kevin threw the folder down, hopped out of his car and quickly made his way to the passenger side of Dave's car. "I'm not even sure what the hell he wants from us, it's a good thing we've got all summer to complete this project."

Dave hastily pushed the button to engage the power locks before lowering the passenger side window. "Sweetie… there ain't no way in hell you're getting in my car looking like that!"

Kevin tried to pull the door open. "What the..?"

"You look like Linus from the freaking Peanuts gang!"

Kevin brusquely patted down his legs and brushed off his shirt causing a cloud of fine dust to surround him. "Is that better," he asked Dave with a stern look.

"You're an ass," Dave muttered as he reached into the backseat and extracted a small blanket to cover up his passenger seat so Kevin could get in. "And wipe that smug look off your face!"

"What's that doing back there," Kevin asked as he turned to look between the two bucket seats. "And what other supplies do you keep back there?" Then he turned around to shut the radio off. "You won't believe what happened…"

Dave placed his large hand over Kevin's mouth. "You do know I'm here doing you a favor, right?" Then he pointed his index finger in Kevin's face. "You know, it's bad enough that I let you climb in my car with those filthy clothes on... But then you messed with my music." Dave flicked the volume knob back up. "You should know better than to mess with a black man's radio? Dude... haven't you ever seen Rush Hour?"

"Quit your bitching... holy shit," Kevin shook his head. "You're going to make someone a fine wife someday."

"And tell me," Dave asked, "what would you know about how a wife should act?"

"I was really close to being married... once. And I've seen how wives are portrayed on TV."

The two men made the short drive over one river, through the middle of town, then across the second river on their way to Omar's. Even from a distance they could tell that this place was going to be something exceptional. From the walls of black glass trimmed in gold steel I-beams to the twenty foot modern art statues of three nude women with lion's heads, it was even more spectacular up close.

Kevin hastily began dusting off his worn, dirty Levis and Pittsburgh Pirates t-shirt again. "I think I'm a bit underdressed for this place," he groaned.

Dave abruptly stopped his car in the entrance of the parking lot. "Seriously Dude! Get your filthy white ass out of my car. You're shedding your dust and dirt everywhere... Get out!"

Kevin jumped out, still furiously trying to beat out the dust that was left on him from the ball field.

Dave drove across the parking lot and pulled up to the front door. A clean cut man wearing a tuxedo approached the driver's side of the car and opened his door. Dave climbed out and handed the keys to the valet. The man jumped into the driver's seat and then waited patiently before driving away to park Dave's car.

Dave glared back at Kevin who was still walking up, "Kev, you better tip this good man!" He looked down to the valet and asked. "How much do you want? Is ten dollars enough?" Then he looked back to Kevin again. "I better not see a scratch in my car tomorrow!"

Kevin tipped the valet before running across the lot in time to meet Dave at the entrance. A bouncer grabbed Kevin's arm as he tried to walk past him.

"Twenty dollars, please," the large man demanded in a deep voice.

Kevin carefully slid a twenty out of his wallet then handed it to the pretty young girl standing beside the bouncer. He raced through the doors down the short hall and into a small lobby where he was quickly stopped by the hostess. "Table for two, please," Kevin requested.

She stood there staring at him.

"Honey, do you not speak English?" Then Kevin looked to both sides of him and noticed there was no sign of Dave. "What now?" He turned around and saw four men dressed in dark suit jackets entering the lobby. "I'm sorry... Did you see an extremely large black man, with just a hint of stubble on his melon, dressed in a pink and blue suit?" One of the men pointed back towards the entrance.

Kevin ran back up the hallway to see Dave standing there with his arms folded and a sour expression on his face.

"Look honey... this is your field trip, not mine," Dave grumbled. "If you want me as back up, you've got to pay the man."

Kevin looked up at Dave while shaking his head. "What kind of strip club has a maître d'," Kevin mumbled as he slapped another twenty in her hand. As the two guys jogged down the hallway toward the lounge, Kevin reached up as high as he could and smacked Dave in the back of the head. "Dude, you've got to quit talking like that. You're supposed to be my body guard, not my fairy f-ing godmother... I'd really hate to see us get our asses kicked before we get a chance to scope out the place."

"Don't you dare worry about that, Sweetie. No one's going to be kicking my ass," Dave said while trying unsuccessfully to hold back a giggle.

A tall, blonde-haired girl dressed in an evening gown greeted them as they entered the lounge. "Good evening, Gentlemen. Would you like to sit in the splash zone?"

Kevin took two steps past her then leaned over the rail that overlooked the main lounge. From his vantage point, all he was able to see was two large U-shaped bars on either side of the dark stage with dozens of small tables in between. He turned back to face the blonde, "What are you saying? There's a water ride down there?"

Dave raised his arm up, "Ooh... I want to get wet."

"Honey, will I at least get a towel," Kevin asked while trying to pull Dave's arm down.

The hostess pulled out two brand new towels and opened one up. It appeared to be three foot by six foot with an Omar's logo covering most of it.

"You can rent the white one for ten dollars," she explained, "or you can buy a blue one for twenty!"

Dave grabbed two blue towels out of her hand. "Pay the pretty girl, Kev!"

The hostess latched on to Dave's arm and softly said, "Come on, Big Fellow." Then she led them past the booths to a small table that was situated right next to the stage. She leaned over Dave wrapping her arm around his broad shoulders then whispered in his ear. "Remember, for ten dollars one of my girls will dry you off when you're finished. And trust me when I say it's an unforgettable experience, Darling."

Kevin took one of the beach towels and wrapped it around his neck. "What do you think she meant by being finished? Finished doing what," he hollered back as she walked away.

The music shut off as the announcer began with the words, "Are you ready to experience the cleanest girls in Pittsburgh?" The silence was broken as the music began with a low rumble from somewhere behind them. Dave sat up in anticipation, turning to look in every direction until all the lights went out. The sound grew louder and louder as it slowly crept around the entire room. Individual overhead lights began flashing on and off as the curtains behind the stage slowly opened up. Then the music and crowd went dead silent as the lights went out leaving the lounge in absolute darkness again... The only sound to be heard was of one man softly crying out.

"Kev... Kevin... I'm a little afraid of the..."

Suddenly the crowd erupted as the stage lights flashed on, temporarily blinding Kevin and Dave, and the bass felt like it was pounding straight through their hearts. Just then the lights softened to a twilight level and a cloud of mist and fog slowly rolled across the stage and into the seating area, at least five rows back. As the fog slowly dissipated, it revealed an enormous shower covering most of the stage.

Dave stood up pointing toward the shower. "Alright...! Now that's what I'm talking about," he screamed.

Kevin grabbed Dave's arm and yanked him back down into his seat. The two men watched in amazement, as every minute or so a man dressed in swim trunks would run up on stage and jump into the shower with all the beautiful girls. Two of the girls would begin the scrubbing process by rubbing him with soapy sponges, and then a third girl would finish the cleaning with her nude body. Next, another pair of girls would take shower wands and begin spraying the man down as well as everyone seated within the first few rows.

Dave reached out and stopped the first waitress that passed by. "Honey, I've had a long day… so I'm going to need a taste of that," he said while pointing at the stage. "What's the going rate, Sugar?"

"A big boy like you," the waitress started rubbing Dave's large shoulders. "I'm thinking fifty dollars, but that includes a pair of Omar's legendary swim trunks. And you'll get to spend two glorious moments with our world famous girls in a shower that you'll never forget."

Kevin watched as the waitress walked away then dried off his face and arms. "I'm going to do some recon work. Can you manage to hang out here and stay out of trouble?"

"Are you shitting me? I want a fifty spot," Dave grabbed Kevin's arm and pointed to the shower behind the stage. "I'm doing my own recon work up there!"

Kevin shrugged off Dave's hold and turned away. "Stay here! If I need you I'll raise my fists above my head and cheer. That's your signal to come help me."

Kevin furtively circled the room, glancing into each booth in search of Greg and his posse. The main lounge branched off into several smaller seating areas, or rooms. He froze in his tracks as an argument erupted in one of those back rooms, craning his neck in a valiant effort to make out what the excitement was all about. Suddenly Kevin froze like a deer in the headlights as two large men, dressed in finely-tailored suits, stood up and quickly headed in his direction. He looked left, then right, frantically searching for an escape route. Before he could make a break for it, the men flanked him and grabbed him by the arms.

"Buddy, I think you're in the wrong place," one of the men suggested in a gruff voice.

Kevin tried to raise his arms to signal Dave. "Yes, Sir… I think you're right, Sir… I'm going back to my table to sit in my seat right now... Right over there." Kevin tried to point to his table by the stage but the men wouldn't let go of his arms.

The large man with the gruff voice twisted Kevin's arm behind his back as he pointed him toward the hallway leading outside. "No, I mean... I think you're in the wrong bar altogether."

Kevin slowly nodded his head yes with a look of terror on his face. As the goons rushed him towards the exit, he thought he heard the sound of Dave's voice screaming over the rowdy crowd.

"Slow down, Cowboy," Dave shouted.

Kevin decided it would probably be wise to spend his remaining time looking for evidence of wrong doing on the outside of Omar's. So he walked around the building only to find Dave sulking on the top step by the loading dock doors.

"Where the hell were you," Kevin hollered. "I almost got my ass kicked in there!"

"Where was I? Where were you," Dave shot back. "I wanted my fifty dollars!"

"Well, there was this larger room in the back..." Kevin explained as they meandered back to the main entrance to retrieve Dave's car. "They got pissed off when I tried to go in."

"You too," Dave squealed. "I tried to get in that room too, but some girl stopped me... So I stood there for just a minute, you know, looking around for Greg. Then she insisted that I either sit down or she would have me escorted from the building."

"And...?"

"And here I am!"

There was no sign of the valet driver, so Dave reached around the wall and pulled his keys off the rack. The two men wandered around the parking lot looking for his car, all the while keeping an eye out for Greg's car. Partway through the lot they discovered a Corvette with a police decal on the back window.

"Kevin," Dave whispered, "you stand up by the front door and keep an eye out for the valet man while I see if any of the doors are unlocked." Dave walked around the Corvette peering into the windows looking for anything that would identify this particular car as Greg's. He gently tried the driver's side handle. "Damn..." He reached into the pocket of his jacket and pulled out a small case. He removed two thin titanium wires and inserted them both into the keyhole, finessing the tumblers until the lock popped up. "I've still got it." Dave lifts the car door handle to the screaming sound of a car alarm. "Shit!" Kevin high tailed it across the parking lot, scurrying after Dave.

"What the hell happened," Kevin shouted.

From the front of the building they heard a man holler, "Freeze Fool!"

The two friends jumped into Dave's car and took off like bats out of hell, screeching tires and racing their way back to Gloria's.

Kevin reached over to turn down the radio, "What a disaster this night has been..."

Dave stared back at Kevin. "There you go again with the radio... And yeah... it was a disaster. Because of your impatience, I didn't get to go on stage."

"When we go back next week, I promise, I'll pay your way up on stage," Kevin said.

"There won't be a next time..." Dave began in a high pitched voice. "Let me tell you exactly what's going on over there even as we speak! First, they're downloading all the video of us from tonight's surveillance tapes. They'll probably send a copy to the local police. Hopefully Greg doesn't get a hold of that. Then our pictures will be hung on the board where the valet stands and displayed inside on the computer where the bouncer takes the cover charge. So don't talk to me about next time," Dave sniffled, "because I lost my one and only chance of being on stage and experiencing the cleanest girls in Pittsburgh!"

"Maybe next we should talk with Coco and Roxy," Kevin suggested calmly. "And don't worry, I'll find away to get you on that stage. I just need to find a way to get me into the back room, because I'm positive there's something going down in there."

Back at Gloria's, Kevin and Dave listened to Coco's description of the typical Saturday night at Omar's when she worked there. "When I first started working there, I spent all of my time in the main area where you were seated." She explained, "After a few years they moved me into the back room. You can't go back there... If I showed up tomorrow, they wouldn't let me back there. The back room is divided into four private areas. Greg's group had the far right side reserved for every other week." She finished up by saying, "That's it. I'm done talking now unless you tell me why you want to know."

Kevin looked over at Dave, "Knowing about the back room before we went over there would definitely have saved us some aggravation."

"And possible some jail time..." Dave chimed in.

"Do us all a favor," Coco pleaded, "just stay away from that place. There's nothing going on over there, at least nothing that you need to worry about."

"Don't worry!" Dave moaned, "After tonight, they probably won't let us back in."

# Chapter 18

**(8:00 AM Monday, July 5)** It's an average Monday morning in the banking industry. Kevin begins his day by sending out a number of emails. Let's see, we'll start with the most pressing question.

**From:** Kevin O'Donnell

**Sent:** Monday, May 20, 2010 8:06 AM

**To:** John.Meyer@PittsburghBankTrust.com

**Subject:** Diane's head...

Is her head on the chopping block? Also, did you hear anything about those loans getting approved? Must know immediately...

The second email was to one of his clients explaining that the board would be voting early next week on his loan. "This is just a formality. I'm sure it'll pass. Please, just have a little more patience." Even though he knew there were no plans to vote this week.

Next, Kevin clicked on an email from Human Resources.

**Subject:** Mandatory meeting at 9:30 in the small conference room.

At nine twenty-five, Kevin made his way down the hall towards the small conference room. Along the way he stopped to speak with a few of his co-workers, just to reassure himself that he's not being singled out for a meeting today.

Kevin hesitated as he entered the room when he noticed that there was only one man sitting at the table. This can't be good he thought.

"Please have a seat." The man continued, "Kevin, I have gone through your personnel file and I must say I'm very impressed. It's not just the quality of your work, but also your loyalty to this company. I know there has been a lot of anxiety and tension among the staff, especially the last few days. So I'm pleased to tell you that you're obviously not going anywhere. The department you work in is actually short-staffed right now. The plan is to temporarily shift personnel into your department for the short term, just to help with the efforts in cleaning up all the impending commercial foreclosures. However, because of the incident last week, there's going to be some other changes in that department as well. Diane's going to fill the void left by Lisa's departure. John Meyer is being added in a supervisory capacity to oversee all the changes, as well as making any additional recommendations for shoring up the stability of the loan department. I expect everyone's full cooperation in this matter. So unless you have any questions, you're dismissed."

Kevin looked up at the man and his lip began twitching its way up on the right side of his face. So he quickly thanked him and scurried out the door then down the hall. On the way back to his cube he noticed Diane talking to her secretary. At first he planned to walk right past them, but he then couldn't help but wonder if Diane had had a similar pleasant meeting with HR this morning. So he paused for a second.

"What now Kevin," Diane growled.

He stood there for a moment debating his options. Which one is better? Should I tell her now so I can experience the full effect of the shock and awe? Or should I just let HR do it? That way she'll have to keep it all bottled up inside her, at least until she leaves the conference room.

"Well, are you just going to stand there staring at my feet, or do you have something to say?" Diane asked in a cranky voice.

Kevin looked up to Diane's chest. "Did you... or do you have a meeting with HR today?"

Her eyes narrowed as she pinned her him with her stare. "What?" Then, as she continued, her voice changed from that of a young preppy girl to what only can be described as a demon from hell. "Did I miss something? Because I didn't get any emails from HR." Diane looked over at her secretary. "Jan? Go over today's emails again... you better not have missed... What's the email about Kevin?"

"Let's just say, I hope you like surprises," Kevin replied with amusement shading his voice before strolling back to his so-called office.

Minutes later, Johnny stuck his head into Kevin's cube. "It's almost four o'clock. What time are we going to Gloria's tonight?"

"Yeah... right! You're a funny guy," Kevin looked at the time. "I can't leave fifteen minutes early. Have a seat and fill me in on how I went from getting you arrested and worrying about getting fired to having the Vice President of the bank apologizing to me. How exactly did that happen?"

"It's all about who you know... right," Johnny explained. "My dad has a standing tee time with one of Fox Chapel's finest. And you know me... So that's how we all live happily ever after. So let's get going! I'm driving."

"You mean you still have a driver's license," Kevin shook his head in disbelief. "I would've thought the police, or at least maybe your dad, would have confiscated it by now."

"Look, Old Man, my dad couldn't afford to have such an incident show up in the news, especially right now that we're so close to finalizing this merger. And wipe that smug look of your face… I'm sure you've made your share of mistakes. Or should I have the police chief look into it for me?"

"Well…"

"Yeah… I didn't think so," Johnny said sarcastically.

Kevin squeezed past Johnny while trying to push him out of the doorway, then turned around to get in one final parting shot. "You won't get in there tonight… I know the bouncer!"

"Oh, is Dave working tonight," Johnny yelled back down the hall. "Tell him I said hello! Or better yet, I'll just tell him when I see him!"

# Chapter 19

(4:50 PM Monday, July 5) Kevin arrived at Gloria's a few minutes early and circled around the parking lot looking for Tony's car. The silver Mercedes was conspicuously absent, so Kevin parked his car at the far end of the back lot, away from the new group of twenty-something kids that are surely going to show up again tonight. He pulled out his cell phone and dialed. He was surprised to hear Tony's ring tone playing behind him.

"Where the hell did you park," Kevin asked.

"Over by Starbucks…" Tony replied.

"What's the matter? You don't want your clients to know you're patronizing this fine establishment," Kevin joked.

"One can never be too safe," Tony answered in a semi-serious tone although he was laughing, "You may have sold your services to your coz!"

As the two men crossed through the dimly lit barroom, they saw Coco standing at the far side, waving them to come over. "I saved you a spot in the corner." She yelled, "It ought to be quiet back there."

Tony's eyes followed the back side of a tall dark Latino girl as she jiggled her partially bare bottom all the way up to the bar. "Nice venue to have a meeting… I just don't want to disappoint the girls 'cause I'm not taking my clothes off tonight," he muttered as his eyes shifted to a large tin plate hanging on the wall behind the bar. "My bartender can kick your therapist's ass… That's a cute sign."

"Dave just hung that up there." Kevin said, "I know… It's lame."

"It's better than that one." Tony pointed to the old wooden plaque down the wall. "Find a job you love and you'll never have to work another day in your life… Now that's lame!"

Tony methodically arranged his notes and a series of grainy photos on the table. He began explaining what kind of information he needed Kevin to gather on the people in the pictures without ever mentioning the name of the person they would be working for.

Dave snuck up from behind them, placing his large black hand over one of the photos before picking it up. "Well, well, well…" he drawled in the deepest voice he could muster. "What kind of games are you playing in my bar tonight, Boys?"

Tony scrambled to stuff everything back in his folders.

"Hold up…" Kevin grabbed Tony's arm to stop him, "Leave everything where it's at. Dave's just screwing with you."

Tony shook his head in disgust as he re-organized the photos and notes. "There's not going to be any other distractions, I hope?"

"Nope, just the three of us, I promise. I just thought this project might need Dave's expertise, if that's okay with you," Kevin asked. "He may be a pain in the ass at times, but I guarantee you, he's a real pro. You drink Yuengling, right?"

Kevin raised his hand to signal Coco to bring a round of drinks.

Tony began his presentation by showing the two guys photos of a man and his wife, and then explained what he needed Kevin to accomplish. Coco placed an ice cold beer on a cardboard coaster in front of each of the men. Tony handed her a twenty and told her to keep the change.

"Wow, big spender," Kevin said. "What was that? Like a ten dollar tip?"

"Twelve... Why? If that's not enough, I have no problem giving her more. She is kinda cute, and it is your money," Tony handed Kevin nine crisp twenty dollar bills. "We had our first new client make the switch to my firm this morning."

Kevin started running numbers in his head, "So you made one thousand... eight... hundred from our business deal? In just one day? You suck!"

The sweat smell of marijuana drifted across two empty tables and into Tony's nose. He took a short sniff followed by a long deep breath and held it.

Kevin rolled his eyes and shot a fierce look at the table full of loud-talking hooligans in their early twenties. "I hate those punks! It's hard to believe they feel the need to bring that garbage in here. You've got all this alcohol... plus the girls."

Johnny came running in and slapped Kevin on the back and shook Dave's hand, "Hey, Old Man! What the hell did I miss?"

The frustration was clear on Tony's face as he spoke through clenched teeth. "Let me guess... another one of your jackass helpers, Kevin?"

Johnny picked up one of the pictures. The man in the picture is clearly too old and out of shape to be Greg. "Who the hell is this supposed to be? I thought we were meeting to discuss how to get even with that piece of crap cop. You remember, don't you Kev, the one who embarrassed you by hauling both of us off to jail the other night?"

Kevin snatched the photo out of Johnny's hand and tossed it back on the stack. "No, he's not my helper. In fact, he's not even twenty-one!" He turned and glared at Dave. "So would you please do your job and kick him out?"

Dave pushed out the fourth chair with toe of his wingtip shoe. "Sorry Kev, I kind of like the bean pole. I vote he stays... But if you want him gone, then go ahead... You throw him out!" Dave gestured toward Johnny who was sitting between them. "I wouldn't mind seeing you try."

Kevin sat there with his head between his hands, glaring at Dave. "That's fine! Whatever... but he's not getting any of my money!" He turned to face Tony, "Assuming that it's alright with you?"

Tony pulled Kevin aside and whispered to him behind his manila folder. "The job I'm proposing is far from legal. I'm not so sure you want a kid involved."

"His attention span is about one hour," Kevin countered, "so I'd expect him to move on to something else before the day is done. Besides, I talked to his dad today... I got the impression that he's spent a lot of time in places like jail and that, so it's probably just a matter of time anyway."

"I'm not sure we want to draw attention to ourselves by having a trouble maker around either." Tony suggested, "But if you think you can handle him... It's your call Kev."

Johnny stood up and waved Coco over. "What's your pleasure young man?" she asked in a soft voice as she sat down straddling the back of the chair. "Would you like me to send over our bad girl police officer? She's equipped with two big badges, one on either side of her huge heart... and let me just say, when she's finished with you, you'll be begging her to cuff you and take you back to her station!"

"Coco..." Kevin whispered as he grabbed her hand giving it a soft tug. "Coco... you do realize the main reason he's here tonight is he hates cops, and wants to think up a plan to get even with one."

"Oops!" Coco put her hand over her mouth. "Sorry, I forgot about the whole cop thing." She slides her chair back and looked him up and down then slowly scanned the room searching for a more appropriate girl for Johnny. "I've got it... a big boy like you might want a sexy farm girl. She's got a lot between the suspenders, and those suspenders are holding up the tiniest pair of tear away shorts... Oh, and let me tell you, she got some moves that would keep even the most dedicated farmer in bed way past sunrise."

Johnny smiled and shook his head no.

"You're so right!" Coco thought about all the different girls and how they looked in their costumes tonight. "Why didn't I think of that in the first place? You look more like a football player! Am I right?" Coco wrapped both of her tiny little hands around Johnny's bicep and attempted a gentle squeeze. "I think Roxy's going to be a cheerleader tonight. You'll love her flexibility and moves so much, that when she's finished with you... you'll be the one doing all the cheering."

Johnny pulled out a ten and smiled a boyish grin. "That all sounds awesome, although I'm not so sure about the farm girl thing... I am definitely intrigued by your description of Roxy the cheerleader. But tonight, I'm just wondering when your shift is over. I'd like to buy you a coffee?"

Coco looked at Johnny with puzzled expression, "That... would be nice... I think. Thank you?"

Johnny put the ten in Kevin's hand, "There, I just bought it. Well, sort of... I mean I paid for it, Kevin's actually going to buy it for you."

She looked over at Kevin with her deep brown eyes. "Hmmm... Alright, I'll see you when my shift is over." Then she smiled and walked away.

"It's your call, Kev," Johnny said as he stood up. "Just remember, I am your best wingman." Then he began swinging his hips, pointing at Kevin and singing the song that the strippers were dancing to. "Should I stay or should I go nowww... If I stay there will be trouble. If I go there will..."

"Fine," Kevin cried out, "Please quit singing... Jeez! You can stay. Just keep your distance from Dave. You're already starting to act like him and, God knows, we can only handle one Dave around here."

After Coco served her last set of drinks for the night, the couple walked over to Starbucks, holding hands like two school kids who just started dating. Coco selected a seat facing the door and Kevin... Well, Kevin sat down and began acting like the typical Kevin all the women hate. But then he remembered the advice that Johnny had given him earlier. He decided to change the subject to something they both had in common. So he asked Coco about her daughter. She told him how much June enjoyed her dance classes. Then he told her about Mark's love of baseball and asked if she'd like to go to one of his games. But then something went horribly wrong and she cut him off mid-sentence.

"I've got to get going," Coco said anxiously. "My daughter is waiting for me at home."

Coco slid out of the booth and grabbed Kevin's hand, pulling him along. He looked back to see one man standing at the counter.

"What... that guy," Kevin asked. "We're running from that guy now?"

They ran across the road to Gloria's parking lot and turned back in time to see Greg's squad car pulling in across the street. "Are you running from all of the police?"

"Nope, just one..." She pointed at Greg stepping out of his car. "That one..."

"How did you...?"

"Simple," Coco explained, "the man at the counter was an off-duty officer. I think he is Greg's new partner or something."

"We can't hide from this guy forever, can we," Kevin asked. "He's an officer of the law. His job is to protect us… You act as if he's going to kill us or something."

Kevin stood there watching Greg through narrowed eyes thinking, there's got to be a way to get that arrogant son of a bitch. By the time he turned around to make his best attempt at kissing Coco goodbye, she had already jumped in her car and was pulling out of the parking lot.

So Kevin did the next best thing and went back inside Gloria's to see if the guys were still hanging out. The four men were embroiled in an intense strategy session about the best approach for their new job when Dave noticed Greg standing at the bottom of the steps. He wasted no time ushering Johnny to the surveillance room in the back. Kevin paused only long enough to grab their drinks before following them into the surveillance room. The three men watched on the security monitors as Greg approached Tony and struck up a conversation.

Tony accessed Greg's portfolio on his smart phone and presented him with some options for some new money Greg recently acquired. As the men concluded their business, Greg moved on and Tony headed for the back room. Dave cracked open the door and yanked Tony inside.

"Please tell me he's not the cop you're all out to get," Tony inquired. "If he is, you can definitely count me out… Most of the officers on the Fox Chapel police force are clients of mine. Plus, if I told you some of the stories that are circulating around about him, you'd piss yourself! Besides, he's one of the wealthier cops I have on my client list. I'd hate to lose him because of your twisted vendetta."

The four men huddled in the little room watching as Greg wandered around the club. "He's obviously looking for someone," Kevin commented. "You know, Dave, you really shouldn't allow cops through the door. I'm sure everyone's on edge while he's here."

"Yeah, how are we supposed to have fun when he's around," Johnny added.

"I'm a bouncer," Dave shot back. "Having the crowd on edge isn't all bad! Anyway, if you don't want him here you get rid of him!"

They all watched as Greg took a seat at one of the corner tables with a trio of guys. He spoke with them for a few minutes, smiling and gesturing with his hands as if they were all good friends. Then the three men abruptly stood up and snuck out the back exit.

The four men stood side by side in the little room watching as Roxy began her set. The provocative choreography combined her cheerleading skills and flexibility with a little pole dancing. She gracefully removed piece after piece of her costume without ever missing a beat of the soft jazz music playing in the background. The frenzied crowd began throwing their hard earned money onto the stage.

"You were right, Kev. She sure is something special," Johnny murmured as he stared helplessly, unable to look away.

"Mmmm, I agree…" Tony added. "Wow!"

Roxy finished her performance and dashed back to the dressing room to change her outfit into something only slightly less revealing before returning to the main room to mingle with the crowd. She systematically worked her way across the room towards Greg, pausing only long enough to visit some of her regular customers and allow them the opportunity to stuff ones and fives under the edges of her skimpy costume which barely covered her lithe form. She perched on the knee of an older gentleman, blowing gently in his ear before flipping her hair into the face of another. By the time she reached Greg she had a roll of bills that would barely fit in her tiny hand. Roxy slid into the chair next to Greg and rested her hand on his shoulder, laughing at his every word. As their conversation progressed, she wiggled her way onto his lap and wrapped her arms around him. Soon the laughing turned into kissing the back of his neck.

The four men stood side by side in the tiny hot room. They stared at the security monitors, their eyes glued to every sensuous move Roxy made. Not one of them was able to look away as she rubbed her foot high up on the inside of Greg's thigh and slowly ran the tip of her tongue along the outer edge of his ear. The room became stifling hot like a large oven causing sweat to roll down the backs and arms of the men as they stood there, elbow to elbow.

"That's enough! Everyone get out! I don't care who is out there," Dave broke the uncomfortable silence. "I'm feeling claustrophobic. This is, without a doubt, the most uncomfortable situation I've ever been in."

Just as Tony managed to squeeze his way out the door of the tiny room, Kevin observed Greg leaving the bar on camera one, which had a clear view of the valet area. Now the rest of the guys were free to make their escape as well. Kevin, Johnny and Dave jostled and stumbled their way out the door and back to the main room.

Johnny watched as Roxy worked the room, straddling the lap of one man while she stroked the nape of another man's neck; picking up cash from every man she encountered. Then the big bills appeared as one patron stuffed a twenty and the tips of his fingers between the small of her back and the top edge of her soft silky shorts.

"That's it," Johnny yelled, "I've had enough man time for one evening. I think I'll go home and take a long cold shower! Maybe wash off the stench left behind from rubbing elbows with you fools."

Kevin decided it would be prudent to begin dividing up the jobs as soon as possible. Since Johnny was leaving, he decided to give him the first assignment.

"Since your dad knows the police chief well enough to help you skirt the law," Kevin suggested, "maybe you could begin by gathering some information on Greg. I'd like to know how much money he makes and maybe the hours and days he works. Anything you're able dig up could be helpful, even the smallest of details might be useful."

The three men swarmed around Roxy, trying to find out what business had brought Greg into their bar.

"Initially, I think he came in looking for Coco." Roxy explained, "We both know him from Omar's. He was always one of my best clients. At the end of each night Greg made certain that I left with enough money. If I didn't, he would hook me up with some of his friends. He's a real gentleman."

"Oh yeah, a real gem," Tony began. "If I told you…"

Kevin stopped Tony by dragging him away mid-sentence. "We need her on our side. Please don't say anything that might piss her off," he whispered. "She probably already knows something that can help us out, and even if she doesn't, we can use her to gather information."

The three guys returned to their table to continue their earlier meeting. Tony opened up his folders and, once again, he began by reviewing the facts he had. After sifting through the photos of Alex and his family, Tony moved on to the spreadsheet detailing Alex's business holdings including partnerships with a number of different shady business men. Next, he spread out the pictures of Alex's known associates. The second one showed him speaking to the CEO of the corporation that Kevin was currently working with.

"This is it," Kevin grabbed the picture and held it up. "I'm in the process of securing approval for this guy's latest venture. This is the person that's going to help us get to Alex. What do you have on this man?"

"Nothing yet…" Tony said. "Why? What makes him so special?"

"I'm going to be contacting him tomorrow," Kevin said. "That'll at least give me a place to start." He began stuffing all the reports and photos back into the folders. "I'm going to look over everything you gave me tonight. Then I'll compile an action list… You know, of what we need and who should try to acquire it. Oh yeah…

our kids have a game tomorrow, so Tony and I won't be able to get here until seven. I'll let Johnny know what time to meet us when I see him at work tomorrow. What do you think Dave?"

"I'm still wondering why your date with Coco only lasted about fifteen minutes," Dave questioned.

"Ummm... things went well, I guess... I don't..." Kevin stumbled to find the right words. "She's a tough one to figure out, and the whole Greg thing seems to be an ongoing problem."

# Chapter 20

**(7:30 PM Tuesday, July 6)**  Kevin arrived at work twenty minutes early so he would have time to send out some emails pertaining to his new found passion, screwing up other people's lives.  Let's see… Johnny first, he thought…. SUBJECT: What…

Kevin heard a sharp knock on the outside wall of his cube.  As he glanced up, Johnny's long face appeared in the opening.

"A police officer in Fox Chapel starts out making around forty thousand a year," Johnny explained as he picked a rubber band out of the desktop organizer on Kevin's desk.  "After five years with the department, they can make as much as eighty thousand, but that's only if they make sergeant or better.  Greg's nothing more than a street cop.  To make sergeant, he would have to score at least seventy-five percent on a written exam and then pass an oral interview.  I'm told there's little or no chance of that ever happening.  So my dad's best guess is he probably pulls in about sixty."  Johnny smiled, "Not bad, huh?  I'll bet you didn't think I was going to help out at all?"  Then he grabbed his long black hair with his left hand pulling it tight together and double-wrapped the rubber band around it.  "Oh, and one more thing, if my dad has his way… 'I'm absolutely not going to be a cop!'  I think those were his exact words."

Kevin leaned back in his chair with his hands clasped behind his head.  "Not a bad start for a kid.  But if you really want to impress me then tell me that last loan was approved."

"Oh yeah, I almost forgot," Johnny pointed his finger at Kevin. "The board is meeting at two o'clock this afternoon. They're supposed to vote on at least six loans. I'm thinking, maybe you should go ahead and schedule an appointment with our client as soon as possible. Ours is high on the list and the plan is to pass all of them. And yeah, I want to sit in when you meet with them. I'd really like to know how the process plays out from here. Impressed now, Fool?"

"I am, I'm very impressed," Kevin gave a silent clap. "If for some reason things don't work out as planned, let me know. As far as you going with me, I'm not that impressed. I just think it might be a little too early for that."

Johnny mumbled something under his breath as he turned to leave.

Kevin jumped up out of his seat and stuck his head out of the cube. "My kid's got a game today! So we're not going to Gloria's until seven tonight!"

Kevin saw Diane entering her office out of the corner of his eye and thought what the hell is she doing here at eight? He crept along the opposite wall until he reached her door opening, then he darted across the opening, glancing in on his way. He stopped mid-stride when he realized she was packing her personal items in a box. His jaw dropped to the floor when he saw her slowly reaching up high trying to pull her framed degree from Penn State off the wall. Inch by inch her jacket crept up revealing her perfectly shaped body, those long slender legs topped off with that small tightly rounded butt, the one that very rarely ever shows itself, peeking out once a year like Punxsutawney Phil on Ground Hog Day. God… What a waste of a hot body he thought.

Then Kevin felt a hand slap his shoulder. He spun around to stand face to face with the new executive in charge of the commercial loan department.

"Dude, quit staring at her ass," Johnny barked before continuing on his way down the hall.

Diane turned her head while still trying to reach the frame on the wall.

"I just stepped in," Kevin stated timidly. "I wasn't standing here staring at you, I promise. Not that I... What are you doing? "

"Good question," Diane snapped back. "Well, let's start with my office. It was just getting a little messy, so I decided to move down the hall to a cube instead of cleaning it. I'm sure you understand?"

Kevin stepped into the room and closed the door, "You're not leaving then, right?"

"Oh yeah... you'd just love that, wouldn't you?" Diane chirped as she finally managed to grasp the frame she had been struggling to reach. "Nope, I'm not going anywhere... except maybe down the hall to a stupid cube."

"Thank God."

"Thank God," Diane shouted. "Do you have any idea how long it took me to get this office? Oh yeah, I guess you have a clue, you've been here longer than me. That punk...!" Diane pointed the heavy frame at Johnny out in the hallway. "That immature dufus is our new boss! I don't know how you can sit there and let management step all over you?"

"He's the VP's son. Did you really expect management to put him in charge of cleaning the toilets," Kevin asked. "Look, summer break will be over before you know it and you'll be bossing me around again just like old times."

"I can't sit in that cube for any extended period of time," Diane whined. "It gives me the creeps. It reeks of mold and I don't know what else... It's simply unbearable! So if you see me wandering the halls like a homeless person, just know that in my mind, I'm in a better place."

Kevin laughed, "Aww, c'mon Diane... Try acting like a big girl and suck it up. Umm... that didn't come out right. Neither did... Maybe I should just shut up."

"Here's something I hadn't considered. When I move into that cube, will I get a cut in pay," Diane wondered. "Because when I moved into what used to be my office, I received a ten percent raise in pay."

"I think if they were cutting payroll, it would have definitely been announced before all the changes were implemented," Kevin hurried to console her. "Look, the good news is, you still have your secretary. You do still have Jan, right?"

"Those assholes better not even try to take her from me. I'll..." Diane choked as her eyes welled up with tears. "You don't understand. You're happy here, working in your little cube as a loan officer. I wasted four good years of my life at Penn State's business school so I wouldn't be stuck in a cube for my entire career. I'm qualified to run this whole bank!" She pulled the heavy gilt-edged frame out of the box and threw it at the wall next to Kevin.

Kevin grinned as he ducked out of the way, "Oh yeah, I'm thrilled with how my life turned out." He decided that now would be an excellent time to return to his cube, stopping in the doorway for one last comment. "I hope I gave you some comfort with my wisdom."

As Kevin sat back down at his desk, he remembered why he went over to see Diane in the first place. So he decided it might be safer to send her an email, rather than risk getting hit by another unidentified flying object.

# Chapter 21

**(4:00 PM Tuesday, July 6)** Kevin pulled on to a half gravel, half dirt road that wound its way along a creek then seemed to almost disappear into the darkness of the woods before popping out to an open valley, where a pristine ball field was located and their next tournament was being held. He parked behind a van to protect his car windshield from foul balls and Mark jumped out, stopping only long enough to get a hug and his equipment bag, before running toward the dugout.

"Peace and quiet... This is the way it should be," Kevin mumbled as he set up next to James. "Is Tony watching from somewhere else? Because he said he was definitely going to be here today."

"Who knows?"

"Maybe we'll get lucky and Ron will be a no show tonight," Kevin rambled on. "I've never met anyone who dominates the conversation like him. And when he cheers, he squeals and whines like one of the women. 'Nice try dear', 'Keep your eye on the ball Honey.' Doesn't he understand that they're ten year old boys now? I swear, if he calls Mark "Sweetie" one more time, I'm going to punch him in the face."

"It almost sounds like your starting to regret getting him removed as manager," James suggested.

"He was a lot less annoying when he was in the dugout," Kevin moaned. "That's a tough one though, because we're at least winning with Dee in charge."

"Are you thinking what I'm thinking," James asked. "We need to do something about Dee as manager!"

"Ummm… I don't know…"

"You can't think of anything can you," James replied, taunting Kevin.

"I'll work up something tonight at Gloria's," Kevin said. "You should come along with us… It'll be like old times."

"Old times, huh," James scowled. "You mean the good old times? Like the night we took the trip in the nice clean squad car?"

Kevin jumped up against the outfield fence screaming at his son to run faster. Then he turned and looked down at James, "Quit being so dramatic, it wasn't that bad!"

"You almost got me thrown in jail," James barked. "I'm just saying… If it wasn't for Kara knowing that one cop, we both would have spent the night in jail."

"Well…" Kevin folded his arms, pouting. "You didn't have to leave me in that dark prison cell all by myself."

"Quit your bitchin'…" James shot back. "You should be happy that all you spent was one night. If it wasn't for Kara's influence over the arresting officer you probably would have lost your driver's license as well."

"Well, it would've been nice if you stayed to keep me company," Kevin whined. "Anyway, Tony and Dave will be there, and you said you wanted to meet Coco. Well now's your chance."

The two stood up and began shouting when Jimmy hit a homerun.

"I'll talk to Kara..." James said, "...after the game, maybe..."

"Shit... I'll tell you what," Kevin offered, "I'll go over and explain to your wife what we're planning to do. Then I'll convince her you need a break. I'm sure she'll be very understanding."

Shortly thereafter, Kevin looked over at the score board and noticed that it was already the fifth inning. With only one out left before the final inning, he decided it was time to face the beast. So he shuffled down the first base line leading to the bleachers located next to the dugout. He saw Kara sitting in the top row of seats, surrounded by all the other mothers. They were laughing and chatting as if they didn't realize we were losing by two runs. With her dark hair blowing in the breeze, it's almost like she's a... Kevin shook his head and closed his eyes. When he opened his eyes and looked up at Kara again, he saw the beast. That's much better he thought. Then he called to her to get her attention and waved her down to the lower corner of the stands.

Kara reluctantly moved down next to Kevin and listened somewhat politely.

"So tell me, do you remember that cop named Greg Handsom," Kevin questioned.

"Why, what did you do this time," Kara stood up and turned to climb back up the stands. "Don't you ever get tired of acting like a child," she whispered harshly as she squatted back down next to Kevin. "And don't sit there looking so indignant. I heard what you did to Ron."

"Shit," Kevin quickly put his hand over his mouth then whispered, "I mean shoot... You should be thanking me for bring that to everyone's attention. Or are you trying to tell me that having a pedophile coaching your son wouldn't bother you?"

"I like to know how you got a hold of that information," Kara continued to whisper while looking around them, making certain no one was in hearing distance. "I checked... I know it had been expunged from his record."

Kevin moved up a row of seats next to Kara. "Speaking of information, what about Greg? I'm sure you know him."

"Why? What did you hear," Kara snapped back at Kevin. "Forget it! If you're in trouble, you deserve it and I'm not going to help you. For the record, I hate your freaking guts. The stupidest thing I ever did was get you off for assaulting that police officer."

"Allegedly assaulting..." Kevin clarified. "Now can you please focus on the question? And forget about me for a second? I'm sure that's a tough thing for you to do. I mean, I am pretty unforgettable."

"I don't know why you're asking, I don't even want to know," Kara began squirming in her seat. "I'm telling you as a friend of my husband, and mostly because your son is my son's best friend... Stay away from him! He's not stable, and his friends are worse!"

"I don't get it," Kevin said in a startled voice. "He's a police officer, right? Are you suggesting he might hurt me?"

"Look Kevin, almost everyone here would like to see you get hurt. You're an asshole. You do realize that, right?"

Kevin slid in closer to Kara, "Go on."

"The thing is Kevin," Kara explained, "they won't act on it because they have principles. Greg doesn't. He has no conscience. I don't think he cares if you have a child, and he's not going to put up with your adolescent pranks."

"Okay, you win! I'll stay away from him," Kevin said as he stepped down out of the bleachers. "One more thing..." He hollered up to Kara, "Tony and I are taking your husband to the bar tonight, okay? We'll be back around eight thirty! Thanks!"

Kevin turned and hurried back up the fence line leading to the outfield where the men were just starting to pack up their chairs.

"Come on, James," Kevin yelled across the corner of the field. "Let's go before the beast... umm, I mean your lovely wife, changes her mind. Oh, and Tony, we'll see you over there whenever you can make it."

## Chapter 22

**(7:30 PM Tuesday, July 6)** James took a deep breath and then followed Kevin through the front door of Gloria's. He stopped at the top of the steps and looked down at the smog filled room below. After an almost ten year hiatus, this place hasn't changed a bit, James thought. I don't get it. They've banned smoking in almost every inch of the city both indoors and out, yet the smoke in this place is so dense I can feel my lungs already trying to escape from my body and fly out the exit without me. James stopped partway down the steps and watched as Kevin scurried across the floor to the far end of the bar where Johnny and Dave sat sharing their latest gossip. As James began his journey across the floor he felt a small hand latch onto his wrist. He twisted back around and saw a cute little dark-haired girl dressed in a bleached-out red and white kimono.

"Hold on Soldier Boy…" She called out, desperately trying to be heard over the noisy crowd. "Twenty dolla make you holla!"

This part I don't miss at all, James thought, as he glanced down at the girl's costume. I swear, I think she's dressed in the same old ragged hand-me-downs I saw back when I was thirty. His eyes slowly worked their way back up her silky smooth legs and with a flick of her wrist she opened up the robe, flashing him a sparkling red lace G-string with a matching red lace Dream Angels® push-up bra.

His eyes stayed locked on her beautiful body. "Damn, this is new."

"What's your pleasure," she asked while stroking back her long black hair. She suggested, "Maybe a private lap dance in back?"

James's eyes finally made it back up to her slightly weathered face. Shit, why can't they hire a real Oriental girl, he thought to himself as he shook his head 'No'? Then he slowly scanned the entire room. All he saw was the typical clash between the young beautiful girls and desperate guys with money. No, sir, this place hasn't changed a bit.

"Sorry about not being able to save you guys a table," Dave shouted. "I tried, but it's this Roxy phenomenon... she's quickly building one hell of a reputation here! Every night seems to be more chaotic then the last. But she'll be finished soon, so things will quiet down and we'll be able to get a table."

Kevin waved James over while Dave set up a round of drinks for the three men.

"It's good to see the struggling economy hasn't slowed down the porn industry at all," James bellowed out.

"It's all Roxy! She's scheduled to perform her second set in less than an hour," Dave hollered across the bar as he poured a beer for a new costumer. "And it's not porn! It's more... it's like... How is this different than the straight guy, who goes to the ballet with his wife and spends the evening drooling over the dancers standing in peculiar positions while wearing skin tight outfits?"

"Or better yet..." Kevin expounded. "What about the dude that belongs to the gym just so he can stare at the hot woman working out in front of him?"

Dave stopped one of the strippers as she passed by. "At least this girl knows why she's here, and she gets paid handsomely for it! So answer me that... if you can!"

James conceded the argument and raised his beer up to make a toast. "To the lovely and talented strippers... God bless every one of them!"

The rest of the men within hearing distance raised their beers in solidarity. "To the sexy girls of Gloria's," someone yelled out from back in the crowd.

James smiled, "What year is it again?"

"Why?"

"I think I made that identical toast ten years ago," James said, "and I got the same reply then. Not only that, but I swear that's the same fake oriental girl from the nineties!"

"Quit your bitching," Kevin shouted over the noise of the crowd. "What's the matter? Aren't you getting your fill of Asian flesh at home?"

Dave grabbed a bar stool out of the back room and slid it behind the bar across from the three men. This way he could continue helping Coco serve drinks and still not miss any of the pertinent information.

"Alright, I'd like to start with what I've learned about Greg…" Johnny said. "After a six year stint in the military, he moved on to the Fox Chapel police force, where he's worked for…." The rest of his words were lost as the place erupted in screaming and whistling. The four men sat there mesmerized by the moves that Roxy made. The way she seemed to glide across the stage, slowly removing pieces of her clothing in a way that was somehow as elegant as it was erotic. Each titillating movement was carefully designed to elicit a frenzied response from the crowd, from slipping off her jeweled G-string while still wearing skin tight shorts, to removing her shorts to reveal the same G-string back in place. All of this while dancing to music she could barely hear over the deafening roar of an out of control mob of drunken men. She snatched up bills as fast as she could, yet somehow she made it seem as if it was just part of the dance. For the entire three minutes, Johnny stood on the rails of his bar stool so he could see over the frantic crowd.

Roxy ended up her routine by dancing across the shoulders of a few of the guys sitting in the front row before gliding across the stage and behind the curtain.

Johnny completely lost control of his senses and blurted out the first thing that came into his mind. "I'm going to marry that girl some day!"

Dave reached over the bar and grabbed Johnny by the collar of his shirt and pulled him back into his seat. "You're going to marry her? If I only had a dollar for every time I've heard some drunk say those exact words about any one of these strippers..."

"What," Johnny hollered across the bar.

"Kids like you don't get hitched to a stripper," Kevin added, "Just sit back and enjoy... you Dumb Shit!"

Tony sat on the steps that led down to the bar. He watched the four men and couldn't believe how they were conducting themselves. He wondered if maybe he picked the wrong group to help him.

"I can see we're going struggle to get anything done again tonight," Tony grumbled as he approached the bar.

Dave quickly cracked open Tony's favorite beer and slid it across to him. Meanwhile Tony dropped a new folder onto the bar in front of Kevin.

"I've gathered everything I could linking Alex to your client at Southside Development Corporation," Tony explained. "I hope there's something in there that can help you."

Kevin slapped Johnny's arm. "Speaking of SDC, I scheduled a meeting with them tomorrow."

"What," Johnny responded while keeping his eyes locked onto Roxy's body as she began to mingle through the crowd. "God, she's amazing."

"I'm assuming you did your part and the board approved the loan today," Kevin questioned.

"The contracts are ready to be signed," Johnny said, "and I don't give a shit what you say… I'm going with you tomorrow. I already went over my schedule with my dad and filled him in with what we were planning to do. But I thought we were here to talk about Greg, not work?"

"I thought we were here to see Coco," James added, "I know that's why I'm here."

"Alright, everyone just shut the hell up for one second," Kevin rubbed his temples while he thought for a moment, then he began to bark out orders. "Dave… you go get Coco! That will shut James up!" Then he backhanded Johnny's arm again. "When you say you told your dad about the meeting tomorrow, did you tell him we were signing a contract? Or did you tell him we were trying to dig up dirt on Alex's business dealings with SDC?"

Johnny's eye's stay locked on Roxy's every move. "How stupid do you think I am," he mumbled.

Kevin shook his head as he turned to address Tony. "I'd like a list of all of the businesses that those two are involved in together. That is, if you have the time."

Tony began going down the list when Dave came back. "Coco said she is way too busy to stop and see you right now. But she did say something about giving you a kiss from her. That, and if you're still here in an hour, she'll give you one herself."

"What about Greg," Johnny asked.

"Greg? Yeah, I think I may have something that might interest you." Tony pulled a second folder out of his slim leather briefcase. "This doesn't leave my sight." He opened the folder to reveal a financial spreadsheet. "I noticed something strange when I was reviewing his accounts. Twice a month, Greg withdraws five thousand dollars out of his money market account. Approximately ten days later, he deposits a much larger sum of money. But it gets better. It appears as if there's a set pattern to all these shifts in money... I'm not sure how he's done it, but he's doubled his money in less than three years."

"Not bad for such a down economy!"

"Let me see those dates," Johnny pulled the sheet out of Tony's hand. "This is what I was trying to tell you earlier! Greg works a nine day work week. You're probably wondering what the hell a nine day work week is? Yeah, so was I. So I had my dad talk with his friend the police chief. Apparently, it's a unique schedule that was set up specifically for Greg because he still had time left with his military thing. It was only supposed to last two years, but years later, he's still on that same schedule."

"Johnny, take those dates of his withdraws and deposits and see how they match up with his five-day weekends," Kevin instructed. "I'll take the other end and try to match the dates up with the weekends that Diane and Lisa went to Mexico with him. Dave, write these dates down and try to match them up with the times that Coco went with him."

"I've got to meet this guy," James laughed and shook his head in wonder.

"I'll check with Coco after her shift is over," Dave said while he finished writing the dates on a napkin, "but I'll go ask Roxy now. I know she's gone with Greg at least once."

"Roxy," Kevin said in a surprised voice. "Do you think...? Maybe that's what she and Greg were talking about yesterday? If you're going to talk to her, try find out if she's thinking about going with him again and when he's planning his next trip."

"I think that's Coco on her way back to the dressing room now," Dave said. "Let me see if she has the time now to talk." Dave ran down the hall after Coco.

"Coco," Dave hollered, "Greg was in here yesterday asking about you... Please don't tell me you two are still a thing?"

"Why doesn't anyone ever listen to what I say," Coco yelled back. "I told you guys to stay away from him!"

"He just showed up here asking about you," Dave calmly replied.

"I swear, I never told him where my new job was," Coco explained, "and I absolutely did not give him any indication that I was still interested!"

"Then why would he stick his nose in here all of a sudden," Dave asked.

"I don't know," Coco replied, "It almost seems almost as if he's following me. And I'm sick and tired of changing my life because of him!"

"Well... It was only one day..." Dave said.

"There's your answer right there," Coco grabbed Dave's arm and spun him around. "You just said the jackass was here yesterday talking with Roxy." Coco pointed across the bar toward the entrance. "And there he is standing right there talking to her again. If you guys keep...."

"Oh shit," Dave said in a panic. "Stay here, I'll be back in a few seconds!"

Dave wound his way through the crowd and back to his seat at the bar. "Holy Hell, Greg's here! You need to break it up and get Johnny out the back door now!"

Kevin immediately began grabbing papers off the table and stuffing them in the folders, preparing to bolt to the back room. "There's no game tomorrow... Maybe if we meet earlier, we'll avoid seeing Greg and the big crowds."

"Say tomorrow at five," asked Tony.

"Whoa!   Hold everything," James shouted as he grabbed Kevin's arm, "I'm not going anywhere!"

"No?  Why not," Kevin inquired with a baffled expression on his face.

"Why should I," James said as he watched Johnny sneaking out the back door. "I didn't do anything wrong and we didn't even discuss how to get rid of Dee as our manager yet."

"I second that motion," Tony added. "How do we ditch Dee?"

"Well, I would usually like to start with her weaknesses," Kevin began.

The four men sat there staring at two nude girls wrestling in a large tub full of jello, until Dave finally spoke up. "Who the hell is Dee?"

"Dee... Yeah, I guess we were talking about what to do with her," Kevin mumbled. "I've got it!  We have a team full of hot mothers!"

"She does look a little like a dude, compared to the others," James commented.

Tony couldn't resist putting in his two cents. "Yeah, she dresses like one too!  You don't think?"

"No!  But just the fact that we're discussing it means other parents may have noticed her manly looks also!" Kevin bobbed his head up and down. "Now we're getting somewhere. All we need to do is come up with a way to use that to divide her from the other mothers. The mothers are the ones who decided to put Dee in charge. They just need a little nudge to rethink their decision."

James stood up. "I think I've seen enough jello for one night. Let's just mull over this Dee thing tonight and maybe we'll come up with a plan tomorrow."

## Chapter 23

**(5:00 PM Wednesday, July 7)** Kevin pulled into an almost empty parking lot at Gloria's and walked over to where James was parked.

"Are you sure they're open," James asked. "Because this place resembles one of those strip bars located in the middle of a ghost town from an old western move."

"Really...? You're going to question *me* on Gloria's schedule," Kevin said as he pushed James along. "I couldn't tell you one thing about my kid's classes or teachers from this past school year; but ask me anything about either Gloria's schedule or the names of the girls who work here and I'm your man."

"So where is everyone," James continued to question Kevin as he followed him through the front entrance. "I mean, really, this place does look like it's closed."

The two men walked into the lounge and all they saw was empty chairs as far as the eye could see. Kevin pointed over at Johnny who was sitting at the bar talking to Dave.

"This is the way it's supposed to be, no one here but us and the girls," Kevin yelled out.

"Two beers, Dave... I'll buy the first round." James slid a ten across the bar. "And I don't see any girls Kev."

"They'll be here soon enough. And when it's time for Roxy to dance, this place will be packed again." Kevin opened up one of his two folders. "I know it bothers Tony when we discuss anything other than that Alex dude, so let's go over what we found out about Greg now. I compared his withdrawals to the dates that Diane and Lisa went on trips with him and they definitely match up."

"And this is somehow breaking news?"

"No…" Kevin added. "But I did pay Lisa fifty dollars to find out they went to an all-inclusive resort. That and she gave me the resort's web site address. Other than going into town to shop for an hour one afternoon, they spent all three days on the beach. Diane absolutely did not want to talk about it, but she eventually described the same scenario."

"I could have told you that," Dave said, as he pulled down the handle of the tap while tilting the large mug underneath. "And it would have only cost you ten bucks!"

"New subject… here comes Tony." Kevin closed one folder then opened the second, placing it on top. "We'll discuss Greg later."

"Can you grab me a beer Dave," Tony asked. "What'd I miss?"

James pushed the change back over to Dave. "I've got the first round."

"Sadly, you've missed nothing…" Kevin replied. "We were basically just getting started. After two days we have no real breakthroughs. Although I did have my meeting with SDC today and I did manage to learn something interesting about our friend Alex. It seems that Alex sold every single share he had held in the company. I'm talking about two million dollars worth of stock. The only thing questionable would be the timing. The timing was too perfect! The value of the company was only down slightly. But less than a week after he sold his last shares, the commercial industry collapsed." Kevin shrugged his shoulders. "You know… probably just dumb luck."

"Do we know where the money ended up?"

"He supposedly used the money to begin his run for Senator," Kevin answered. "I would imagine that it's a matter of public record and therefore easily verified. Regardless, both men from SDC had nothing but praise for Alex. In fact their exact words were, 'I'd let him back in today if that's what he wanted.' But I'll keep digging. At least until we find a different avenue to explore."

"Someone needs to start looking into his family life," Tony demanded. "No one is that squeaky clean. Come on Guys! Don't embarrass me here. We only have two months to find something. That's not as much time as you think!"

"I'd love that job!" Dave raised his arm up. "I always wanted to be in on a real stakeout!"

"You sort of do that every day. Don't you, Dave," Tony said pulling out a cigar to light. "You know, back in your little surveillance room..."

James stepped back from the corner table so he could look over the end of the bar into the main part of the lounge. He saw that the room was almost full and the line of men walking down the steps seemed to have no end.

"I don't know what they pay that Roxy chick," James yelled back to the other men, "but it's probably not enough."

"Are you kidding," Kevin shouted. "Stick around... when she finishes her first set, she'll leave this room with two fists full of money. There's a very good reason why Dave has to escort her out every night."

"I can't believe the clientele she brings in!"

"I hate to be the voice of reason here, but can we get off Roxy and focus on the job at hand," Johnny grumbled.

"Sounds like Big Boy here has got a thing for our little Roxy," Dave slapped Johnny's shoulder. "A little jealous… are we?"

"No, I just have a great idea," Johnny stated in a firm voice. "What if I sign up as a volunteer for Alex's campaign? My father donates big money to both sides, so he's got to know someone high up that can get me in."

"Well alright…" Tony shouted. "Now that's the kind of idea I expected out of you, Kev!"

"Besides, the more time I spend on the campaign trail, the less time I'll have to spend at that boring office with those mind-numbing people," Johnny observed. "I don't know how you can stand working there, Kev!"

Roxy strutted her way out onto the stage and the boisterous rumbling of the crowd immediately turned into a deafening roar. She pulled the curtain in front of her then she poked her head out and after blowing a kiss she disappeared again. The place went dead quiet for a few seconds then she suddenly reappeared behind everyone at the far end of the lounge. Dave grabbed her just below the hips then lifted her up, placing her on the bar top. She slowly danced her way down the forty foot counter while the men pulled their drinks away from her shuffling feet. The crowd turned around and began pushing their way in closer to the bar area where Kevin's group was having their meeting. The four men silently sat while their eyes followed Roxy's every move. As the crowd pressed closer, they found themselves smashed against the bar rail, now sitting mere inches from the most beautiful girl they had ever seen. She danced from one end of the bar to the other, collecting money every time she dipped down. Coco circled to the back side of the bar to pour a trio of beers which she slid down the bar to rest in front of the guys.

Kevin latched onto Coco's wrist when she reached for the twenty in his hand. He pulled her over one edge of the bar as he leaned over the other side, his lips nearly touching her ear.

"What time are you getting off work tonight," Kevin whispered to her. "Maybe we can take our kids out for ice cream or something."

Coco nodded her head in agreement then gently attempted to pull her hand out of Kevin's grip. She looked up just in time to see Roxy do a short spin followed by three sharp steps with the last one getting lodged into Kevin's shirt sleeve. Her four inch heel snapped off as she gracefully spun twice landing onto Johnny's lap. Johnny stood up spinning her around one more time before gently placing her on the edge of the bar trying to make it appear as if it was all planned. Dave reached over the bar top and picked her up by the waist then spun her around like a top placing her down behind the bar so she could take her hard earned money back to the changing room.

Just like a sunny day in Pittsburgh disappears all too quickly, so did Roxy. The entire crowd stood around for the next few minutes finishing up their drinks. Some men stuck around for her second set and the others raced home to their wives and children. Before you knew it, the place was quiet enough to hear a beer bottle shatter on the concrete floor.

"Damn... that Roxy is so freaking hot," Johnny blurted out while bobbing his head back and forth trying to get one more glimpse of her. "Did you find out if she's going to Mexico with that asshole Greg this weekend?"

"I can't get anything off her," Dave said as he giggled like a ten year old, "and she won't tell me anything either."

Johnny watched as Roxy reappeared at the other end of the lounge. "You should never send a man to do a boy's job," he told Dave as he slapped him on his back. "Give me five minutes. If I'm not back, just stand up and give me well deserved round of applause." Then he glanced at the mirror behind the bar to check out his hair. "Perfect."

Johnny strutted his way over to the other side of the room and sat down at one of the tables in the area where Roxy was currently mingling.

"Thanks for catching me earlier," she leaned in close so she could whisper in Johnny's ear. "My name is Roxy."

Johnny just sat there with a foolish grin on his face.

"Are you looking for dance... or just looking," she asked, running her fingers through her long blond hair. "It'll only cost you twenty dollars." Then she winked at him as she slowly gyrated in place.

Johnny's smile faded as the blood drained from his face. His friends stood up and began clapping in support of his daunting task. "Go Johnny, go Johnny!" He propped himself up as his composure began to creep back. As the color began to seep back into his face, Johnny pulled out a hundred dollar bill and edged it across the table.

"I'm sorry, friend..." Roxy declined in a disappointed voice, "dancing is all I do. I can go find someone else for you. If that's want you're looking for?"

"Nope, I think you'll do just fine. My name is Johnny." He introduced himself as his smile returned in full force, "That was just a test, and the good news is you passed." He pushed a chair out with his foot, "Please, have a seat."

Roxy perched on the edge of the chair with one hand on each of Johnny's knees as she leaned in closer to him. "I should be up mingling with customers, it's the only way I make money," she replied in a husky whisper.

Johnny picked up the bill and gently placed it deep in the plunging V of her lacy semi-sheer teddy. "There, that should buy me at least five minutes of your time. I would just like... I'm hoping... maybe if you're not doing anything this weekend, we can go out?"

Roxy reached up with her right hand and brushed Johnny's hair out of his eyes. "You're really cute, but I'm sorry, I'm not allowed to date the customers." She shrugged her shoulders. "It's Gloria's policy."

Johnny's smile wavered again. "Okay... wait. Don't go anywhere. Okay... problem solved. If I leave right now and never come back, is that enough time away for us to go out on Sunday?"

"Well Mr. Johnny, first of all, you don't have to go anywhere tonight. I won't be in town this weekend, so the earliest we could go out is on Wednesday. That doesn't mean I'll definitely go out with you though. You'll have to pass my test first."

"A test? Hmmm..." Johnny smile began to slowly creep back. "I hope you don't mind me asking, but where are you going?"

"I'm going to Mexico on business."

"Let me guess... there's not enough strippers down there," Johnny clapped his hand over his mouth. "I'm sorry. Did I just say that out loud?"

Roxy leaned back in her chair away from Johnny. "That's okay. It's actually kind of funny. No, I'm going with a guy and it's his business trip so he's paying. I couldn't pass up the offer."

"A guy..." Johnny paused to gather his thoughts. "Mexico... That's nice."

"Yeah, we're going to an all-inclusive resort in Cancun," Roxy noticed Johnny's upbeat demeanor beginning to disintegrate. "Oh, it's not what you're thinking. We're not romantically involved. Greg's like a big brother to me. That and he's a customer."

"So your brother watches you strip," Johnny asked, his voice dripping with sarcasm.

"Alright, funny man," Roxy chirped as she pointed her right index finger right at Johnny's face. "Do you want that date, or would you rather just sit here making jokes?"

Johnny flashed her his best frowny face, "Sorry."

"Ooh! He's supposed to be here around eight tonight. You should hang around and meet him?"

"Maybe, if I'm still around… " Johnny replied as he stood up to leave.

Roxy grabbed Johnny's hand pulling him around. "Just so we're clear. I strip… that's all. So don't think…"

"I got it. Or should I say, I won't be getting it…" Johnny took in the beautiful golden hair framing her delicate features and the pearly white smile which ended in two little dimples. He looked back down at the table. "I'm sorry," he looked back up and gazed into her killer baby blue eyes, "but I must say you are the most beautiful girl I've ever laid eyes on."

"Thanks, but there's nothing to be sorry about."

"No, but I just don't get it…" Johnny asked, "Why a stripper?"

"Hmmm… It's all about time and money," Roxy explained. "I need money to pay my college tuition. And time? Well, I only work two hours a night and I'm always scheduled after classes."

"You go to college? Hmmm, I'm impressed."

"Don't sound so surprised, most of the girls who work here attend classes," Roxy pointed to the two girls on stage. "Rachel and Angela are in a couple of my classes. Gloria is happy to schedule around our classes if need be. I can study in between sets if I have to. And the money… what can I say? The money is awesome."

Johnny began walking backwards. "I should go back over with my friends. Maybe I'll see you tomorrow. If not, enjoy your trip and I'll see you when you get back."

Roxy pulled the hundred dollar bill out of her cleavage and stuffed it back into Johnny's hand. "Good news! You passed my test. I'll go out with you next week as long as you're willing to take your money back.  The rules are the rules, so when I get back I can't date customers."

Roxy began working the room again while the guys bombarded Johnny with questions about her.

"Alright, enough... you guys sound like a bunch of school girls," Johnny bellowed as he pushed the men away.  "Next thing you'll want to know is if she has a friend for you."

"But is Roxy going away with Greg this weekend?"

"With Greg?  Oh yeah, that's right," Johnny stumbled for the right words.  "Well, she did say Greg would be stopping by here in a little bit, so I better to get going."

"Hold it," Kevin throws his hands up.  "What about..."

"Alright," Johnny yelled.  "Yes!  Are you happy?  She's going to Mexico with him this weekend.  But she said they were just friends.  I'm going out with her when she gets back."

"Yeah, just friends..." Kevin snorted with laughter.  "It's actually kind of funny.  Our girls have a couple of things in common.  Let's see, they're both hot and they both went to Mexico with Greg.  Oh yeah, and they were both *just friends* with this awesome six foot plus guy who's packed with muscles and good looks... right!"

Tony slapped the counter in frustration.  "This whole thing with Greg is bullshit, and it's taking up way too much of our time.  If you don't want this job that's fine, I'll gladly find someone else.  If you guys are so certain he's crooked, then turn him into his superiors.  I'm sure they can sort that mess out."

"I'd like to tap his phone," Kevin said, "or I don't know, maybe bug his house."

"Who the hell are we even talking about now," Tony ground out.

"I don't think it matters."

"Yeah... Screw it! I say we tap both phones."

"I agree," James jumped in. "Did you guys ever consider just going back to your own simple boring lives? I mean, just leave those two poor boys alone."

"I can get you whatever you need," Dave offered with a serious look on his face, "I mean I've got some great connections."

"You," Johnny spat out. "You're nothing more than an out of shape has-been who works as a bouncer at a strip bar. Who in the hell do you know?" Then he rolled his eyes. "Just shut up and get me a beer."

Dave reached down and pulled a dark beer out of the fridge. "I have no doubt you all heard the rumors about me working for the CIA?" He opened it up and slammed it down on the bar. "Well, the rumors may be partially true." Suds bubbled up through the open top and down the sides, spreading around the beer like molten lava. Dave stood there glaring at Johnny.

"Which part," Johnny shouted as he stood there facing off with Dave. "Was that the part where you got kicked out for acting like an overgrown child?"

Dave held up his middle finger. "Watch what you say, Boy. I can kill you with this one finger." He boasted as he switched the upheld finger to his index finger. "First I'll poke you in the eye! When you reach up, I'll jam it into your skinny little neck, collapsing your wind pipe. If that doesn't kill you, then I'll sit on you and fart in your face." Then he started giggling.

"Can we get back to reality, please," Tony begged.

Dave lifted up his shirt. "Look at this. This is reality."

Johnny smirked, "What's that, your man boobs?"

"No, the scar... look," Dave pointed at a perfectly round scar about three inches below his left shoulder blade. "This almost killed me." Dave pulled his shirt down. "I was only twenty-four years old, fresh out of the academy. It was just my second time out in the field." He sat down and took a deep breath. "I was in... Well, they called it a safe zone." Dave shook his head and took a swig of beer. "Let me tell you, it wasn't very safe! One second, I heard shots being fired. I had no idea where they were coming from, or what they were shooting at. Next thing you know, I felt my legs giving out and I hit my head on a concrete wall as I collapsed under my own weight."

Johnny laughed, "That's a lot of weight"

Dave patted his stomach, "Well, I've put on a few pounds since then."

"Finish the story; I want to hear the end. Did you live or die?"

"Hmm, where was I," Dave thought for a second. "I blacked out, and the next thing I remember was waking up with tubes sticking out all over my body. The doctor had already made the decision not to operate. He felt that I wouldn't last through even ten minutes of what was sure to be at least a four hour operation. Between the extensive damage to my one lung and the fact that even if I was somehow lucky enough to survive the operation, he was certain that I would probably have severe brain damage from the massive blood loss and lack of oxygen. The doctor felt it was best to just let me die in peace. Luckily someone told him that I was a federal agent, because then he was required to use whatever means necessary to try to save me. Between my time in the hospital and my time in rehab, I lost more than one year of my life." Dave took a swig of his beer as the other men stared at him anticipating his next words. "I spent four years in high school, four year in military college and one year in special ops training, all for the sole purpose of preparing me for my dream job. And it was all gone in the blink of an eye. I wasn't coherent enough to see it, but I was told they shot that asshole twenty-three times."

"Are you kidding me," Kevin said. "What kind of CIA training do they have in high school?"

"I needed to speak three languages to have a chance to even qualify for the training," Dave explained. "So I started in high school... by the time I finished college, I was fluent in eight."

"No shit," James said, "which eight?"

"Obviously you have your standard three; German, French and Spanish. I'm pretty damn good at those three. My Russian, Japanese, Italian are better than passable. I also speak two different Chinese dialects, Mandarin and Cantonese. Those two are a real bitch."

"You speak Spanish," Kevin asked enthusiastically. "That's tremendous! You never know, it could be a very useful thing to know if this job takes us to Mexico."

"You're incredible," Dave blurted out. "I just got done telling you that I wasted seven years of my life training for a job that almost killed me. Plus I speak eight different languages. All you got out of that is I know Spanish? You're screwed up in the head."

"Don't let him get to you," James said, "he has trouble just speaking English. I'm very impressed. In fact, I usually call a temp agency when I need a translator, but lately I've been thinking of hiring one full time. Obviously, it would involve a lot of traveling and you should be aware that most of the places you would go to are business districts rather than tourist areas." He handed Dave a business card. "Give me a call if you're interested."

"I hate to break up your love fest," Kevin said, 'but we've got to leave now. Sorry, but the boys... umm, I mean the boys and girl have a double header tomorrow. That reminds me, James... At the last game, I started operation 'divide and conquer' against Dee. I have no real updates on that front. Finally, on Friday night I'm taking Coco and the kids out so I'm not certain when we can meet again."

"What's going on Saturday," Johnny asked.

"Saturday night is no good. The baseball boosters are holding their annual gun bash. It's their biggest fundraiser of the year and every parent is required to attend and work the event. How about we meet on Sunday?"

Johnny stepped in front of Kevin. "Wait, hold everything. What in the hell is a gun bash? Let me guess, you're all anti-hunting? And you have a big party to destroy guns?" Johnny pounded on the table. "I love it! You can count me in on that."

"I take it you hate guns. Also…?"

"Hell, yeah," Johnny replied. "My dad is a hunter and he's good friends with Dick Cheney. When I turned twelve, they tried to push that barbaric sport on me. I hate everything about it."

"Then, you'll fit right in with this group. I imagine most of them are Clintonistas."

"If I can't find a gun to bring, will someone supply one for me," Johnny asked.

"I'm sure you're going to love this party, Johnny," Dave added. "In fact, I'm going to personally pick you up and drive you there. That way you won't have to worry about being pulled over by the police again."

"Are they going to have beer there?"

"There's going to be all the food and beer you can consume in a day, and since I'm driving you'll be able to drink as much as you want. Oh yeah, there will be plenty of guns there, so please don't bring one."

# Chapter 24

(**5:00 PM Friday, July 9**) As Kevin crested the hill that led down to the first river, he could see the entire city below and it was truly a thing of beauty. The three rivers glistened in the sunlight, and just like the traffic, they never seemed to go anywhere. The tall buildings appeared to rise right out of the confluence, only to block traffic at every intersection.

Kevin pulled out his TomTom and started typing in Coco's address as he inched along painfully behind an endless line of cars. Cutting through downtown Pittsburgh at five o'clock without getting seriously bogged down in traffic is impossible on a good day. Attempting it around five o'clock on a Friday is borderline insanity.

Kevin's thoughts drifted along at a snail's pace, much like his car... Having never visited New York City, I'm not sure what they mean by 'the city that never sleeps' but having spent my entire life in Pittsburgh I know exactly what they mean by 'you can't get there from here.' Added to the fact that I have no idea where I'm going... Well, let's just say this has disaster written all over it.

Kevin zigzagged his way through traffic like he's playing a real life game of Frogger. Then he started across the first of the two bridges that stood between him and his dream girl. He made it about half way across before the traffic stopped him dead in his tracks. Sitting on the bridge, he could see the entire length of road leading to the other bridge. There's nothing but bumper to bumper traffic. I'm never going to get to her house on time he thought frantically.  So he pulled out his phone and began texting while inching his car ever so slowly forward over the river.

**"I'm stuck in town.  It doesn't make sense for us to try to meet tonight?"** ☹ Kevin clicks 'send'.

**"Where are you?"** Coco replies.

**"7th Street Bridge - bumper to bumper traffic!"**

**"Kev, why are you doing this to me?  Get your ASS over here now!"**

**"What?  What did I do this time?"**

**"I spent the last two hours getting ready!!!   And now you're telling me you don't want to see me tonight!!!"**

**"No I'm telling you when - if I ever get there we'll have less than an hour together!  Love you?"**

**"But I bought a new outfit just for this evening!!!"**

Mark picked up the phone when he heard the next text come in.  "Dad…!  You're not chickening out on another date are you?"

"Give me my phone," Kevin growled.

**"You went shopping for me?"**

"To answer your question Mark, no… we're still going out, I'm just playing a little hard to get."

"Dad, at your age, I'm not sure playing hard to get is such a good thing.  You know, you sound a little bit like the girls at school."

Kevin picked up the phone when another text came in, followed by three more in rapid succession.

"First I went to Macy's and tried on this beautiful dress. When the sales lady told me the price I was so upset that my hands started shaking uncontrollably and I had to ask her to help me take it off."

"Then I went to Penneys and found three dresses I liked, the third one was close to my price range so I bought it. It is baby blue, your favorite color!

"Then my best friend from work who helps the girls with their hair and makeup came over to fix me up just right! And Roxy loaned me a pair of her high heel platform shoes that go perfectly with my purse and I know how much you like tall women!!!"

"PS  I also got a surprise from Victoria's Secret!!!"

"Anyways Dad, I'm sure she already figured out by now that you're desperate," Mark added.

Kevin typed 'Dairy Queen' into his Tom-Tom and he found there was one located just on the other side of the second bridge.

"I am not desperate," Kevin countered.  "Why would you think…?"

"That seems to be the consensus of all the mothers at baseball," Mark butted in.

"Is there any way you can meet me at the DQ in Station Square?" Kevin asked in his next text to Coco.

"YES!!!"  ☺

Twenty minutes and one more bridge later the two boys pulled into the parking lot.  Kevin saw Coco standing across the street holding her daughter June's hand.

"There they are right there in front of Hooters," Kevin said to Mark as they walked briskly through the parking lot.

"Holy cow, Dad... really?!? I'm proud of you for trying, but you need to start dating women more suited for you. She's way out of your league!"

"Shhh... try not to embarrass me," Kevin whispered.

"Don't worry Dad... I'll do my part."

"I hate driving in this city," Kevin hollered while they waited to cross the road. "I don't know whose dumb ass idea it was to build a city surrounded by water but I'd like to punch the man right in the face." Kevin groused as they swiftly crossed the street to meet Coco and her daughter. "I mean, jeez... we passed by six or eight bridges on the way over here and every single one of them had a string of cars just sitting there, stretched from end to end."

"Umm, Kevin dear, I think you're scaring my daughter.

"Oh, yeah, sorry about that..." Kevin mumbled as the four newfound friends walked along the storefronts on their way to the takeout window of the ice-cream shop.

Kevin ordered one large twist cone and three small twists. He handed the large one to Mark before snatching the first small one for himself as soon as it was handed out, leaving Coco to grab the last two.

"I must say, Kev, you did okay with the ice-cream idea," Coco hollered as she handed June her ice-cream. Then grabbed June's other hand, hurrying her along, trying to catch up to Kevin and Mark who were already walking toward the water feature that's dancing to the sound of jazz music playing in the middle of the courtyard.

"I've got one more surprise for you three..." Kevin said as he took Coco's free hand and led the way down to the asphalt hiking trail by the river. "Now this is the great outdoors at its best. We have trees, the river and ice-cream. What more could anyone ask for?"

"Kevin, I'm thirty-one now…" Coco began.

"I didn't know it was your birthday," Kevin exclaimed.

"No… what…?" Coco shook her head. She pulled on Kevin's hand to stop him. "Listen, I'm thirty-one and not getting any younger, so if we ever managed to fall in love and…"

"Awww geez," Kevin began tapping the side of his face, "I'm not sure I like the direction this is going. This is our first date!"

"Unofficially it's our third date, but I'm just saying… If we ever got married, and you were given the power to change one thing about me, what would it be?" Kevin continued walking ahead trying to keep up with the kids. "Come on Kev, I'm serious." Coco ran up, grabbing his hand and pulling on it.

"Well, for starters, I don't think I like your line of questioning. You're already sounding like a wife, or worse yet, a lawyer." Kevin stopped Coco by pulling her hand up in the air and then he slowly spun her around. He looked up and down every inch of her amazing body. Her long auburn hair flowed down her back like molten copper, contrasting the crisp white sundress which showed off her slender legs beautifully. "Yeah, not bad, but you'd look better if you were two inches taller. What happened to the high heels and the blue dress?"

Coco pulled her hand away from Kevin's, "You're such an ass!"

Kevin grabbed her hand again pulling her along, trying to catch up with the children.

"What about secrets," Kevin suggested. "I don't think you can have a successful marriage if there are secrets."

Coco laughed, "Who do you think you are? Dr. Phil?"

"Secrets will kill a marriage," Kevin added, gasping for air.

"Well, if that's going to be your attitude, our marriage will be dead before it's alive," she stated emphatically, "because in my world, I think it's the secrets that make a marriage great!"

"So, somewhere in your twisted mind…" Kevin paused to rethink what he was about to say. "So, I can go out and have an affair as long as I do a good job of hiding it from you? And you view this as a good thing? I think this is going to be an unusual marriage, at best!"

"Please! You're going to have an affair," Coco exclaimed while delicately choking back laughter. "If Bo Derek was a ten that would mean I'm at least a strong eight. I'll give you a six, although you're probably more like a five. You're the math major. Does that add up?"

"Well, I'm not sure…"

"Do you really think you're going to do better than this," Coco gestured down the length of her body. "Oh and another thing… What's all this about me being twisted? And you already think I'm going to marry you! You've got a lot of work ahead of you before I say I do!"

"Well, what am I missing then," Kevin asked.

"I'm talking about the little secrets. You know… the good ones." Coco explained. "…The ones that make you crazy, but crazy for me. You're never really going to know exactly what I'm thinking. You should always be trying to figure out who I am or what I want and every time you get close I'm going change"

"It sounds to me like being married to you is going to be a full time job," Kevin replied in a dejected tone.

"You know what they say, 'Find a job you love and you'll never have to work a day in your life.'" Coco took two steps back and pointed at her almost flawless body. "The question you have to ask yourself is this. How badly do you want this job?"

Kevin slowed down while Coco walked out ahead of him. "Well, the fringe benefits promise to be a lot sweeter at this job than at the bank." he yelled as he admired the swing of her hips.

Coco paused and spun around, "Doesn't the thought of two girls invading your manly lifestyle scare the hell out of you?"

"No," Kevin stopped for a moment trying to think up something witty to say. "Nope, I'm at the point in my life where nothing really scares me. Except, maybe, the first time... making love... to you."

After a quick snort of laughter, Coco shot back, "Yeah, good thing you don't need to worry about that any time soon!"

"Alright, smart ass, what about me," Kevin asked.

"What about you," Coco snapped.

"Change, what would you change about me? That is, assuming I would let you."

"Kev, there are so many things. I wouldn't know where to start, so why even bother trying." She yelled back before racing out ahead.

Kevin stopped as he reached the edge of the park and leaned against a tree, trying to catch his breath. He watched in amazement as Mark gently picked up June and placed her in a child's swing. Then he ran around behind her and began pushing the swing gently, as if he had been playing with her ever since she was a baby.

I don't quite understand what just happened to me this week, Kevin thought. I spent the last ten years of my life looking for that special someone. In fact, for Mark's sake, I probably would have married just about anyone the last couple of years. And now that I've finally given up, Coco comes out of nowhere. Almost like my own personal angel or maybe she's a devil, at this point I'm still not sure and I don't know that it even matters.

Kevin snuck up alongside of Coco and lowered his left hand to the bottom edge of her sundress slowly pulling it down while still looking at her chest.

"Stop that, you jackass," Coco whispered harshly while slapping at his hand. "The kids are playing right there." Then she leaned in close to him, sliding one arm around his waist and hooking her index finger in to the vee of her top slowly pulling it down to reveal the top edge of her new black and gold satin bra. "There, is that what you were hoping to see? Jeez, one would think you'd seen enough of that at the bar."

Kevin face turned a ruby red as his eyes slowly drifted down from Coco's eyes. "Speaking of secrets," Kevin began as they both sat down on one of the many benches outlining the playground, "I know you don't like talking about Greg but..."

"It's not that at all," Coco interrupted, "I just don't know him that well. Except that he's just like all the other jackasses I've dated. You date a man for a few weeks, and he seems like a nice normal guy. Then before you know it their real personality comes shining through like a switch blade knife... that cuts out your heart."

"Yeah, but you went with him to Mexico... Not just once but four times."

"Is this going to be a problem Kevin," Coco asked as her patience grew thin. "I did go with him, and no, I don't regret it. What I do regret is falling in love with him. He had me fooled. So I made the choice to suck it up and move on. Something you should learn how to do."

June started running up the other end of the path and the three chased after her. They followed the path that lead to the bridge and began to cross the river.

"It's actually the trips to Mexico that I wanted to talk to you about," Kevin said. "We think he may be involved in some sort of illegal business deals and the trips are part of it. Look we're walking faster than the cars."

"So you think the people he meets at Omar's are somehow involved in it also? Well, whatever you think is going on, it certainly wouldn't surprise me."

Whoever designed the roads in this city should jump off one of these stupid bridges, Kevin thought. "Well, you went with him four times. Is there anything you can think of that may have seemed at all unusual? I talked to two other women…"

"What," Coco yelled. "What do you mean you talked with other women? Don't tell me you're some kind of undercover cop?" She grabbed her daughters arm and walked swiftly away from Kevin. "I knew this was going too well! What about the boy? Please don't tell me he's not your child! You pigs…"

"Hold on," Kevin took her hand. "What the hell are you talking about? Mark is my kid, I'm not a cop, and I'm definitely interested in you. I'm just trying to find out what Greg's involved in. Holy shit! You're a bit of a wacko, aren't you? Mark, if you're done eating that cone just throw it into the river."

"What exactly happened last week when Greg pulled you over? You act as if this man has stolen you're… Hold on, did you say he took other women there? Because I'm certain he's unstable. And if you're saying there were other women? Do you think it's possible that he might have killed one of them? Forget it… let's change the subject. The kids are too close, they can probably hear us."

The four turned around and began walking back across the bridge.

"Do you think you'll have time to stop by and see me at the gun bash tomorrow," Kevin asked hopefully.

"Yeah, but I won't be able to stay all day. I'm scheduled to work at two. Maybe I'll have Roxy fill in for me for a bit. I should only be an hour or so late."

"I guess she didn't tell you..." Kevin said in a somewhat surprised voice. "She's with Greg this weekend, in Mexico."

"What the hell? Why didn't you guys try to stop her? Or at least tell me so I could try," Coco called Roxy but only got her voicemail. "I'll send her a text... Hopefully she'll call me back. What time is your stupid thing tomorrow? Because... apparently Greg is going to force me into telling you everything!"

"What's everything," Kevin asked.

"Everything I know! Look, let's just focus on whatever kind of criminal activities he's involved in and quit focusing on my relationship with him. Nothing happened between us."

"I don't understand? What do you mean," Kevin stammered, obviously baffled.

"It means I didn't sleep with him," Coco stated emphatically.

"Why," Kevin asked with a confused look on his face.

"How the hell do I know? He said he just wanted to be friends!"

"I didn't... know... huh," Kevin struggled for the right words.

"I know, right? Look at this. I thought I was every guy's type!"

# Chapter 25

**(11:00 AM Saturday, July 10)**  There are two sure signs that the tournament season is well underway, Ron's team party to kick off the season and the FCBA's annual gun bash.  Most of the revenue required to finance the baseball organization comes from this one fundraiser.  With almost a thousand tickets sold it's of vital importance that the men keep the beer flowing and the women do whatever it takes to sell as many raffle and  instant win tickets as humanly possible.

Tony stepped outside the fire hall doors and saw a line that stretched through the parking lot and down the street.  "I don't get it, Kev.  They've been lined up there for hours."

James stood on the top step, sporting an old stained apron, looking down at all the hungry men.  "Oh yeah?  I get it.  After eating my flaming hot wings last year, I think word just got around.  So this is what you get, a long line of hungry men."

Kevin pointed down at the line about one hundred people back.  "There's Dave and Johnny, one of us should sneak them in through the side door."

"Good idea, Kev," Tony said, "I'm going back inside to check on my bed pans full of pasta."

Kevin walked down and waved the two men out of line.  "Meet me at the side door and I'll let you in.  You guys will need to go straight down to the basement and, whatever you do, don't draw attention to yourself. They'll be carding everyone who goes upstairs where they're serving the beer. The best thing for you to do will be to lay low for the first couple of hours. Once the place is full, they'll quit carding people."

Kevin rushed back inside to sneak his two friends in through the side door. He handed Johnny a pitcher of beer and quickly ushered them down the steps.

Johnny looked around in amazement, "Holy shit! There's got to be at least a hundred people down here already. Are there this many upstairs?"

"Not yet, but I think we sold well over nine hundred tickets. Oh, and make sure you save that," Kevin said, pointing at the pink ticket with a three digit number on it. "And remember what I said earlier. Just keep spending your daddy's money."

"Do I get a gun to destroy," Johnny asked.

"What you do with it if you win one is your business," Kevin pointed to a line of tables in the far corner of the room. "The food is over there. Why don't you guys pour yourself a beer and grab something to eat? Because once they open the doors, the line for food will be a consistent hour or more wait. Coco should be here in a few minutes… That should give us enough time to get everything set up for a short meeting."

Kevin rushed back up the two short flights of stairs to look outside for Coco. As he opened the door for the main entrance, men of all shapes and sizes began rushing in to get a seat near the food. He stood on the inside edge of the open door trying to look past all the rude people but quickly decided to call Coco instead. He could barely make out the word hello then her voice was drowned out by a loud roar.

"Turn down the music," Kevin yelled.

"What," Coco screamed.

"Do you have a car load of kids!?!"

"I don't think June's in my car! Why," Coco asked.

"What?" Kevin stepped into the storage room.

Kevin heard the sound of the announcer calling out numbers in the background of Coco's phone.

"I'm going into the ladies room with Kara so I can hear you better," Coco shouted into the phone.

"Noooo," Kevin screamed as he ran up the third flight of stairs. He frantically scanned the room as he attempted to weave his way through a crowd that was tighter than elbow to elbow. "Pardon me. Sorry." Then he saw her in the hall way standing with his arch enemy Kara. "Oh no…" he cried as he ran toward the ladies' restroom waving his hands above his head.

"Stop, get away…" Kevin yelled. "You're going to ruin her!" He crawled under two sets of tables. "Excuse me!" Then he sliced his way through the line of ladies waiting to use the women's restroom and quickly stepped in between the two. "I'm sorry. Coco, this is Kara… Kara… Coco," Kevin politely said while trying to push Coco away from Kara. "You're better off not talking to her." He whispered, "She's damaged goods. I'm sure you know what I'm talking about."

Kevin grabbed Coco firmly by the hand and dragged her away as fast as he could, disappearing into the mob.

"But… she seemed very nice," Coco protested. "She insisted that I sit with her at the game tomorrow."

Kevin continued pulling her along.

"Where are we going," Coco asked. "I want to meet the rest of your friends!"

"Yeah, most of the people here would never qualify as my friends," Kevin shouted back to Coco as he led her towards the stairs.

"Besides which, the guys are waiting for us downstairs." He saw Tony starting down the steps with a tray of food. "Can you show Coco where we're sitting?"

"It is twelve o'clock so let's get started with our first winner. We're looking for number 4-3-5. Please come to the prize table to select your gun," the announcer called out in an excited voice.

Coco followed Tony and his tray full of hotdogs and sauerkraut through the downstairs crowd and over to the line of buffet tables that outlined the stage.

"Everything looks and smells so great," Coco said as her eyes continued to scan the tables full of food. "The hotdogs and the hamburgers... Oooh, look there's pasta on that table over there. I love pasta." She picked up the serving spoon and scooped up some pasta then dumped it back in. "This is the way all Italian food should be made... thick rich sauce... and lots of it."

"I had no idea," Tony said trying his best to flirt with her, "not only are we blessed by your beauty, but obviously you're also a true pasta connoisseur. I'd love to get your opinion of my sauce."

"It smells like it was shipped over straight from Italy."

"You're close," Tony smiled and explained. "It's my mama's grandmother's recipe on her mother's side. She was born and raised in Sicily. I start with whole San Marzano Roma tomatoes, peeled and seeded... after a few seconds in the food processor I throw in copious amounts of fresh basil and garlic. Oh, and don't let the baseball size meatballs scare you, 'cause they'll melt in your mouth."

"Well, my granddaddy was the executive chef at one of the finest Italian restaurants on the Southside," Coco said enthusiastically. "He passed his secret recipes down to me. I've tasted some of the so-called best pasta in Pittsburgh and still haven't found a contender. So we'll see where your great- grandmother's sauce ranks."

"I made the world famous chicken wings," James hollered over while replacing an empty tray of salad. "They have a few pinches of cayenne pepper and gobs of Frank's Red Hot Sauce, so make sure you've got a beer on hand ready to chase it down!"

Tony put his arm around Coco and guided her away from the food. "You'll want to eat the pasta first." He whispered both in warning and explanation. "After one bite of his stupid wings, you won't be able to taste anything else."

"Well, after hearing you both describe your food," Coco said, "I'm feeling a little like one of those snobbish judges on the Food Network. I can't wait to chop one of you."

"Come on, Coco. I'll show you where we're sitting," James sidled up and smoothly pulled her away from Tony. "Then I'll get you a plate full of food, with lots of wings."

"I talked to my boss yesterday…" Dave said as he stood up to shake James' hand. "I told her about the job offer, she seemed very happy for me."

"Great!"

"Yeah, the only thing she had asked was that I finish out this month," Dave added. "I hope that's not a problem?"

"No, the timing should work out very well," James suggested, "I'm flying to Mexico in three weeks. Maybe you can go with me."

"I'm actually thinking about switching jobs myself," Johnny asked, "What exactly do you do there?"

"Pick of the table number three… 6-3-1… and we're still looking for 4-3-5 on the pink ticket."

James pulled out a chair and sat down next to Johnny. "We build an electronic device that's installed in every phone that's sold all over the world." He pulled out his BlackBerry and held it out. "It enables your phone to go from making a call to taking a picture, than playing music, to emailing and the device is about the size of a spent staple."

"Do you think you can talk to someone for me," Johnny asked. "I really hate working in an office and I don't think the college life is for me."

"You're not even twenty-one yet..." James looked at Johnny and sighed. "Put your time in at college than give me a call. I'll get you set up with a great job in sales."

James stood up to leave and Johnny grabbed his arm. "I'm serious, I need a change."

"Look, if you were to get a job with my company fresh out of high school, you'd make around twenty to twenty-five thou to start, with a top end around fifty. And that's after working there for the better part of your life. You kids are all the same." James said as he sat back down. "You want to have everything right now. I'm just glad I wasn't like that when I was a kid. Or I'd probably be working at a steel mill somewhere in Smalltown, Arkansas."

Johnny laughed, "So, does this mean you'll help me out or not?"

"What's your major Johnny," James asked.

Johnny flinched at the loud clicking sound of pump shotgun being engaged close by. He turned around and saw a large hairy man sitting behind him with the barrel of a gun sticking up toward the ceiling. "Huh?" Johnny looked back over at James, "What am I studying? English writing, it's actually a very difficult curriculum. But I've almost completed my first book. Maybe when I'm finished I'll let you read it."

"A writer," James shook his head. "You freaking kids and your silly dreams, no one writes anymore. You should major in business. If you do that, I'll guarantee you a job when you get out. It might not make sense to you now, but the stupid shit you do when you're in your twenties, will impact you and your wife and kids for the next twenty years!" James voice grew louder and more intense.

"What the…"

"Let me ask you this. Do you have any brothers or sisters," James asked.

"No, I'm an only child… why," Johnny replied.

"The twelve fifteen number is 6-1-8… and we're also still looking for 4-3-5."

"Well, let's pretend that Dave is your brother for a moment," James explained, "and let's say that I did hire both of you tomorrow. Because of his extensive education, ten years from now, he's going to be making about a hundred fifty thousand a year and he'll be living in a half million dollar house. On the other hand, because of your lack of education, you'll be making around forty. And here's the bitch, you'll have to explain to Roxy why you're still renting. Plus, when you have family get-togethers, your kids will be swimming in his pool and they'll be asking you why they don't have all the nice things that their cousins have. Instead of taking them to Disney, you'll take your kids to the Pittsburgh Zoo for vacation. Is that what you want for your kids?" James yelled, his face turning red. "Well, is it?"

"Whoa! What the hell are you talking about," Johnny shouted back. "I don't have kids. Did you forget to take your medication this morning? And there's no way I'm marrying a stripper." Johnny pulled Kevin aside and whispered, "I think your friend is delusional."

Kevin opened up the folder and began separating the information they had compiled on Alex so far. "Before we get started Coco has some information about Greg that she wants to share with us."

"We're drawing 'pick of the table' for table number four... the number is 7-5-3... and we're still looking for 6-1-8 and 4-3-5," the announcer's voice droned on in the background.

"I think we're all in agreement that Greg is capable of almost anything, right," Coco said in a commanding voice. "Apparently he was going on these trips with other women, right? Well, if you put..." She paused when Kevin slid a few photos out onto the table. "Yeah, that's the guy," Coco exclaimed as she pointed at one of Alex Cooper. "How did you get his picture?"

"Who's picture?"

Coco reached over to the stack of photos in front of Kevin and pulled out the photo and held it out, "This one! This is the creep that would show up with Greg at Omar's." Kevin opened the folder and spread all the photos across the table. "Yeah, that's him! Who is he?"

"That's Alex Cooper.  He's running for senator," Kevin explained. "Why would... why's he going to a strip bar?" Kevin rolled his eyes. "Well, yeah... dumb question."

Coco stood up with a hand full of photos, "Who took all these pictures for you?"

"Forget asking who or why," Tony cut in enthusiastically. "I think we've finally gotten our first break.  Maybe we can catch him fooling around with a stripper or something."

"Yeah, but...  What the hell would he be doing there with Greg?

"Oh shit," Dave slowly looked around the table at everyone involved, "I've got the best question..." He drawled with a sinister grin. "I wonder what's on those surveillance videos at Omar's.  And, more importantly, how can we get our hands on them?"

"Don't forget, I worked there until just three short weeks ago. I still know most of the employees," Coco offered.  "They may be willing to help me out, especially when I tell them Roxy could be in trouble."

"Well, we're going to be working here most of the day," Kevin began. "Why don't we…"

"Work… shit…" Coco cried as she stood up, "I've got to get to work soon." She gave Kevin a kiss on the check. "Damn it… I didn't even get a chance to try Tony's pasta or James' hot wings."

"We'll save you some," Tony and James shouted in unison.

"Fantastic! I'm going to the ladies room to freshen up before my shift. I'll call you after work Kev."

"We're now looking for 3-6-7… and 4-3-5…"

"Are they still calling 4-3-5," Dave asked. "Johnny, Honey, let me see your pink ticket."

Johnny threw his ticket out on the table.

"You've got 4-3-5," Dave squealed, jumping up out of his seat. "Let's go see what you won."

The two men grabbed their beers and headed up stairs to the prize table to see what Johnny won. Dave stood there looking at a table full of brand new shiny guns. There was an over and under, three 30:06s, at least seven hand guns and a dozen pump shotguns.

"I think I'll take that one," Johnny said, pointing at the Browning 22-250 rifle.

Dave picked up the gun and aimed it at the back ceiling. "Nice weapon. What are you going to do with it? Maybe do a little groundhog hunting?"

Johnny pulled it out of Dave's hand. "I don't hunt! That's a disgusting sport! Who knows, maybe I'll give it to the animals. So they can protect themselves."

"It's too nice and new to just destroy," Dave commented.

"Maybe I'll just give it to my dad for Father's Day."

Meanwhile, Kevin checked the status of the food in the buffet line and noticed the tray of pasta was almost empty, so he raced back into the kitchen to bring out another.

"Something doesn't feel right," Coco said while squeezing her purse.

"What doesn't feel right?"

Coco looked inside and saw there was something missing, "How about this? Something doesn't look right either!"

"What?"

Coco quickly scanned the room and saw at least a dozen men rifling through their wallets. She frantically ran from one guy to the next ripping the wallets out of their hands to inspect them to see if it was hers.

"Hey! You crazy bitch," Coco heard one man scream as she ran to the next guy who was pulling a small stack of bills out of his. Finally she stopped in disgust.

"What kind of guy would steal from a single mom," Coco softly said to herself as she slowly walked toward the man on stage calling out the winning numbers. She stood there watching him finish up announcing the most recent winning number. Then he turned off the microphone before going through the doors behind the stage. Coco paused for a moment staring up at the mic. She carefully cut her way through the first line of men getting food and then scooted under a long table. When she popped out from under the table, she found herself at the feet of a large hairy man holding two large styrofoam plates full of food.

"Hello... can you please set me up there," Coco asked as she pointed to the stage. "Thanks," she hollered back as she ran across the stage toward the microphone. She pulled it down to her lips and squeezed the button to make a bold announcement, "We have a thief among us!" She looked across the room full of drunken hillbillies and noticed not one person looked up at her. "Didn't you hear what I said you, you dolts? My purse was sitting right there!" She pointed at the table where Johnny sat. "I left it there, for just a minute, and now my wallet is gone!" And yet no one responded to her cry for help. So slowly she pulled up the bottom edge of her blouse revealing her tight abs then her lower ribcage until one old man sitting alone in the corner grunted out, "Take it off baby!" Then two or three men joined in until the whole mob of drunken men were chanting it in unison. "Take it off... take it off!" Coco raised her hand with the microphone in it and the place became dead silent. "There's a thief in this room! Someone stool my wallet, right out of my purse..." she announced again while pointing back at the table where Dave and Johnny were sitting, waving their hands up high. "I was sitting right there! Did anyone see anything?"

Johnny looked around the room at all the pathetic men staring up at Coco. He wondered if the men were thinking about Coco and her missing wallet, or just thinking about Coco and how much more of her shirt she's going to lift up.

Kevin carefully walked backwards through door marked exit as he left the kitchen with a tray full of pasta. He heard the announcements over the loud speaker. I know that voice from somewhere he thought. He made the turn into the large banquet room and saw Coco standing on stage with a microphone in one hand and her shirt partially pulled up with the other.

Johnny looked back towards the steps and saw Kevin standing like a statue staring across the long room at the new love of his life.

Johnny bent down next to the largest drunk man sitting at his table. "That's him," Johnny whispered as he pointed back at Kevin.

"The jerk with the apron on and the silver tray in his hands, he's the thief. I saw him."

The crowd erupted in a unified chant, "Take it all off! Take it all off!"

Kevin began to sprint across the room in an attempt to save his damsel in distress when he heard the grunting sound of a man's voice growing louder.

"There's that son of a bitching thief," the large drunk man yelled.

Then Kevin felt his knees buckle as he was blindsided by the large man. The tray of pasta exploded to Kevin's left, spraying sauce and noodles ten feet in the air and covering everyone within a twenty foot radius.

"I got him... I got the thief!" The man shouted while sitting on Kevin, "WooHoo! What do I win?" he screamed as he pounded on his chest before quacking like a duck.

Coco pulled her shirt back down and jumped from the stage onto one of the buffet tables. "He's no thief," she yelled as she jumped across to the next row of tables leading to where Kevin lay on the floor covered in pasta and rich red sauce.

"That's my boyfriend," Coco cried out in defense of her man. Then she ran down the six sections of tables spilling drinks on everyone sitting there. "Get off of him, you dumb shit!"

The man rolled over off Kevin as Coco rushed to his arms.

"Coco, is that you," Kevin asked as she began scraping hot pasta and sauce off his face.

"Yes. It's me, my dear Kev."

"I think I may have pissed myself," Kevin whispered in her ear.

Coco reached down and rubbed her hand up Kevin's inner thigh then licked her fingers. "Nope, it's just spaghetti sauce," she said, "and I must say, it's very flavorful."

"That's good to know because it's beginning to burn my leg... a lot," Kevin explained, "and, well, I was concerned there might be a more serious problem down there."

Coco leaned into Kevin's arms and licked some more sauce off his neck. "Tony," she hollered, "where's Tony?"

Tony ran over pulling Coco off Kevin.

"I'll give your great grandmother's sauce a top two," she said as Tony helped Coco to her feet.

"Just a top two," Tony asked in disappointment.

"Yes, well..." Coco shrugged her tiny shoulders, "Maybe someday, if you're nice enough to me, I'll have your family over to try my number one."

Kevin put his arm around Coco and walked her back over to the table. "You know, you should probably watch what you say in a room full of drunken men with guns. Someone could have gotten seriously hurt." Kevin looked down at his shirt and pants. "I gotta go wash this crap off me. Do you think you can find me some aspirin? 'Cause my heart's beginning to race again, and I'm told aspirin is good for a heart attack."

Coco dumped the contents of her purse out on the table, searching for aspirin. Then she shoveled everything back in and ran upstairs to ask the other mothers if they had any aspirin. After striking out with the moms, she went out to check the glove box. She reached in with both hands and pulled everything out and threw it all on the passenger seat.

"Let's see..." She said, speaking aloud to herself, as she systematically placed it all back in, item by item. "Sunglasses, driving gloves, pepper spray, hand lotion, hand sanitizer... wallet, small flashlight... tissues, and... Did I say wallet?" She rifled back through until she found it again. "What the hell? Who stuck that...? Damn it anyhow..." she mumbled as she stared at the wallet in her hands. "Should I go back in and let them know I found it? Or do I...? Oh, what the hell," she pulled out her cell phone and started texting.

**"Sorry Kev... I just got a call from work. I'm going to have to leave now. See you soon. XOXO"**

# Chapter 26

(9:00 AM Sunday, July 11) Kevin parked his car along the street that leads to the ball field. Mark jumped out with his bag in hand and started down the road toward the visitor's dugout. Kevin hollered to Mark's retreating back, "Hit one over the center field fence for me!"

Coco followed that great advice with some of her own. "Yeah, and walk down there," she said while pointing at the fence that parallels the first base line, "not on the edge of the road."

Kevin walked with Coco about halfway down the road and pointed toward the third base side bleachers. "There's Kara sitting over there. I'd go all the way down with you, but the women don't like the men entering their zone. You understand right?"

"I do understand. You're terrified of them, as you should be."

"Sure, something like that..." Kevin mumbled while glancing back in the parking area for James. Instead, he saw an old friend who was pulling umpire gear out of his truck. So Kevin gave Coco a quick kiss on the cheek and then ran over to try and schmooze him.

"Hey Paul! You got home plate today," Kevin yelled out.

Paul sat on his tailgate strapping on his shin guards. "Bad news Kev, I'm it... At least until the other ump finds his way to the field."

Kevin smiled. "Yeah, that's too bad."

Paul stood up and grabbed his chest protector. "Hey, there was this rumor being spread at the last umpire meeting. Did you guys really go and recruit yourselves a woman manager?"

"Yeah, unfortunately…" Kevin replied in a disheartened voice.

Paul picked up his face mask and began to waddle his way toward home plate. "Does that mean I'm in for a calm peaceful afternoon?"

"Yeah, you're freaking funny," Kevin growled out as he jogged to catch up with his buddy. "Can you do me a small favor?"

"I'm not calling a big strike zone for your son again," Paul whispered fiercely, "The last time I did that the other manager threatened to kick my ass."

"Oh yeah, I never did thank you for that. Thanks," Kevin whispered back, "but he's not pitching today…"

Paul stopped and looked around, checking to see if anyone was in hearing distance. "Okay, sure… but make it quick Kev."

"Do you remember the story about the umpire we had in the Delmont tournament? The one that was calling the base runners out if they weren't standing on the base when the pitcher returned to the mound with the ball?"

"Yeah, I still don't believe that actually happened but…"

"Well, it did… and it's going to happen again today," Kevin suggested urgently.

"It is, huh," Paul asked.

"Yeah, you'll need to do this before the second ump shows up. Manager Dee is very competitive, and a stickler for the rules. I'm hoping she'll run out to argue the call. When she does you'll give her the first warning. When your help shows up you can fill him in on the out of control woman manager. Then, for the rest of the game call our kids a big strike zone when they're up at bat and a small strike zone when our kids are pitching."

"And when she argues a call on a ball or a strike she's out for the game." Paul added. "League rules… one warning, then ejection… but why," he asked.

"Simple, I learned a valuable lesson when I got ejected from that game," Kevin explained, "and that's if she gets kicked out of a game, she's gone as manager. That's Fox Chapel Baseball Associations rules." he added.

"Is she that bad as manager?"

"They're ten year old boys," Kevin explained, the frustration clear in his voice. "They need a man managing the team!" Then he glanced up and saw Dee hitting soft ground balls to the infielders. "She has them singing in the dugout for crying out loud!"

"That's okay, dear," Dee yelled out to her son who's sitting on third base crying because he missed a slow ground ball. "You'll get it next time."

"These boys will only be ten once," Kevin moaned. "I'm not going to sit on my ass all year, wondering when or if I should do something!"

"This has got to be a first," Paul mumbled to himself as he turned toward the backstop. "He's asking me to throw the game the other way.

Kevin grabbed his arm. "Just remember, Mark is number ten."

Coco waved back to Mark as she walked past the concession stand. "Nice try honey, you'll get it next time," she yelled when she saw him trip over his own glove after missing a ground ball. Then she climbed up to the top row of the bleachers to join the mothers.

"Good morning Ladies," Coco called out as she sat down next to Kara. "I was hoping you'd be able to help me out with a few things?"

"Like what," Kara asked.

"First, and most importantly, I've never actually watched a ball game. So I'm going to need to know which team I should be cheering for. And you know, when am I supposed to cheer?"

"No problem, our team's dressed in burgundy with black trim. The other team is a deep red and has navy blue trim."

Coco looked out to where all the kids were playing. There was a dozen out in the grass chasing the balls they were throwing at each other. Then she glanced across the dirt area twice. She saw four lines of kids and Dee standing in the fenced-in section. Dee would hit the ball in the dirt and the kids would take turns chasing it out into the grass area. Then she noticed one tiny kid sitting on a white bag crying. "I'm confused. They all appear to be wearing the same costumes."

"Just follow my lead," Kara replied. "If I stand up and cheer, then you stand up and yell… Oh, and make sure you yell loudly enough that the men hear can you out in centerfield. The guys like it when we make a fuss over the boys and their silly games."

"Sounds easy enough… thanks," Coco said.

"What else did you need," Kara asked.

Coco slid over closer to Kara and spoke quietly. "Well, I'm not sure if I should talk to you about this. If Kevin finds out we talked, he'll surely over react."

"I'll be the judge of that," Kara responded in a firm voice followed by a soft giggle. "Sorry, but that was some great magistrate humor. I couldn't resist. Anyway, go ahead… If I can't help, I've got some friends on the police force, maybe we can just have Kevin put in jail."

"That's kind of what I wanted to talk to you about," Coco explained. "There's this Fox Chapel police officer, his name is Greg Handsom."

"Oh no... not you too," Kara interrupted in an exasperated tone.

"Well, unlike the men and their childish antics, I think I might have some real... I'm just concerned for my friend who's with him now and possibly our men if they continue on their witch hunt."

Kara slid over closer and prompted Coco to continue, "Okay, I'm listening."

"Well, for starters, I'm assuming our men filled you in on the things they found," Coco explained, "like the discrepancies between his pay and his lavish lifestyle."

"Yes, go on."

"And then, of course, there are the trips to Mexico..." Coco added.

"What about them," Kara snapped as her face began to redden.

"Well... Ummm..."

Kara watched as the ump called a strike on a pitch that was clearly out of the strike zone. "Hold on one sec, Coco!" She stood up and circled her hands around her mouth like she had a mega phone. "Where was that pitch, Blue?!?" Kara sat down and leaned close to Coco, whispering behind her hand, "That wasn't even close to the strike zone."

Coco rose and mimicked Kara's mega phone stance. "Yeah, what the hell were you looking at Blue," she yelled out in an unsure voice before returning to her seat next to Kara.

The umpire snapped his head around looking straight up at Kara and Coco, then turned and glared at Dee who was quietly sitting in the dugout. "Consider this your first bench warning," he yelled in before looking back up at Kara. "I won't put up with coaches or parents questioning my calls and cussing is clearly grounds for ejection!"

Kara smiled at Coco, "Look dear, I don't want to sound like one of those dumb ass prosecutors, but the men are all going through their midlife crises at the same time. Add to that Kevin's…" Kara paused briefly as she tried to find the right words to describe Kevin. "Alright, let me think about it. For now, let's just watch the game."

Coco took a deep breath and sighed, "I don't think I'm doing a good job of explaining this."

"I'll tell you the same thing I told the men," Kara explained. "I know he's not a good person and the people he associates with are trash. That doesn't make him a criminal. Go back to raising your daughter and living your life. If there's something going on, the police will find out."

"But I think I know something they don't." A tear ran down the side of Coco's face. "He was dating a friend of mine from work. They started dating right after he split up with me. I know they went on at least one trip to Mexico together. The day after they broke up she was fired. One week later, she was found dead. The news reported it as a hooker being in the wrong place at the wrong time. But I knew her really well; she was a friend of mine. She was clean, no drugs, and certainly not a hooker. She was a junior in college and she made the dean's list every semester. Stripping was just her way to buy books and earn a little spending money… Maybe she found out what Greg was into?"

Kara watched her son hit a double. "Go Jimmy! Run! Run," she screamed. "I'm sorry what were we talking about?"

"Greg," Coco said in a frustrated voice. "I was telling you…"

"You think he killed your friend," Kara said, interrupting Coco. "Fine, I'll tell you what… Not that you've convinced me, but I'm willing to listen to whatever you have. I'll help you on two conditions... Number one, I don't want my husband involved. If he is, I'm done helping. Second, I definitely don't want Kevin involved. When you get all their info and gather your thoughts, give me a call. Now, can we please watch our kids play?"

"I have everything out in my car," Coco explained. "I don't think it will take more than a few minutes to convince you. I'll get rid of your husband and Kevin while Dave explains to you what we have."

"I'm sorry, but who the hell is Dave," Kara asked stiffly, the annoyance clear in her voice.

"Dave is... Well, I think he's some sort of retired CIA agent. Anyway, he's going to tell you what to say and how to behave when you confront Greg. He also has a wire for you to wear. That way he can monitor the situation from anywhere."

Kara stood up and started walking down the bleachers. "I'm not sure I'm ready for all of this."

Coco hurried after her. "I think you'll do just fine. Dave will explain all the details. You'll be in a public area, so it'll be safe."

Kara walked far enough away from the bleachers so she was sure that no one else could hear her talk. "So you went with Greg on one of these trips. What was your opinion of him?"

"Actually, I went four times. Greg was really one of a kind and the resort was like paradise."

"Four times," Kara mumbled. "That's nice."

"Have you and your husband James ever vacationed at one of those all-inclusive resorts," Coco asked. "It's truly a magical experience"

"I'll keep that in mind, but my husband's really not much of a vacationer," Kara replies politely. Then she watched as the umpire called her son out at second for not getting back to the base before the pitcher had the ball on the mound. "What the hell are you talking about, Blue?" Kara screamed as she ran through the opening in the fence right out onto the field. "You can't call my boy out," she shouted. Then she broke the heel of her Nine West shoe as she did her best attempt at kicking dirt onto the ump. "He didn't do any..."

Dee ran out and grabbed Kara, dragging her off the field, but the damage was already done.

The ump followed Dee into the dugout to remind her of their policy. "I'm sorry ma'am, but I have to eject you. You not only have to leave the field of play, but you'll need to vacate the park property.

Kevin turned to James and gave a half-hearted smile. "Sorry."

"Sorry? Sorry for what," James asked while trying to hold back his smile.

Kevin sat there searching for the right words. "Well, for starters, your son getting called out at second. Plus, your wife getting..."

James let out one short laugh. "Why would you be sorry about that?"

"I talked the ump into making a few bad calls. I was hoping Dee would argue them and get ejected," Kevin explained. "Why? What's so funny?"

"What," James laughed again. "You think you're the only conniving son of a bitch here? Kara and I planned this out yesterday. I just can't believe how the ump played right into our hands."

"Yeah, well, I kind of helped too," Kevin muttered.

# Chapter 27

(2:30 PM Tuesday, July 13) Dave stood staring out the floor to ceiling windows watching an AirTran 727 land. He watched the plane as it taxied to the gate and then he walked over and sat down next to Kara. "Alright, just take a deep breath and relax. I've done this dozens of times. Just stick to what we discussed... And remember, you be the aggressor. Make him answer all the questions," he stated firmly. "But most importantly, I need to go through his carry-on." Dave stood up and put his foot on the seat next to Kara. "Think of this bench you're sitting on as if it has the same power as the one in your court room. And remember, I'm going to leave you when he shows up, but I'll be close by, listening... So if you need me, you know the signal, right?"

Kara glanced up at Dave with an unsure look on her face. "I'll be fine."

"Here they come," Dave whispered as Kara stood up to greet Greg.

"Kara! Dave! If I'd known you were coming to pick us up, I wouldn't have paid sixty dollars for parking," Greg joked as he looked down at Kara who was standing there with her arms crossed and an irate look on her face. "Okay, then... I give up. What the hell are you both doing here?"

Kara grabbed Greg by the arm pulling him away from Roxy. "We need to talk."

"Come on Roxy," Dave said, "let's go wait in the baggage claim area."

Greg stepped in between Dave and Roxy. "Thanks Dave. But all we've got are these carry-ons."

Dave turned toward the stores. "Then I'm sure you're up for a little shopping trip… Right, Rox?"

Dave reached his hand out and Roxy latched on as they walked away.

Greg looked down at Kara who was still glaring up at him with her arms folded.

"Well, I ain't got all day, Sweetie…" Greg said with an arrogant edge to his voice.

"I have a mountain of evidence," Kara whispered, "that at the very least makes you appear to be a drug smuggler or maybe something like that. Between your regular trips to Mexico which coincidentally happen to coordinate with the movement of large sums of money in and out of your accounts, and the pictures of you and Alex Cooper exchanging envelopes every month, the evidence is very damning." Kara paused a moment looking for a reaction from Greg but got nothing. "Look, it's just the two of us, tell me what the hell is going on and I'll do everything I can to try to help you. Please Greg, I thought we were friends."

Greg stood up and slowly walked down the hall. "We're friends, huh?"

Kara jumped up and followed after him. "Of course we are."

"Well, I thought we were friends too... Now, I'm not so sure. On the one hand, you've just accused me of being a criminal. But on the other hand, you do seem sincere about helping me."

"I am," Kara quickly blurted out.

"And I do appreciate that," the two continued down the hall away from everyone else then sat down. "However, you're not even close."

"I'm listening..." Kara said in her sweet voice.

"Let's start with the money..." Greg explained. "With the stock market going up and down like a yo-yo, moving my money around in a certain pattern seems to be working for me... at least for right now." Dave and Roxy finished their shopping and walked back to stand behind Kara.

"Greg, please," Kara replied in an aggravated tone, "I've worked in the criminal field for over twenty years. I know when a person is hiding something. What do you think we would find if Dave looked through your bag?"

"Well, let's see..." Greg picked up his small suitcase and slid it between his legs and the bench that Kara was sitting on, "before Dave could even unzip it I would most likely break every one of his fingers!"

"What? This finger," Dave stuck out his index finger. "I could kill you in seconds with this one finger! First, I would stab you in the eye. Then, I would shove it into your wind pipe, collapsing it... which would eventually kill you."

Greg picked up his bag and walked over to stand face to face with Dave. He narrowed his eyes and spoke in a steely tone, "Look, you're an easy guy to like Dave. But don't mistake my kindness as a sign of weakness, because I'll shove that finger right up your..."

"Alright," Kara interrupted, "that's enough! Dave why don't you take Roxy over to Seattle's Best and get a cup of coffee or something? This is going to take a bit longer than we thought." Kara waited until Dave and Roxy were out of sight. "Greg I'm not going to ask again… please."

"If you would've let me finish…" Greg continued to explain, "I've already told you why I was moving the money around. Everything thing else I tell you has to stay here in the airport."

"That's fine, assuming it's within reason."

"Alex Cooper is being blackmailed…" Greg expounded. "Apparently screwing around with one of the staff members in a certain five star resort can be very costly. Unfortunately for Alex, he found this out the hard way. He was vacationing with his wife two years ago at this particular resort, one that you may have knowledge of." Greg smiled as he softly elbowed Kara. "Anyway, each night after his wife would pass out in bed, Alex would sneak out of the room to hook up with this hot little senorita. They were very active, very creative and apparently very careless. They hooked up in the halls, the bathrooms and even once in the lounge. The problem is this… the Mexicans take the security of their guests very seriously because tourism is so important to their economy. They have cameras everywhere at this particular resort and caught him in all the best positions."

"That's great! He's a real player, I get it," Kara said impatiently. "Move on."

"Do I have to spell it out for you," Greg barked, losing his patience as well. "It's simple. He's just planning to pay them off until after the election. He got his first extortion notice a few days after he announced his candidacy for senator. They must keep a database, just waiting for the chance to blackmail people. So remember, if you ever decide to run for office, it won't be a shock that photos of us show up." Greg smiled. "So you might wanna keep that in mind the next time you get this crazy idea of accusing me of… of whatever your imagination digs up next… Sorry."

"I'm not here to dig up dirt on anyone," Kara said with a furious look on her face. "And as far as we're concerned, that's all in the past."

"That's what I'm trying to tell you, there is nothing in the past to them. As soon as you make a reservation they start to compile a dossier on you. After you check in, they watch every move you make. They cross reference photos of you and whoever you're with. Then they Google your name, check your facebook photos and compare all the pictures just to make certain you're actually there with your spouse. They have an entire team of investigators that spend countless hours going over videos of every person. They pump as much alcohol into you as they can, then they sit back and watch you while you do things you're going to regret later. And remember, it's all on video... Please tell me you remember having sex on that beach bed?"

Kara stood up. "Alright," she cried out, "that's enough!"

Greg started gently rubbing his chest. "And the wet t-shirt contest... damn you looked great! I still don't know how you didn't win."

"I said enough," she shouted.

"Is it," Greg asked in a stern voice. "Because you know I could go on."

"Enough of us," Kara replied firmly. "What else do you have on this blackmail crap?"

"Before you leave," Greg explained, "they compile all this info on a disk and store it away until they have a use for it. When your name shows up on the internet, it's automatically forwarded to them. And that's when they pull out the disk on you. If they think there's any chance of blackmailing you successfully, they try. It's apparently one hell of a money maker.

"Why go to all the trouble and fly to Mexico? Why not just wire transfer the funds," Kara asked.

"Come on, what about those twenty years of criminal law you have under your belt? What does that tell you? How about... follow the money. I'm sure you've heard that saying before? Well, good luck following this money. It's all about protecting the resort. They set the price and the time frame. If you don't agree, they have all the connections they need and they guarantee it will come out. Once you agree to their terms, then they give you the opportunity to either shorten the timeframe or pay fifty percent off. All you have to do is fly down and pay cash. This does two things for them... First, you're down there spending money at their resort. Second, it gives them new potential clients to extort. You know... someone much like yourself."

"Why not pay them off all at one time," Kara asked.

"Great question! Now you're starting to sound like the Kara I remember," Greg replied sarcastically. "We tried that, and I certainly don't recommend it," he sneered. "You should have seen me trying to explain why I was going on a weekend vacation by myself to Mexico and taking three suitcases. I had twenty-five grand stuffed in socks. If I'd gotten caught, I probably would've been in jail for at least a decade. The worst part of that trip was before I got back to the states they had already sent Alex an email saying they had decided it wasn't quite enough. What's he supposed to do? He is supposed to pay just one thousand dollars per trip, at least until the election is over. It's only a year and a half now... That's a little over one hundred thousand dollars. He'll make that up in less than one year of retirement pay if he gets elected senator."

"Yeah, I don't know."

"You don't believe me," Greg asked.

"I just said..."

"It does sound a little out there I know," Greg suggested, "but I can easily prove all this... I'm living it and sometimes even I don't believe it. I have copies of all the emails they sent him and I kept some of the better photos for my own records. Why don't you come over tonight and we can look at them together? You know, for old time's sake."

Greg picked up the luggage and they started walking towards Dave and Roxy. "I'm married. You do remember that, right? I would like to see what you have though. You did offer... I mean the pictures and the emails only. I have no interest in the rest."

"Look, I'm done playing Mr. Nice Guy with you," Greg lashed out. "I'll gladly show you all the photos and emails, assuming that's what it's going to take to get you off my back. But if any of this shit gets out, you can say goodbye to that rich husband of yours! There'll be pictures of us plastered all over every paper in the city!" Greg handed Roxy's carry-on to Kara. "Tell Roxy I said thanks for a great time!" Then he turned and started walking away.

"You saved photos of us?"

"I keep telling you..." Greg hollered back down the hall. "*They* have them, and you'd be surprised what a thousand dollars will buy you in Mexico! It's their new billon dollar industry!"

Kara pulled out the wire and talked into it. "Dave, did you get all that?"

"Yeah, don't worry your secret is safe with me," Dave said. "I won't tell a soul."

"No not that. Well, yeah... that too. But what I mean is... I think there's someone else involved. Greg said one thousand per trip for about two years. Then he said that adds up to about one hundred thousand. He only goes twice a month. I don't care how bad your math skills are, that doesn't add up."

Dave paused to consider her words. "So does that mean there's someone else besides Greg going down every other week? We need to find out who that person is."

Kara spied Dave and Roxy inside the gift shop. She walked in and pulled him aside. "We're going to get those two and when we do, I'm going to... Well, I'm not exactly sure what I'm going to do yet, but I'm doing something. Do you have any connections with the media?"

"Kevin has friends both at the Post-Gazette and KDKA TV news," Dave answered.

"I can't believe I'm going to say this. Wait a minute! I can't believe Kevin actually has a friend. Alright, the first thing I need to do is find out what kind of photos that resort has of me," Kara said. "Have Kevin call his friends in the media and start a rumor that I'm running for State Attorney General next fall. If what Greg said is true, then I should be contacted within a day or two."

Dave picked up a shirt and held it in front of his face, "I don't like the sound of that. It doesn't make sense for you to put yourself at risk."

"You're right. Let's start by trying to find who Greg's helper is and go from there. We have to go over every photo again. Only this time, we need to look at the people he's meeting with outside of the strip bar. I'm guessing that the men Greg is meeting at the bar are also being blackmailed. Coco told me that he has a regular meeting room reserved at the bar. If Greg is gone every other week, then we need to know who has that room on his off week. He may be Greg's helper."

"Maybe you can go down to Omar's," Dave suggested, "and ask to see their security footage."

"Move that shirt, Dave," Kara said as she pushed it away from his face. "I can't talk to you this way. Why don't you go down to Omar's tomorrow?"

"We tried Saturday night..." Dave groaned. "They kicked us out before I could go on stage and take a shower."

"Wait... what," Kara hesitated for a second trying to imagine why there would be a shower on stage. "Anyway, when you go to

Omar's ask for Stan. Tell him that you're working with me and you're looking for a person of interest. He'll take care of you. If he has a problem with that, give him my cell number. That's all it will take, he'll show you whatever you want to see."

Dave looked down at Kara, who was clearly overwhelmed and shaken. "Thanks for all your help, but I think I can take it from here."

"I have a few people I can talk to. I'm not helpless, you know…" Kara replied a little defensively.

"Please… don't talk to anyone," Dave advised. "Just trust me to handle it."

"Call me as soon as you get anything. Oh, and Dave, this is just between you and me… no Kevin and no James."

Dave flashed a small grin, "I'll take care of this, trust me." He grabbed her hand and reassured her in a strong confident voice. "Kara, please stop fidgeting and look at me. This is my job; I'll take care of this. Greg is right. Go back to your life and forget this ever happened."

## Chapter 28

**(6:30 PM Friday, July 23)** One by one, Kevin shuffled his feet down the steps and into Gloria's main room. He scanned the room until he saw Johnny and Tony sitting at the bar. Kevin made his way around the crowd and wondered if he finally lost his touch. He pulled out a bar stool and stood beside it.

"We were so close, I just don't get it," Kevin lowered his head in disgust then hit it off the top of the brass bar rail. He moaned softly, "Owww... that hurt."

"I looked at the surveillance videos from Omar's for freaking hours and hours..." Dave replied in a disappointed voice. "There was nothing but hot-looking girls hanging all over Greg."

"I can't believe we wasted two whole weeks chasing after a cop whose biggest crime is being a jackass," Kevin muttered.

"I told you..." Tony smirked. "Trying to bring down a dirty cop is like chasing after a ghost. A, they don't exist; and B, no one wants to help you... especially the police. Plus, there was no money in it for us. I hate to say this, but we really should be concentrating on our real project, digging up something on Alex Cooper."

"Yeah, well, I'm at a loss with him also," Kevin lowered his head again, softly banging it on the rail. "I mean, I thought we had the smoking gun when we found out he was associating with Greg."

"Now what the hell do we do?"

"It's funny you asked that Johnny." Tony pulled Kevin's head off the bar top. "I have a friend in the real estate business. Let's just say, she wants to get even with her ex-partner."

"Getting even…" Kevin groaned. "I use to love getting even with people, now it's just not enough."

"It's easy money," Tony said with a smile.

"Well, I still need money, and easy money is the best kind of money." Kevin began to perk back up. "If it's so easy, why aren't you doing it yourself?"

"At one time, I knew both parties quite well," Tony explained, "so I thought I should stay as far from this one as possible."

"I'm guessing that one of them was a recent client of yours," Kevin asked.

Tony pulled out a cigar and began tapping it on the bar top. "Yeah and when the partnership dissolved, she not only pulled all her investments from my firm, but she also tried to convince some of the clients that she had brought me into leaving."

Kevin shook his head. "This sounds more like you getting even than it does her old partner. So you don't want to be seen anywhere near the action, just in case something goes wrong?"

"Absolutely!"

"Does this demon of yours have a name," Johnny asked.

"Chris Patrick…" Tony answered.

"Okay," Kevin perked up a little more, "I know her. She's a real estate agent, right? She deals in residential more than commercial, and she can certainly be a pain in the ass at times."

"Anyway, Pat was known for giving kickbacks to anyone who helped her get a listing," Tony explained. "I know this for a fact because I got my share. I would also get paid if I helped with a sale. You just have to…"

Kevin jumped in, "I have to tell her that I'm willing to sell a list of prospective clients that applied for a pre-loan and are looking for a house. Then…"

Tony interrupted, "Then call the PA Real Estate Commission and inform them that Pat initially contacted you. Tell them that you would gladly help them set up a sting."

"Hey! Speaking of ex-partners," Dave interjected, "my old partner from the CIA is stopping by tonight to pick up the equipment I borrowed. Why don't you guys stick around? Bill is one of a kind, and I'm sure he'll have some great stories to share."

Kevin jumped up on the bar stool. "Speaking of stories Johnny, you never told us how your date with Roxy went. Please, give us all the details. Maybe even some pictures, I'd love to see her nude. Oh yeah, that's right… I'll see that in ten minutes…" Kevin said enthusiastically.

"Oh shit, I've got to go," Johnny answered in a panic. "Sorry guys, but if Roxy finds out I was here she won't go out with me tomorrow. Oh, and by the way… You suck Kev!"

Kevin started to smile just a little bit, "Did you say Roxy will be around on Saturday because…"

"Yeah, we're going out," Johnny snapped as he turned to race up the steps towards the front door.

Dave cleared off Johnny's drink from the bar and threw the five dollar tip in Coco's jar.

Johnny cleared the last step on his way to the front door. "I'm sorry…" he said as he bumped into a strong, older man dressed in a very conservative suit, wearing a crew cut and dark glasses. "Are you sure you're at the right bar?" Johnny asked, looking down the steps then back at the man.

The man smirked as replied, "I'm meeting a friend."

"Oh, you must be Dave's friend," Johnny stated in an eager voice. "Are you Bill from the CIA?"

"Hmph," Bill grunted, "if I told you, I'd have to kill you. Why are you asking?"

"This is clearly none of my business, but I'm just afraid that Dave may be getting in way over his head," Johnny explained, "and if he continues investigating this case of extortion, he's going to get someone hurt."

"He's playing a private investigator now," Bill asked in a condescending voice.

"Yeah, he is…" Johnny replied, "He really seems to enjoy chasing after men with guns."

"He does, huh?" Bill grunted. "We'll see about that."

Bill paused on the bottom step to analyze the situation. First, he saw a girl seductively dancing on stage, with at least three more walking the floor dressed in sleazy costumes. They appeared to be begging for money from a gang of filthy old men or some punks with more shit hanging from their faces than the average woman has in her jewelry box. What an absolutely revolting environment, Bill thought in disgust. Then he saw Dave waving him over to the bar.

"So, this is what moving on looks like," Bill asked in a snooty voice. "Are you certain you have the qualifications for such a demanding job as this?"

"It pays the bills," Dave responded as he handed him the large bag of equipment.

"Yeah... So, how did your little stake out go last week," Bill asked. "I trust no one shot themselves?" Then he let out a deep laugh.

"We got to bug someone's phone," Kevin explained enthusiastically, "that and we placed a few cameras in a house. You've got some cool gear in that bag."

"I'm sorry, but who are you," Bill inquired. "It doesn't even matter. I just need five minutes alone with Dave." He grumbled as he turned his back on Kevin.

Kevin wandered into the back looking for Coco.

"What's going on Dave? I want to know right now," Bill demanded. "Because the last time I checked, you retired a few years ago."

Dave quickly explained all the information the five men had compiled over the last few weeks while Bill pulled all the equipment out of the case and separated it out on the bar to take inventory.

"That's some serious accusations you're throwing out there and about a fellow law officer to boot," Bill said. "And you say you have pictures to validate your story?"

Kevin sat back down at the bar. "What'd I miss?"

Dave poured two beers and slid one in front of each man. "Nothing Kev, we were just going over old times."

"I'm going outside to make a phone call," Bill said with a grimace. "I expect you'll both be here when I get back. If not, I know where you live, Dave. And as for you," he pointed at Kevin, "I'll hunt you down."

The two men watched as Bill disappeared into the crowd.

"I think your friend's been chasing serial killers too long," Kevin observed, "because he appears to be taking on some of their more intimidating traits."

"It's all for show," Dave explained. "He feels more comfortable when everyone around him is on edge."

"Maybe he won't come back..." Kevin said. "What do you think? Should I leave?" As Kevin started to get up, Bill walked back in. "I was just going to the men's room, but I think I'll sit back down instead."

Bill began packing his equipment back in the bag. "It looks like everything's here." Then he stood there looking back and forth between the two men. "This asshole here I understand," Bill said, slapping Kevin on the back. "He looks too stupid to comprehend!"

"Hey! That's not right..." Kevin interrupted.

"There's nothing to be ashamed of Kevin. But you, Dave..." Bill put his arm around Dave. "What the hell were you thinking? You should know better!"

Dave pushed Bill's arm away.

"You may have been interfering with an ongoing investigation," Bill explained. "At the very least, you definitely put a civilian in harm's way. I know it's been a while since I trained you..."

"I didn't break any rules," Dave barked.

"Did you forget everything I taught you," Bill shouted at Dave while staring down both men. "So, here's how this is going to work... You two have one hour to bring me every little thing you have on this guy. I don't care how insignificant you think it might be. I want it all. And then you'll forget we ever talked. And when you see your friends, you better fill them in on..." Bill shook his head. "Just tell them to keep it to themselves if they know what's good for them." Bill grabbed his bag and stormed out.

# Chapter 29

(5:50 PM Wednesday, July 28) Coco pulled out the chilled bottle of champagne and handed it to Dave to pop the cork. Then she lined up five champagne flutes and poured a continuous stream from one to the next, barely spilling a trickle down the sides of the glasses. She carefully wiped off the edge of one before smoothly handing it to Kara.

"Who didn't get one," Coco yelled as she raised her own glass high.

Dave tipped his glass against Kara's then leaned over close to her, "It's all taken care of..." He whispered in her ear, "I told you to trust me, didn't I?" As he sat back in his seat, she smiled and lightly tapped her glass against his before taking a long sip.

Dave stood up and whistled as loud as he could. "Okay, quiet everyone! It's almost seven o'clock..." he shouted.

Gloria, the owner of the bar, stepped out onto the stage to make an announcement. "I'd like to apologize to anyone that's here to see our favorite girl, Roxy." A few men began chanting Roxy's name. Gloria raised her arms up trying to quiet the crowd as Dave jumped up on the stage and handed her a microphone. "Alright, I appreciate how you feel about Roxy. Don't worry, she'll be out shortly," Gloria explained, "but for now we have a different kind of show... a very special show." She pointed over at Dave on the edge of the stage. "Go ahead, Dave, lower the screen."

Dave started the mechanism to lower the projector screen as Coco dimmed the lights.

Kevin hurried through the front doors of Gloria's. Since there was no bouncer collecting a cover charge, he raced straight down briefly pausing on the bottom step. "What the hell is going on," Kevin asked in a surprised tone. "Did they turn this place into a movie theater overnight?"

Coco ran over and gave Kevin a quick kiss on the cheek. "You're late," she said as she grabbed his hand pulling him over to an open bar stool. "I promise, it'll be a short movie, dear." As he took his seat, Coco picked up her glass of champagne and handed the last glass to Kevin.

Kevin glanced over at Coco with a confused look on his face. "What is this? Don't tell me you're proposing," he asked in a cautious voice.

"No, Dumb Ass! Just wait a minute and you'll see." Coco sat thinking for a few seconds. "Proposing? Hold on. Are you saying that *me* proposing to *you* would be a problem? Because…"

"Not a problem at all…" Kevin replied calmly. "I'm one hundred percent for women's rights and all that other feminist crap!"

"Shhh… It's starting!!!"

"Why in the hell are we watching the CBS evening news," Kevin asked as he looked around the room. "This place has hit rock bottom."

"With the economy still in a free-fall and the value of houses continuing to drop," the newsman began, "we will be interviewing an economist later in the broadcast to get some ideas on how to stretch your dollars."

"Turn it up." Someone yelled out from the back.

"Also, we'll be speaking with a home builder to see how you can save money when you build your new dream home. But we lead off the day with breaking news… The FBI and CIA, in a joint task force, have uncovered one of the biggest extortion rings in recent history. It apparently all started with one Pittsburgh police officer..."

The crowd went crazy when they showed a picture of Greg being lead away in hand cuffs.

"Less than two years ago, on a seemingly harmless vacation with his best friend Alex Cooper..."

The crowd lets out another roar.

"Greg Handsom was able to obtain video of his friend, Alex, who was having an affair with an employee of the resort. He patiently saved the video until last year when Alex announced his intention to run for the US Senate. That's when the blackmailing began… From there, it quickly escalated, spreading across the nation. Greg compiled video of some of the biggest names in the country, from sports figures having homosexual encounters, to politicians engaged in threesomes; not to mention, the forty-seven year old lawyer acting like a twenty-two year old girl on spring break. Our reporters are working to obtain photos even as we speak and we'll be certain to bring you more on this story as the information comes available. Coming up next… The housing industry, is it still in turmoil?"

Dave reached over and flipped on the lights. Everyone in the bar stood up and raised their drinks high in the air. Then the crowd erupted as Roxy slowly danced her way across the stage.

Kevin grabbed Johnny's arm as he was walking past. "What the hell is this?"

"Don't look at me that way," Johnny snapped back. "You got what you wanted!"

"I don't know what's going on here," Kevin replied as confused as ever.

"Look Kev, I'm not the person you think I am. Can we just leave it at that?"

"No way," Kevin said to Dave who had just walked over. "There's more to it than this, I want to hear it all!"

"Come on. We'll talk in the back where we have some privacy," Dave suggested. "I'll tell you what I can, but then you'll have to drop it!"

The two men took their drinks back to the surveillance room and sat watching the customers either celebrating the good news or just simply going crazy over the sensuous moves being put on display by the stunningly beautiful Roxy.

"Okay, let's hear it," Kevin demanded.

"Alright, but what I say can't leave this room," Dave stated emphatically. "Because number one, this investigation is still on-going; and number two, if this gets leaked to the media, then I'll never get help from my friends at the CIA again."

"Alright, already," Kevin shouted as he sat at the edge of his seat in anticipation. "Now tell me, how did we go from rock bottom to seeing Greg in handcuffs? Plus there's the added bonus of smearing Alex, possibly to the point of him stepping down?"

"You remember that night we talked to my friend Bill from the CIA," Dave asked. "You know, we handed over all the photos and documents."

"Sure, I never forget the way that psycho stared at me."

"Well, it must have been enough to peak someone's interest down there at the CIA, because they decided it was worth looking into. So Bill acquired Greg's work schedule and made flight reservations for himself and one of his colleagues. They decided to go under cover posing as a married couple and even flew down on the same airplane as Greg. When they arrived at the resort, they did the standard installation of cameras in Greg's room and bugged his phone. They followed him around the resort for two days, and saw absolutely no sign of Greg engaging in any type of suspicious criminal activity. At this point, they just assumed this was nothing more than a case of false allegations. Then around twelve o'clock on the third day, Greg went back to his room and reappeared shortly thereafter dressed in an employee's uniform. They followed him to the resort's surveillance room just outside of the lobby. I imagine their equipment is a little more complex than this stuff."

Dave and Kevin watched through the two way mirror, as drunken men made complete fools of themselves in the hopes of impressing the sexy women in the room.

"As you can see we're also videoing everyone," Dave explained, "and everything that goes on in here tonight." Dave said as he pointed at the four screens around them. "The thing is there's really no one out there wealthy enough to blackmail."

"I wouldn't say that. I know James has money."

"Well," Dave continued, "imagine a resort full of filthy rich people like James, or even more money. It's a place where they can drink all they want, when they want; a place where they do this all day and all night. The more one man drinks, the more the next guy feels he has to... When one couple does something crazy, the next couple tries to outdo them... All this going on and they all think that no one's watching."

Kevin shrugged his shoulders. "I still don't get it."

"You might not, but they do," Dave said in a direct voice. "They capture every move. Everything you do, they see. And it's all on video, and worse, it's all saved and catalogued in an elaborate database."

Dave slapped Kevin's arm. "Can you focus on what I'm saying and not on that little girl out there dancing? Now where was I?"

"The last day…"

"Right… So, Bill watched as the security man behind the wall of glass walked out to take his lunch break, passing by Greg who was walking in. Greg slipped him a roll of cash… five hundred dollars," Dave continued enthusiastically. "Greg sat in there, making copies of all the video taken over the previous two weeks. Next, he would download all the private information the resort had on each guest from the resort database. Then, he would take everything back home with him to Pittsburgh where he would review the videos, forming his next list of potential candidates to extort."

The two men sat in their chairs watching their friends celebrate and noticed Tony talking to Coco. She turned around and pointed at the two way mirror. Tony walked over to the wall of glass and pulled out a roll of money, slipping out a hundred and smashing it tight against the glass.

Kevin tapped back on the other side of the glass. "I'm guessing its payday," he said to Dave.

Tony busted through the door, emptying his pockets out, placing three fat rolls of hundred dollar bills on the counter in front of Kevin. "That's your first installment…" he exclaimed. "Rumor has it that Alex has scheduled a news conference to announce his withdrawal from the Senate race."

Kevin slid a bundle of money down the counter in front of Dave.

"Thanks, but that's yours," Dave said as he flipped it back over to Kevin. "I don't want your money. I was just doing my job."

"But you earned it," Kevin protested.

"Yeah, maybe… But…"

Johnny walked through the door, immediately followed by James. "Am I interrupting anything," Johnny asked.

Kevin tossed one of the rolls up to Johnny. "I know he'll keep it," Kevin said.

Johnny grabbed it out of the air and popped the gum band off. "Nice. What have we got here?"

"That's your first installment for helping me," Kevin explained.

Johnny dropped the stack of money scattering it all over the counter in front of Kevin.

"You guys did as much as me to earn this money," Kevin insisted. "You don't want it either?"

"Don't want! Don't need! Don't care," Johnny said as he looked out the window at Coco who was picking up a tray full of beer mugs and champagne glasses. "Think of it as an early wedding gift!"

Kevin looked out at Coco and smirked, "Who's getting married?"

Johnny's eyes slowly shifted around the room at Kevin's so-called friends and thought about their childish antics. Dave... whom God graciously provided with all the brains and talent to help people who are in dire need, yet he would rather waste his life hanging out at a bar feeling sorry for himself. Then you have Tony... who instead of learning his job so as to help better the lives of his clients, would rather destroy the reputation of his closest competitors with the hopes of being nothing more than mediocre. Then you have James who has what every man wants and needs, and he would rather spend his time helping oust the manager of his son's ball team instead of just helping the man manage the team. Lastly you have Kevin... Johnny thought to himself, he's counting money he earned by smearing a man's reputation for no other reason than financial gain. He glared down at Kevin impatiently waiting for results.

Johnny picked up a handful of hundreds and threw them across the room. "Don't you ever wonder what life could be like," he shouted. Then he paused for a moment trying to regain his composure. "I don't give a shit what you do with your life! You can grow up... or don't! All I know is this; I'm done wasting my time on you!" He stood there, looking around the room again, glaring at each man as they stood there silently staring back at him. "You have a woman who's looking for a husband and a father," Johnny pointed through the glass. "Or you can hang out in a bar full of... It's time for you to decide which direction you want your life to go!" Johnny walked back out the door, stopping only long enough to give Coco a final hug goodbye.

"The kid has got a good point," Dave suggested. "Might we see a wedding in the near future?"

"I'm going to have to think that one over," Kevin said as he stared out at Coco who was wiping down the table in front of the window. "Johnny turns twenty-one in a few weeks. Maybe we should all go to Mexico for his birthday?"

Dave laughed, "How ironic would that be?"

"Well, what about you Dave? I guess congratulations are in order?"

"What? Me? I'm not getting married..." Dave exclaimed.

"No, I heard you're going to work for James soon."

"Oh that..." Dave shook his head. "I think I'm going back to the bureau. After these past few weeks, I realized that catching bad guys is what I was born to do."

The four men watched as the crowd's demeanor quickly changed from the standard screaming and yelling to completely silent, staring up at the TV on the wall.

"Now this place really does resemble a church," Kevin said with a laugh.

Dave changed one of the monitors to match the channel the crowd was watching. The three men watched in disbelief at the breaking news scroller running across the bottom of the screen.

"In an apparent suicide, Alex Cooper was found dead today from a single gunshot wound to the head."

# Chapter 30

(**2:00 PM Tuesday, August 31**)  Professor Chapman walks down a poorly lit hallway, glancing up now and again at portraits of some of the most gifted people to ever walk the face of the earth. He carries with him a stack of folders. Each of those folders is filled with the summer activities of each and every child in this year's writing class. The top folder slides off the stack, scattering all over the cold hard floor. The Professor kneels down and his hand begins to tremble as he slowly reaches out to stuff the papers back in to their folder. He glances up slowly and finds himself kneeling in front of the Blessed Mother Mary's statue. Tears begin to seep out of the corners of eyes. He reaches up and carefully wipes off his face with the sleeve of his suit coat then he softly prays. "Dear God, please give me a sign. Could this boy be the one I've been praying for?" He promptly does the sign of the cross then stands up and hurries down the hall leading to the class room.

Johnny sits on the edge of the Professor's desk staring out at the elite group of fifth grade students. Sitting before him is supposed to be some of the most intelligent students in their age bracket. He wonders if the next nine months spent as a student teacher will really make him qualified to teach a group of this caliber. Then he thinks back to the morons he found himself working with this past summer at the bank. Is there really a difference between the so-called geniuses with their one fifty IQs and the complete idiots we all seem to find ourselves surrounded by every day?

Johnny spies a piece of crumpled paper on the floor near the trash can. He walks over to pick it up and carelessly stuffs it into his pocket. Then he steps out the door to look up and down the hallway. "I guess the Professor's going to be late again," he grumbles as he shuts the door behind him. He notices a new stack of papers sitting on the podium, so he picks up the papers and prepares to hand them to the little boy sitting in the front left corner of the room.

"Hand them out yourself, you overgrown freak," the little boy said in the nastiest voice an eleven year old could muster up.

The young man sitting behind him promptly jumped out of his seat and walked over to stand in front of Johnny. "Don't let Greg get to you, Teach. He's just an a-hole," he mumbles as he stares down at his feet. "Like I told you before, we're going to get even with him one of these days."

"Thanks Kevin," Johnny replies politely as he writes a few words on the bottom of the last sheet. "But what did we talk about this past summer? Staring down all the time projects a lack of self-confidence... I'm way up here Kev." Johnny said in a commanding voice as he crouches down a little. "You need to begin looking people in the eye when you address them."

Kevin glances up, "Sorry Sir." Then he quickly looks back down at the floor.

"No, you don't need to apologize..." Johnny responded softly followed by a long sigh. "Kev, you need to be a stronger more confident boy."

"Stronger, Sir? I don't understand," Kevin mumbles.

A chill runs through Johnny's veins quickly covering his whole body with goose bumps. "God has big plans for you Kevin. I can't explain how I know, but you're going to make a difference in the world someday... you just need to work toward the goals we've set."

"Yes Sir... why me, Sir," Kevin asked still looking down at his shoes. "Why does God have plans for me, Sir?"

Johnny looks down at this awkward eleven year old boy with fair skin and long, thin blond hair that surround his thick black glasses and thinks... I've been asking myself that same freaking question all summer long. "Please, just hand out these papers, Kev."

"Yes, Sir... Sorry, Sir..." Kevin replies in a timid voice.

"Oh... and class," Johnny announces in an authoritative voice, "please quit giving Greg your lunch money. There are no dangerous children attending this school, so you don't have to pay him for his protection."

Johnny watches Kevin as he hands out the new project sheet. He begins writing in his notepad as he observes and analyzes each student's behavioral makeup.

Kevin places one on Greg's desk and Greg complains immediately. "Shhhhoot... Not another stupid book assignment! This Professor is such a piece of shhhh... crap!"

He hands the paper to Jan without incident. Sitting across from Jan is the bossiest child in this room. She's a thin, almost brittle, girl named Diane who's holding back her long golden curly hair with one hand while applying makeup to her tiny face with the other. "Jeez, Kevin! Would you kindly quit staring at me?"

Next, Kevin hands a paper to the only black child in the room. His name is Dave. He has a body that's clearly too large for an eleven year old and a mind that's more suited to a Rhodes Scholar. "Th-an-ksss dear... Kev...inn... you're a true ffffriend." He speaks with a slight speech impediment which makes him an obvious target for a few of the children to pick on. But all the girls seem to adore his fun-loving personality.

Then he hands one to Ron. Ron seems to be nothing more than a stuck-up rich white boy with a small kid complex. "Here Kev...

here's a dollar for your efforts. Maybe you can go buy yourself a real haircut!"

Kevin quickly snatches the bill off of Ron and quickly turns to hand a sheet to Dee. He pauses for a moment before dropping the next paper at the feet of a cute little Asian girl with long black hair. "Oops," Kevin said followed by a long exaggerated sigh. "I'm really sorry Kara," then he kicks it under her desk, "how clumsy of me."

The next one goes to Tony who seems to be more cunning and devious than even me, but acts as if he's dumber than a door knob. He is a gangly youth with brown frizzy hair and a spastic personality. He definitely needs to learn to be less assertive.

Then there's Joe, who is supposedly Kevin's cousin. But other than them both being eleven and wearing the same nerdy glasses, they appear to have absolutely nothing in common. Joe is easily a foot taller and at least forty pounds heavier than Kevin. And not only does he look Italian but he also acts as if he's part of the new Mafia. On the other hand, Kevin appears to be one hundred percent Irish right down to his fair skin and freckles.

Next comes Jess, who is so shy, she won't associate with any of the other students. I wonder if she's hiding something or maybe it's because she's two years older than the other students and still not smart enough to attend a school of this stature. I think I'm going to need more one on one time with her.

Roxy is sitting behind Jess. Her sheer beauty at twelve can be intimidating to even a twenty year old man. "Thanks Kev... you're a sweetheart." She spoke softly as she sweetly batted her eye lashes.

Then there's James who appears to be the most popular child in class. He's also Kevin's best friend and seemingly the only person who can understand his complex personality. "Go get her," James whispers his encouragement as he takes the paper from Kevin's hand.

Next is the new girl, Jules. She just recently joined the class. I'm going to have to schedule some time to meet with her privately to get to know her a bit. And it probably wouldn't hurt to also meet her parents.

Kevin saves the best for last... As far as he is concerned, she is the sweetest little girl in the whole wide world. He steps forward with the last sheet of paper and holds it half way out then slowly glances up to her long auburn hair. His eyes slowly skip from one freckle to the next, pausing only a second on her soft red lips then stopping to stare deep into her brown eyes.

That's right, Kevin, make her meet you half way. Johnny mentally coached him as he watches Kevin's face turn from a pale white to a slight red while his hand begins to shake in anticipation.

Coco glances up to the front of the room at Johnny and winks at him. Then she looks back at Kevin and her lips begin to twitch as she tries to hold back that million dollar smile. She slowly reaches out to take the paper just as it begins to violently shake in Kevin's hand. She touches the edge of the paper and it slips out of Kevin's fingers. They both watch as it drifts back and forth until finally finding a place to rest on the floor between them. They both bend over to pick it up and Kevin softly bumps the crown of his head off of Coco's forehead.

"Oh my Gosh," Kevin said as his face turns a deeper red, "I'm so sorry." Again, he reaches down to pick up the paper and notices there's a hand written note on the bottom. He sets it on the desk in front of Coco as they both read the short note.

"Would you like to sit together at lunch," signed Kev.

Kevin glances back at Johnny with a confused expression on his face. Then he looks back to see Coco's sparkling white teeth covered with bright shiny chrome braces rapidly bobbing up and down with the rest of her head. He reaches out to brush the hair back out of her eyes and the two are startled by the sound of the door slamming from behind.

Johnny quickly walks to his seat in the back of the room while Kevin sprints back up front to his desk behind Greg.

"You dork ass," Greg whispers to Kevin.

"Quiet please," the Professor barks as he taps the bottom edges of the folders simultaneously on the desk to straighten the stack compulsively. He places the neat stack of individual folders which are stuffed with each student's short story on the corner of his desk.

Johnny unfolds the crumpled paper and begins to read the scribbled, random thoughts of a truly distressed man. He wonders what kind of horrific thoughts must be running through the Professor's mind as he watches his every move. From the continuous shifting in his seat and the rapid blinking of his eyes to the uncontrollable tapping of his right index finger into his ear, these are all signs of a disturbed man Johnny thought. I've mastered almost every gift that's offered, but the talent for reading one's minds definitely continues to elude me.

# Does Hell Have Room for One More?

### Book Two of

## Breaking All the Rules

Rule #2: Friendship can open many doors but anger will change a person's mind much faster.

## RICK GRASINGER

## *Prologue*

**(2:15 PM Tuesday, August 31)** The Professor returns eleven of the twelve folders by placing each on the desk of the child who wrote the story. He returns to his podium, slamming the last folder across the top of it.

The Professor begins speaking in a stern voice, "It was a pleasure to see most of you young adults took your summer project seriously. In fact, all but one of you followed my rules to a T." With that comment, he glares down the first row to where Johnny sat in the last seat.

"Was this your idea of a joke, Son," the Professor asks as he begins walking down the aisle towards the back of the room.

Johnny jumps up to meet the Professor halfway. "No Sir... No joke Sir," he replies calmly, looking down in to the Professor's eyes. Johnny mentally reviews the last three months and the disturbing news he learned about the Professor.

The Professor steps up closer to Johnny in hopes to glare him down. "Son... each student was supposed to write a story based on their *own* summer experiences."

"You've got it Old Man." Johnny thinks back to Kevin's advice on how to read a person's mind, so he tries to draw some type of reaction from the Professor. "That was my summer. My father is the vice president of some stupid bank and I worked there as an intern. Kevin's dad let him tag along with me a couple of days a week so I could have more one on one time with him." He pauses briefly, but the Professor fails to respond. So Johnny lowers his voice to finish. "You know, because of his mother's recent death."

"Johnny... will you please follow me up to my bench?"

Johnny shrugs his shoulders, "Sure, why not?" Then he struts his way to the front as the class begins giggling and whispering among themselves.

The Professor pulls a gavel out of the top drawer and slams it across his desk. He glances out at the room full of children sitting at attention before whispering harshly at Johnny. "There's no way this story resembles your summer activities. If your assignment is not redone, and redone correctly, by the end of the first semester, then I'll be forced to have you removed from our student-teacher program!"

"You can't kick me out," Johnny said while glancing back at Kevin then to the front of the room, "my father donates like one million dollars each year to this crummy institution."

"I don't care who your daddy is," the Professor snarls as a bit of drool slides down into his short beard, "and I could care less about how much he donates!"

Johnny glances back at all the young students whose eyes are locked on to his every word. Then he turns back to the Professor. "Listen to me Old Man, no one's rewriting anything." Johnny thinks over some of his previous jobs... he wonders if this erratic behavior is the Professor's way of reaching out for help. "If you have questions regarding the authenticity of this story, then I recommend that you schedule an appointment with my father to discuss it with him."

"Son, it's not your work at the bank that's the problem here and you know it," the Professor retorts in a stern voice. "I don't know how, or why, you decided to dig through my past. But if you think you're going to sleep through your year of student teaching with the intention of blackmailing me into giving you a passing grade... it's not going to happen!"

Johnny smiles briefly before taking another swipe at the Professor's patience. "I wrote a story following your stupid rules. If my story happens to resemble your shady past, then that would be your problem, Sir... Not mine!"

"We both know the problem with this story and I'm telling you right now that I absolutely refuse to put up with you childish pranks," the Professor shouts back.

"Bravo! You nailed it... Old Man," Johnny claps loudly two times. "Obviously, I based the story on your sordid past... It's really quite ironic, but in the process of writing your silly summer project, I came across some juicy information about you and your lovely wife. She was a stripper at a bar you frequented. That was not only easy, but also very valuable info to obtain. So then the next question became... what would drive a person from that life to one of such strong religious beliefs, as well as helping troubled children?" Johnny leans in close to the Professor and tries to whisper. "Feel free to stop me if what I'm saying isn't true... Let's put aside the fact that your sweet wife sold her body to sleazy guys like yourself. But you also learned of your best friend's affair which, of course, you tried to benefit from. Only your plan backfired and he killed himself because of your actions."

"You bastard," the Professors slams his chair into his desk knocking over the picture of his wife.

Johnny waggles his finger. "Now now Professor, no swearing in class... Not even you." Johnny struts his way back to his seat then kicks his feet up on the desk beside his.

The Professor clears his throat as he steps up to the podium. "You all have a copy of your fall project. The subject of this paper is where you see yourself and how you imagine your life will be ten years from now." He looks straight out at Johnny. "Please take note of rule five.  Although I still want your life intertwined in this story, you will be given a lot more leeway in using your imagination.  Just keep in mind that it's supposed to be a story based on your own life... not someone else's."

Johnny pulls out his pen and notebook than began writing down his thoughts and notes on everyone in the room.  Profiling a person has always come easy for me, determining their needs; well that's a different story.  I seem to find myself constantly bending rules.  For instance rule three, 'You must not get personally involved with your client or anyone close to them'.  I understand why the rule is needed, but it's nearly impossible to avoid at times.  I found that if I start the job with my client hating me, then the chance of developing any type of relationship is minimal at best.  But when the jobs start out undefined and you don't know the person, you don't always know what they need. Helping people to move forward in a positive way is what keeps me coming back for the next job.  Helping people who are destined for some type of tragedy in the near future is tougher but it can definitely be a much more rewarding part of my Job.  I guess some time in the next nine months I'll know exactly what the Professor needs from me and hopefully I'll be able to come up with some kind of plan to help him.

The Professor stands up and slowly walks toward the door.  His face is a ghostly white and he staggers as if he were drunk.  "Class, I need to step outside for a moment.  Please continue going over your fall project and I'll answer any questions you may have when I return." Then he quickly steps outside and the cool fall air hits his pale white face.  Thoughts of his ignoble life slowly drift through his mind as if it was playing out right in front of him.  He sees himself as a boy playing shortstop with his best friend Jimmy on the Tigers.  Then there's the first time he laid eyes on his beautiful wife and how he had to coax her into dating him.   But then he sees himself and his friend Alex arguing. "Why the hell did you tell her," he shouted at me.  Then Alex pulled a gun out of his jacket and slid it up under his jaw.

The Professor's hands begin to tingle as he gets light-headed and falls to his knees.  I don't understand... only Stacy and I knew that

Alex was cheating on her. It's as if he knew my whole life, from the Mark character in little league to Kevin who met his wife in a strip bar. And how the hell did he know about those other women I took to Mexico, and what about the eight languages I know? "Oh dear God… Am I dead?" The Professor begins pinching his face. "Is this what they mean by seeing your life pass before your eyes? Am I dying soon?"

Johnny stands inside the full length glass doors watching the Professor as he pinches and pokes at his face. Yeah, this guy's definitely more screwed up then I originally thought. Why the hell is he kneeling down outside? Is he praying? Doesn't he see those dark clouds moving in?

A large rain drop hits the sidewalk in front of the Professor and he stands up and he quickly spins around. He finds himself staring through the glass door into Johnny's eyes. The fear of dying runs through every inch of his body as he opens the door separating himself and Johnny. "Are you the one," the Professor softly asks. "Please tell me… are you the one that's been sent to kill me?"

"Me… kill… you…? No…" Johnny hesitates for a moment trying to find the right words to say. "I'm not sure… I believe I was sent to help you."

"You say you are sent to help me," the Professor asked as he suddenly felt the pressures of his life released from his tormented body. "Well, that's what I'm asking for!"

"What do I look like, a freaking Genie in a bottle or something," Johnny said, laughing. "Either way… you don't need me, go jump off a bridge. There's plenty in this city to choose from."

"I believe it's a sin…" the Professor explains, "so if I did jump off a bridge, then I wouldn't go to heaven."

"It's nice to know you've thought this thing through," Johnny said with a smile, "I don't know… maybe… we'll have to see…

Look… if I'm supposed to kill you, then… I don't know… I'm not going to make any promises."

Johnny watches as the Professor disappears into his classroom, but then his attention is quickly diverted as the driving rain begins to beat harder on the glass door in front of him. Johnny thinks about his new job and the Professor's unusual request. *I continue to cross that line separating good and evil in an attempt to fulfill someone's needs. But when their desire involves death, then I believe it's time to come up with a few new rules.*

Johnny's mind wanders back to his last job, Kevin. And he wonders if Kevin will ever realize his potential by working toward the goals they set together. Then he pulls a pen and small notepad out of the inside pocket of his jacket and continues to write down his thoughts.

*I find myself being bombarded by fools who believe the world is at its lowest point ever… Maybe it's the economy… maybe it's the next generation of punks and thugs that are moving in down the street… or maybe they just find comfort in thinking they're surviving the worst the world has to offer… The simple result is an endless supply of new clients these days… If you find yourself spending every minute of your short life getting lost in an endless cycle of doom and gloom, then I'll be here at the ready… just patiently waiting to welcome you into my world.*

Made in the USA
Charleston, SC
19 April 2012